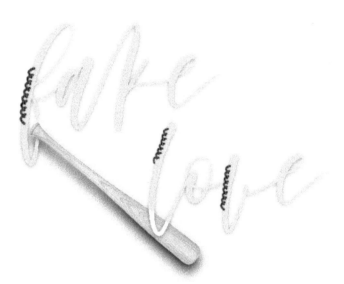

JOCELYNE SOTO

FAKE LOVE

JOCELYNE SOTO

Cover Design by Enchanting Romance Designs

Special Edition Cover by Opulent Swag and Designs

Edits by My Brother's Editor

Proofread by My Brother's Editor

Paperback ISBN: 978-1-956430-15-8

Special Edition Paperback ISBN: 978-1-956430-16-5

I had everything going for me.

Drafted right out of college. Signed a multimillion-dollar contract. Slated to become a Hall of Famer.

All my prospects were looking up... Until a diagnosis caused me to ruin everything.

It took me a season to destroy my career, and now I have to work to repair it.

Step 1: Get clean.

Step 2 : Show my new team that their investment isn't a waste.

Step 3 : Find a woman and convince her to be my fake girlfriend and make my mom happy.

1 and 2, I got a handle on. Step 3 is turning out to be a lot harder than I thought. Finding a woman was a piece of cake, convincing her is a different story.

Jen Zaragoza is hardheaded, feisty, and a pain in my behind. But even with her being all those things, I start to fall for her.

And hard.

This started out as something to make my mom happy, and it's turning into me planning our future together.

Jen is my grand slam and there is nothing fake about it.

CONTENTS

PLAYLIST

Swim - Chase Atlantic
Kiss Me - Ed Sheeran
I was never there - The Weeknd
Me and Your Mama - Childish Gambino
Dress - Taylor Swift
Reflections - The Neighbourhood
Heaven - Julia Michaels
'Tis the damn season - Taylor Swift
Love on the Brain - Rihanna
I wanna Be Yours - Arctic Monkeys
My Love - maye

To all my baseball fans that go to games just for the pants.

AUTHOR'S NOTE

This book touches upon the subject of drug use and addiction. This book also touches upon gun violence and a possible shooting event.
Some scenes are explained with detail.
If that is something that you are not comfortable with, please do not read.
If you would like more information, please follow the QR code below.
Thank you.

BREAKING NEWS

BAUER TO SAN FRANCISCO
February 8, 2022

STRAIGHT FROM THE Chicago front office, Maddox Bauer has been traded to the San Francisco Miners.

Bauer, who was drafted from Chicago at the age of twenty-two as a first-round pick, has been suspended from the league since August after a drug test resulted positive for a banned substance. It was later revealed that Bauer tested positive for cocaine. At the time, the front office in Chicago stated that Bauer had tested positive for a banned substance before, but it was the first time he had tested for cocaine. This has been the longest suspension that Bauer has endured. Serving a ten-game suspension back in May.

Rumors have been circulating that Chicago has been

wanting to cut ties with Bauer since October but had yet to find a team to take over the contract.

At the start of the 2020 season, Chicago signed Bauer to a ninety-five-million-dollar contract over eight seasons. The contract came after two spectacular seasons in 2018 and 2019, 2018, ending with Bauer being named Rookie of the Year.

Bauer was slated to be a Cy Young contender this past season but after a few mishaps, the positive drug tests, and the ninety-game suspension, that went out the window.

There are still a little over forty games left in Bauer's suspension and if everything goes well, he should be playing by mid-May.

Here's hoping that The Cove is a better place for Bauer, and he comes back to his old self.

Good luck in the city, Bauer.

1

MADDOX

TRADED.

Throughout my career, I had an irrational fear of that word. Of what it would mean if I heard the word and my name in the same sentence.

In the five years that I've been playing in the minor and major leagues, that word has been traumatizing for me.

If I had to guess, it might stem from having men on the same team as me one day and then the next, they're playing across the country.

Or it could have stemmed from my wanting to play nowhere else but my hometown team for all of my career and be within a ten-mile drive from my mom.

Whatever it stems from, the word has terrified me for years. It's as if it has a death grip on me.

Since I've been called up to the big times, every time I hear the word, I jump a little. That happened a lot during my first season when I was just a rookie, a nobody.

Even when my first season was over, I would sweat

profusely thinking that I was going to be sent to another city.

There was always a thought floating around my head that my team didn't want me, even with the Rookie of the Year title in my back pocket.

That fear stayed with me even after I signed a multi-million-dollar contract.

A ninety-five-million-dollar contract to be exact.

The second that my name was on the dotted line and dried, my fear of the word disappeared. It was only going to disappear for eight years, but for the time being, it was gone.

I was at the top of my game, in the city that owned my heart, and the fear of being traded was nowhere in sight.

And it was like that for almost three years.

Then I got a call from my mom's neighbor, a call that shattered everything in me. A call that put the fear of the word 'traded' to shame.

It was the worst news of my life and within days of hearing it, I started to throw everything I had built away.

I started to do things that never in my life did I think I was ever going to do.

Actions that had words like traded and suspensions being thrown around, but in those moments, I didn't care. I was going to lose everything, anyway. Why not lose the sport that has been in my blood since I could walk out too?

I didn't care when I started to throw everything down the drain. I didn't care when I got my first ten-game suspension. I sure as hell didn't care when my last drug test came back dirty, and I received a ninety-game suspension and a hefty fine.

I didn't care until I was face down on a couch inside a strip club.

I didn't care until I had the club owner knock some sense into me with his words.

I didn't care until it was almost too late.

Now all my fears were coming true and there was nothing that I could do about it. Because it was my decisions that got me here. Decisions that I'm now paying for.

I've been suspended.

I've been traded.

I'm away from my mother when she needs me most.

All because I couldn't keep my nose away from the small baggy filled white powder.

The suspensions, I knew were coming. I saw them from a mile away. I knew my tests were going to come back dirty, so I didn't fight it.

The trade, though, took me by surprise. I should have expected it, I should have seen it coming like the suspension, but it still blinded me.

Even more so when the first call I got as I walked out of the rehab facility I was in for six week, was from my agent telling me that Chicago had traded me to San Francisco.

I thought that the team that had built me from the ground up had my back, I couldn't have been more wrong. I guess when you have two suspensions under your belt for illegal substances, the non-trading clause that's in your contract goes out the window.

So instead of leaving Utah and heading back to

Chicago to see my mom and get shit squared away, I'm currently trying to deplane a flight in San Francisco.

"I have places to be!" the lady in the row behind me exclaims as we wait for the people in front of us to start moving.

I look at my watch and see that we've only been waiting for four minutes. I let out a snort at the lady's eagerness, damn sure she's what my mom would call a Karen.

After three minutes of Karen's annoying complaints of getting off the plane faster because she has dinner reservations, the people ahead of me finally start to move.

The woman behind me exasperates loudly. "Finally."

I hear her shift from right behind me, the pleasure of having an aisle seat, and when I look at the mom that is sitting across from me, I know I need to make Karen's day a little more worse.

My seat gets pushed forward and I take that as my signal to go through with my plan.

Shoving out of my seat, I stand to full height in the aisle, blocking anybody behind me from taking another step.

As I wave for the mom and her two kids to go, as well as my seatmates, I receive an earful from Ms. Karen.

"Excuse me, I was supposed to go. I have reservations."

"I think everyone on this damn plane knows you have reservations," I grumble under my breath, turning to face the lady and giving her a smirk.

She has the audacity to gasp. "Who do you think you are? I have a right to get off this plane."

Giving her another smirk, I turn and grab my bag out of the overhead compartment before making my way out of this metal tube.

I hear the woman complain the whole way off and continue to hear her as we make our way out of the gate.

If I hadn't just gotten out of rehab and was still high out of my mind, I would have blown up on her.

Putting the lady and her childish tantrum behind me, I make my way through the terminal and out of the airport.

This isn't my first time in San Francisco, but it is my first time being here while not traveling as a part of the Cubbies.

It's definitely a different feeling.

When I make it over to arrivals, I look around for any sign of the team representative that Cole, my agent, said was going to pick me up.

I see nothing at the baggage claim, so I make my way outside onto the curb. When I don't see anyone, I'm about to call Cole to tell him the person is late when someone lets their horn rip, not even thirty feet away from me.

After jumping a bit and letting my heart settle back in its place, I look up to find an enthusiastic kid jumping out of a dark SUV and waving me over.

I guess this is my ride.

Kid doesn't even look old enough to drive and he's the team representative?

Letting out a sigh, I walk over to the SVU.

"Mr. Bauer, sir, I'm Jai. I will be taking you to the stadium today." Jai holds out a hand for me to shake, which I do.

"Thank you for coming," I say to him.

"It's my pleasure, sir. Do you have any other bags with you?" Jai looks around as if I may have left my bags somewhere unattended.

"Just this," I say, holding up my duffel.

I'm only in San Francisco for a night to meet with my new team manager and agent to get everything squared away. As soon as possible, I will make my way to Chicago to see my mom.

I owe her a huge apology and it's better I do give it to her in person.

Especially with all the stress I've put on her over the last six months.

"Okay, then. Should we head to the stadium?" he says enthusiastically, throwing a thumb over to the waiting car.

I give him a nod and soon we are both in the SUV leaving the airport and making our way to the stadium in Bay Area traffic.

"What do you do, Jai?" I ask, as he merges onto the expressway.

Is it an expressway in California or is it a highway?

I should figure that out.

"I'm a sports management student at Stanford. I'm interning at the Miners' front office this semester." he answers, his face almost splitting into two with his huge smile.

"Do you like it? Working for the team, I mean?"

When you play in the major leagues, you come to hear quite a bit about certain teams. You learn who the bad managers are, who has a horrible front office, who cares way too much about their players and who doesn't.

In all my career, I've only heard good things about San Francisco, and I can't help but to think that it's all a ruse.

"If I had a choice, I would never leave. Best job I've ever had." He sounds sincere.

Maybe everyone is right, and San Francisco is one of the places to be.

I stop my inquiry of the intern and for the remainder of the twenty-minute drive, I try to take in as much of my surroundings as possible.

The cars, the streets, the highways, the buildings, everything. Even with the short drive, I know it will take me a while for me to get the way of the land here.

Within minutes of entering the city, we make it to the stadium and are pulling into the back parking lot.

Getting out of the car, I marvel at the red brick and try to take in all the fine details that the building has to offer.

This is home for the foreseeable future. Or however long it takes this team to also throw me to the curve.

"This way," Jai states, waving me over to the giant door leading to the inside of the stadium. No, not stadium, park, if its name is any indication.

With duffel in hand, Jai guides me through until we reach the front offices and enter a conference room.

As I step foot into the room, I see that not only am I meeting with my agent and new team manager, but also the big guns.

The team's general manager and president are also

here to welcome me. I'm surprised that the owners aren't here too.

"Maddox, you are right on time," Cole greets me, trying to give me a smile to ease some of the tension flowing through the room.

Cole may be happy that I'm here but if the expression on the executives' faces are any indication, not everyone feels the same way.

I push every emotion that I'm feeling down and mirror Cole's smile. "Happy to be here." I say as genuinely I can, shake his hand then turning to my new manager.

Ben Kipper is supposed to be one of the best managers this team, or better yet this league, has ever seen. Every player and coach that has played with him has said that they would work with him again in a heartbeat. The man may have only started his managerial career eight years ago, but he already has a great reputation.

From what I hear, he's well-liked by all, including the fans. His age and his looks might be a factor in that though, given that the man is a good-looking dude. He can be the face of the team all on his own.

"Maddox," Ben says, holding out a hand to me. "Welcome to the team."

I shake his hand. "Thank you, Ben. I'm happy to be here and to hopefully be in your bullpen."

Hopefully, because even though I was traded it doesn't mean that I will be seeing the pitcher's mound anytime soon.

"Glad to hear it."

After shaking hands with Darryl Mann, the team's

general manager, and Von Douglas, the team president, the four of us all take a seat at the conference table, my contract in front of us.

Without any hesitation, Von starts the meeting. Getting right to work.

"The reason the Miners were willing to take on your contract was because Cole here informed us that you were completing an addiction program." Von states.

They were *willing* because I was getting clean.

Not because of the work that I have done as a pitcher in for Chicago but because I was getting clean. Great.

If I wasn't already feeling like a piece of shit, that would have certainly caused me to.

I give him a nod. "Yes, sir," I confirm. "I just finished six weeks at a facility in Utah."

"And?"

What kind of question is that?

Squaring my shoulders, I looked at Von straight on.

"And I realize what my mistakes were. I understand that what I was doing to myself was wrong. What I was doing to my team was wrong. I was dealing with some things in my personal life, still dealing with them, and I decided to handle them the wrong way. I'm clean if that's what you're asking, and I will stay clean. I can promise you that my head is straight now. I won't slip," at least I will try not to, "and I certainly won't let your investment go down the drain."

Von looks at me with hard eyes. It's as if he is trying to figure out if he should believe me or not.

"It's your mother, correct? The stuff you're dealing with."

I wouldn't label my mom's sickness as 'stuff' but I still give him a nod.

"How is she?" Ben asks, sincerity in his tone.

Talking about my mother these last few months has been one of the hardest things that I've had to do.

I swallow down a lump that is starting to form in my throat. "Doctors are hopeful. She has monthly appointments to keep an eye on the growth of her tumors. Hopefully if it all goes well, she will be able to have surgery to remove them."

In February of last year, a little over a year ago, my mom went to the doctor because she was having these painful headaches. Her vision was also getting blurry, and at times, she felt like she didn't know how to speak.

It was right before I had to report for spring training, so because I wasn't going to see her for two months, I decided to go with her.

I was in the waiting room as she was getting checked out. when a nurse came to get me. The second she said my name, I knew something was wrong.

I thought that maybe my mom had fallen or something along those line but when I walked into the doctor's office and saw tears running down her face, I knew it was something bad.

When I sat down, I took my mom's hand and listened to the doctor tell a bunch of things that I couldn't comprehend.

Turns out my mom had gone to the doctor a few weeks

earlier and had to get some tests done to find out what was going on.

The appointment we were at was to tell her what they had found.

According to the doctor, one of those tests was a brain scan. A brain scan that came back abnormal.

The scan had found several brain tumors that at the time looked like they were going relatively slowly.

When I had asked what they were going to do about them, all the doctor said was that they were going to keep a close eye on the tumors. A close eye he said, followed by hope that they wouldn't grow.

Both mom and I left that appointment feeling numb.

I didn't know how to take the news, so I just jumped into work, hoping to forget about it until it was necessary.

For six weeks they kept a close eye on the tumors and the day before I was slated to start our first game of the season, mom went to the emergency room because she couldn't handle the head pain.

That's when things became necessary.

That's when we found out that the tumors had grown and things went from being malignant to cancerous.

Somehow, I was still able to pitch the next day. I pitched like shit that day and as soon as the game was over, I started to spiral down a hole that would take me close to a year to escape from.

"If you need anything, anything at all, let us know and we will take care of you," Daryll tells me, giving me a curt nod, taking me out of the drive into memory lane.

I clear my throat. "Even if I have to fly to Chicago in an emergency?"

I may not be playing anytime soon but there may be time where something going on with my mom may interfere with the game.

Both Ben and Daryll nod.

"Even if you have to fly across the country. Whatever you need, you will get. You're a part of our family now and we take care of our players," Daryll answers.

Take care of their players.

I've heard that before, and now look at where I'm at. With a new team across the county.

Let's hope that *their* words hold actual power behind them.

I look at the three men that now have a very large say in what happens next in my life.

One of them may hate me, but the other two, the other two are on my side. Just from looking at their faces, I know that they will do everything in their power to make me the player, and the man, that I once was.

So, I give them a nod.

"Should we sign this contract then?"

If these men believe I can be the individual I once was, so can I.

For the next three hours, we go over every single thing on my new contract with a fine-tooth comb.

What I can and cannot do while serving the remainder of my suspension.

When I will be able to be in the dugout for a game.

When I can actually take part in a game.

Everything is laid out for me in black and white, including a drug test every single week.

The Miners want to protect their multi-million-dollar investment and if me peeing in a cup every seven days does that, then so be it. The team is going to take over the reminder of what was promised to me by Chicago. Which means I'm now the highest player on the Miners roster at a little over seventy million dollars for the next six years. Of course they want to protect their investment.

After the meeting is over, I'm given a tour of the field, training center, and clubhouse by Ben.

By midafternoon, I'm exhausted and want to jump on the next flight out to Chicago.

"You have your drug test tomorrow morning. Be here at the park at nine," Ben announces, throwing my plans to catch the next flight out the window.

I nod. "I will."

"Listen, Maddox," Ben says, placing a hand on my shoulder. "I know this is a big change for you, an unexpected one at that, but I think it would be a good thing. You'll continue training and once your suspension is up, you will be better than before."

But what if I'm not, I want to ask but I don't.

Before all of this, I was on the top of my game. What if that is all gone? What if my decision to sleep with the little white substance caused me to lose the ability to even hold a ball correctly?

I don't show him those insecurities though.

"Thank you, Ben. Means a lot to know you believe in me."

"We all believe in you, kid. You just have to believe in yourself. Now, go. Explore the city and I will see you in the morning. Give me a call if you need anything."

With that, me and my duffel bag are left to our own accord.

I guess it's time to explore the city that I now get to call home.

Fingers crossed it treats me better than the last one.

2

Jennifer

YOU WOULD THINK that a coffee shop's busiest time of the day would be the morning hours. Because that's when people need coffee the most, right? To be ready and energized for their working day, right?

Wrong. In a city where most individuals work remote and can work from almost anywhere, afternoons and evenings have started to become the busiest times for coffee shops.

How do I know this?

Well, I'm currently elbows deep in espresso at four in the afternoon, so I think I'm qualified to say when people run to get their coffee.

That and I've been working at this hipster hot spot since my college days. I know a thing or two.

And right now, I know that this crowd of afternoon coffee drinkers can go suck an eggplant. I want to go home and forget about this place even existing, but no they keep coming in and we don't close until eight.

Yippadi fucking do.

I should have never agreed to work a double, I would have been out of here already.

But instead, I'm making Barbie Karen her latte for the eighth time because it doesn't taste like a latte.

Maybe if she wasn't chewing gum it would taste like one.

I didn't tell her that, but I did think about it.

Finishing up the flower design at the top of the milk, I cross my fingers as I call her name.

"Latte for Barbie," I call out. Yes, her name is indeed Barbie, and she is not the first one today.

"It better taste like a latte this time," she says, chewing her gum obnoxiously loud.

I want to strangle her.

"It does, ma'am. I promise." I give her my sweetest smile, the one that my best friend tells me is evil at its core.

Barbie approaches the counter, her eyes narrowed at me as she reaches for her drink and takes a sip.

If she tells me it doesn't taste like a latte, I will quit right now.

After she finishes her sip, she takes another as if she can't find the taste of it.

Finally, after her third sip, she gives me a nod.

"About damn time you got it right," she spits out, throwing an eye roll in my direction.

I swear my eye twitches as she flips her hair and leaves the coffee shop with her stupid latte in hand. Without a doubt I will be having this same conversation with her by the end of the week.

Just thinking about that is making me cringe.

Ignoring all the other coffees that are waiting to be made, I head to the back and pull out my phone, making plans to look forward to when I get out of this hellhole.

ME: Tell Hunty that you're mine tonight and I don't want him to cockblock my girls' night.

I HIT send and instantly the little typing bubble starts to pop up. My anger starts to dissipate and gratitude for having my best friend in the same city washes over me.

Her message comes in within seconds.

SELENA: Bad day at work?

THIS GIRL KNOWS me all too well.

Selena and I have been best friends since we were little girls. What with us being in the same elementary school classes together and our dads working together at the same construction company. She has been one of my constants in my life, even when we went to different colleges, and she started building a life with her professional athlete of a boyfriend.

Or should I say fiancé, since they got engaged last month when San Francisco's own football team won the Super Bowl.

Selena lives within a thirty-minute drive from me, I take any time with her that I can.

I shoot her a reply.

ME: I had to remake a latte 8 TIMES!!! 8 TIMES, SELENA!!!! All because it didn't taste like a latte. So I'm initiating the BFF card!!!!!!!!!

SELENA: I'll make him disappear. Come over whenever you're off.

ME: I LOVE YOU!!!!!!

WITH MY SALVATION SECURE, I pocket my phone and head back to the counter. The second I step through the double doors and see that the line of cups has increased, I feel like crying.

I try my hardest to hold in a groan at the sight, but I fail. So much so that my second lead, Annaleigh, lets out a chuckle at my frustration.

"I swear I hate four o'clock coffee runs," I grumble as I make my way back to my station of the day.

"Hey, at least you don't get yelled at for telling them that mocha indeed has chocolate in it," she says with an eye roll.

I swear there are some people that think that mocha is

this magical thing.

"Let's hope these last few hours move along fast," I say, going back to my hell.

For the next two hours, it's non-stop coffee making for me and taking coffee orders for Annaleigh. It's as if all of San Francisco decided to come here to get their caffeine IV to be able to survive.

By the time seven comes around, the shop is dead, not a single customer coming in for a good twenty minutes, and both me and Annaleigh are dead on our feet.

It's days like today that really make me hate my job.

"You can go ahead and go home early," I say to Annaleigh as I wipe down a table. "I think I can handle an hour on my own."

"Are you sure? I don't mind finishing up my shift."

As much as I want to tell her that she should stay and I leave, I don't. That's what a manager does, right?

I give her a nod. "Yeah, I'm sure. Go ahead, one of us needs to get out of here and I have to close anyway."

"Thanks, Jen," she says as she takes off her apron and grabs her stuff from under the counter.

I go to clean a different table as she rounds to the other side.

"Alright, I will see you tomorrow," Annaleigh says as she heads to the door.

"If I don't suffocate in espresso in the next hour." I grumble, which causes her to laugh.

"I'll make sure to check on you to make sure."

"Please do."

With a smile and a wave, Annaleigh is out the door and I'm left in the shop all by myself.

It's times like these, when I'm alone at work, with no coworkers or customers that I really think about the direction my life is currently taking.

I graduated from San Francisco State five years ago with a degree in digital marketing. I had a few internships under my belt and once I had my degree, I thought I would have no problem finding a job. One that would let me quit my part-time job I had started a few months before.

I was so sure of it. I was so sure that within weeks of me getting my degree, I would be working with some big company and handling their social media presence. Yet, even as I applied to hundreds of jobs throughout the years and have gone to a handful of interviews, I'm still at that part-time job from college.

Have I had a few offers from places I applied to? Yes, but there was always something that had me saying no.

Exclusivity clauses.

No personal time off.

Insane hours expected to work throughout the week.

There was always something, and now I can't help but wonder where I would be if I had said yes to one of them.

Would I be working in a high rise with my own office?

Would I be living in a different country, taking pictures and finding a new meaning in life?

Or would I have left that job and come right back here to serve coffee, because what I was doing was causing me to be miserable?

I don't know, and now it's a little too late to figure it out.

I wipe down the remainder of the tables and the chairs before moving to the back to the other side of the counter to clean out the display case of its pastries. Usually any time after seven, we don't get a whole lot of customers that want pastries that have been sitting out all day.

I'll give them to the homeless people that I pass every night on my way home.

It's as I'm pulling the last of the chocolate croissants that the shop door opens, causing me to look up.

I don't know if it's because of how tired I am or the coffee fumes finally getting to me, but the second I see who just walked in, my lady bits start to tingle.

My eyes land on a broad chest and shoulders that are covered in a black long sleeve and then move to where his sleeves are rolled up his forearm.

Forearms that look like rods of rope that took some effort to get that big and can hold a girl up with no problem.

My mouth is watering at the sight which is causing my imagination to run wild.

The heavenly daydream of being pinned down by those forearms is rudely interrupted when I hear a clearing of a throat.

"What?" I ask, my mind coming back to the present.

I involuntarily take my eyes off those delicious forearms and look up to meet the gaze of their owner.

Their hot delicious owner. His eyes look like they have a green and blue tint to them. His jaw looks like it would be sharp under that small beard he's sporting and his hair is this rich dark brown color that shines in the light and is long enough to run your fingers through.

He takes a step further into the shop and I can't help but follow each of his movements.

"I asked if you were still open. The sign says you are," he says, his voice rough and making my lady bits even more uncomfortable.

Damn this man is perfect.

Somehow, I'm able to compose myself enough to form a complete sentence.

"Yes, sorry. Yes, we are still open," I say, walking over to the register. "What can I get you?"

Forearm guy looks over at me with what looks like a smile trying to escape for a second before he steps up to the counter.

"Can I have a large dark roast?" he says, pulling out his wallet.

"Just a large dark roast, nothing else?" I ask.

He gives me a nod. "No, just the coffee."

If I wasn't impressed by the man's simple coffee order, I would be getting lost in his eyes for sure.

"Why are you looking at me like I have two heads?" forearm guy asks.

I shake my head a bit. What is it about this guy that is making me forget how to speak to people?

"Sorry, it's just that usually people have some crazy request when it comes to their coffee. I think your order was the first normal one I had since this morning."

"Really?" He lets out a small chuckle and I swear my lady bits cry.

I nod. "Yup. Earlier today, I had to redo a lady's latte eight times because it didn't taste right. Another wanted a hot chocolate with caramel and no chocolate."

Why did I feel the need to tell him that?

Whatever my thought process was, I will thank it because my rambling causes forearm guy to give me a smile.

"You're joking, right?"

I shake my head. "I wish I were. So, large dark roast?"

He nods. "Large dark roast."

I get his order ready in two second flat and when I turn back to hand it to him, he hands me a five-dollar bill.

"Keep it. It's on the house for being a simple customer."

Again, he looks at me like he is studying me, before taking his coffee and placing the five dollar bill in the tip jar.

I watch as he steps back from the counter only to look around the shop, probably noticing how empty it is.

"Are you here all by yourself?" he asks, taking a sip of his drink.

I give him a nod. "I am. It got a little slow, so I sent the other girl home."

He takes another sip of his coffee. "Was that a safe choice?"

The hairs on my arms stand up at his question. "Why? Are you going to try something?"

Here I thought this dude was one of the good, sexy ones. Now all I can think is that he's probably the zodiac killer's son and I'm going to be chopped up into little pieces.

I could reach for my phone and try to call Selena and if she hears my screams, she'll call the cops.

He lets out another laugh. "No, I'm not going to try anything." That's what all the killers say. "I just think it's odd, leaving one person to close down a business this late."

"It's not even eight o'clock and not fully dark yet," I state and it's true, now that April is near, the sun is going down a lot later.

I honestly can't wait until summer, yet again living in San Francisco, we don't really get a summer.

"Something can still happen," forearm guy tells me.

I could argue with him. I could tell him that it's completely safe for me to stay here at the shop by myself after eight, but I would be lying.

There has been a string of robberies lately all over the city, people breaking into business and cars in broad daylight. People have gotten hurt and frankly, I'm always terrified when I walk home, which is why I have a taser and pepper spray in my bag.

"You're right, but I'll take my chances."

He gives me a nod. "Alright then," he says, holding his arms up in surrender. "Do you mind if I hang out here for a bit? Don't really want to go back to an empty hotel room."

That means he's either in the city as a tourist or for business. And if this is the last time that I see this gorgeous man, who am I to deny him where he spends his time?

"Go right ahead," I say to him with a nod.

He gives me one back and goes to sit at one of the tables by the window.

I wonder if he's staying because I'm alone. Or if it really is because he doesn't want to go back to an empty hotel.

Not wanting to bother him, I don't ask and do all my closing duties for the night.

I get one more customer before I close out the cash register. Right at closing time, I look over at the forearm god, who is finished with his coffee and is doing something on his phone.

"I'm sorry about this, but I have to kick you out. We're closed and I would rather not walk when it' s pitch dark outside."

His hazel eyes meet my brown ones and I try my hardest not to melt into a puddle and ask God for forgiveness as I beg this man to fuck me in every way possible.

He gives me a nod as he stands up. "Thank you for the coffee."

"Of course," I say, giving him a smile.

With a nod and a smile of his own, the forearm god is out the door without a backward glance or even a name.

College Jen would be having a heart attack right about now if she heard that I didn't ask this man back to my place.

I'm sure he has better things to do than to bang a barista.

Forgetting about the man, or at least trying to, I finish out my closing duties and right at eight twenty, with a bag filled with food in one hand and my stuff in the other, I close the shop for the day.

Tomorrow will be the same shit all over again.

I really need to get a new job.

Making sure I have everything, I lug the bag of food over my shoulder and make my way over to my apartment.

Only a few blocks in the dark, drop off the food and then I will be making my way over to Selena's for our girls' night.

I'm twenty feet away from the shop when I get stopped in my tracks.

Why?

Well, because the forearm god is leaning against the brick wall a few feet ahead.

"Need help finding your way back to your hotel?" I ask, jokingly, raising an eyebrow at him.

The next words he speaks take me off guard. "Let me walk you home."

3

MADDOX

IF THE SUN WAS SHINING, I bet that her light brown eyes would look almost translucent. They did when she was under the florescent lights of the coffee shop.

Her eyes are what drew me to her, what had me captivated by her and what ultimately made me want to be near her. So I stay at the coffee shop when I didn't need to. For longer than I needed to.

Did I lie when I told her I didn't want to go back to an empty hotel room? No, that was the truth, but I still wanted to find what was so damn intriguing about this woman.

Staring at her for close to an hour without saying a word, didn't help with answering any questions and when she told me my time inside the shop was up, I felt defeated almost.

Why? I have no idea. Never, and I mean never, have I felt that way about my proximity to a woman.

So, I got up and left, but the second I stepped through the door, I finally put together what she said.

She was going to be walking home, by herself.

The hairs on my arms instantly stood up. This may not be Chicago, but you still hear of some bad shit happening on the streets of San Francisco.

That was my reasoning for staying behind and waiting for her. I was going to order her an Uber and make sure she got home safely but no. Here I am offering to walk this strange woman home.

Who the actual fuck am I?

"You want to walk me home?" she asks, looking at me questionably.

I honestly would look at myself the same way.

"I do. You shouldn't be walking by yourself, especially in a big city."

For all I know, this was a bad neighborhood and someone might be waiting at the next corner to get her alone. Half the store fronts on this street have metal bars covering their doors and windows for crying out loud.

"But you don't even know my name. For all you know, I can be a barista, but still a serial killer. I can be the zodiac killer's daughter."

Jesus. This girl watches way too many crime shows. Is she always like this?

"Are you related to the zodiac killer?"

She shrugs, the bag she has on her shoulder moving in the process. "No, but I could be. You don't know."

"I know your name is Jennifer."

It took me by surprise that a girl that has the lightest

brown eyes that I have ever seen and looks as if she belongs on the cover of a fashion magazine, has such a simple name.

I think that's one of the reasons why I'm attracted to her, because other than her name, there is a simplicity to her. A simplicity that I didn't have in my life for a great while.

What with drugs, baseball, and rehab and all that.

Jennifer takes a step back as if I were a stalker and she was scared. I'm a strange man that knows her name. She rightfully should feel that way.

"You have a nametag on," I say, pointing to the plastic rectangle attached to her shirt.

She looks down at the name tag like she completely forgot that she was even wearing it.

"Fine, but I don't know your name," she throws out, her lips ending up in a pout that I want to kiss.

Seriously, what is wrong with me?

"My name is Maddox," I say.

As I say my name, I watch her. I watch her to see if maybe she's a baseball fan and recognizes me. Maybe she knows that I'm the new pitcher for the Miners. I watch to see if she debates in her head about revealing that she knows who I am.

But as I watch her, she gives nothing away about even recognizing my name.

I think I like her even more.

"Well, Maddox, it's nice to meet you. But knowing your name, still doesn't tell me why you waited outside the coffee shop to walk me home."

Do I tell her? Do I tell her that something about her woke something in me up?

I'm only in town tonight and it's not like I'll see this girl again when I come back into town the second week of April.

Might as well give her all my cards.

"Honest truth?" I say, giving her a smirk.

"Obviously."

"I don't know what it is, but the second I walked in and I saw you, I was captivated. Maybe it was your eyes or your voice, but whatever it was, made me feel the urge to spend more time around you. And when I walked out, it felt like I needed to stay behind and make sure that you got home safely. Like it was my duty or something."

I'm seconds away from telling her to forget that I even said anything because of the way she is looking at me, when something shifts.

Jennifer goes from looking at me like I have three heads to giving me a full-blown smile that brings one of my own.

"I thought I was the only one that felt it," she lets out enthusiastically, the smile reaching her eyes.

Not words that I expected her to say. I for sure thought that she was going to call me a creep.

"You felt it too?" I ask like she didn't just say she did.

She gives me a nod, coming slightly closer to me. "When you walked in. It was like this pull. I couldn't explain it, I just thought it was the coffee messing with my head."

"Definitely not the coffee." I give her a smirk before

breaking the distance between us. "So what do you say about me walking you home?"

"You're not going to end up in my bed."

I nod. "I just want to make sure you make it safely."

Jennifer looks at me with narrowed eyes and a smirk playing at her lips for a minute before she answers.

"The independent woman in me wants me to say that I don't need you walking me home, but your eyes are too pretty to turn down."

She doesn't have a filter, and I like it a little more than I should.

"Pretty eyes, huh?" I smirk, waving at her to start walking.

With an eye roll in my direction, she guides me past the coffee shop.

"Like you didn't know you were gorgeous," she states.

"I never had someone say it so bluntly," I say, my eyes going to the plastic bag she has slung over her shoulder.

Is that food?

A shrug gets thrown in my direction as we cross the street. "I've been told more than once that at times I don't have a filter."

We cross the street as Jen hikes up the plastic bag on her shoulder some more.

"Do you need help with that?" I offer, already reaching out to take it from her.

Without hesitation, she hands me the bag and rolls her shoulders in relief of no longer feeling the weight.

"Thank you. Who knew that pastries could be so damn heavy."

"Is there a reason why you have a garbage bag of pastries?" I ask, looking at the contents of the bag.

Is she taking these home because she can't afford to eat? If that's the case, I will buy her food before we get to her place. No way am I going to let her survive on just pastries.

I'm about to pull out my phone to look for the nearest grocery store when she answers my question.

"I feel bad every time I close and there is a ton of food left over, because there are people out there that really need it. So, when I can, I get everything that was supposed to be thrown out and give it to the homeless on my way home. The food is still good, so why not give it to someone that really needs it, you know?"

Am I stunned by her kindness? A little. There are a lot of generous people out in the world and at times you find them in the most unexpected places.

A coffee shop.

A strip club.

"That's very admirable of you," I state.

When I was first drafted, I made it my mission to give back to my community and to the people that watched me play since I was in t-ball. I gave back any chance I could, but when my mom's diagnosis came and I shut down, it all stopped.

It may be time to start it back up again.

"I'm just giving them food. There are people out there that do so much more for them."

"Is that what you're passionate about? Helping the homeless? Or is it making coffee?"

I added the last part to lighten the mood a bit, but I already know that she could give two shits about making coffee. I saw the way she looked in the cafe, and she hated every minute of it.

A snort escapes her. "Coffee was just a steppingstone that I got too comfortable with," she says, turning to give me a small smile. "I like helping people, sure, that will always be something I do, but not an ultimate passion."

"So what is?"

"Digital media."

Now I'm the one letting out a snort. "So you're one of those social media influencers?"

"There is nothing wrong with being an influencer, but no. I'm talking about using digital media to send a message. A good message and use the world that you have in the palm of your hands for something great."

Interesting.

Being a professional athlete, I always have to be conscious of what I post on my socials. It can't be anything too personal or even something that can be taken the wrong way. I never posted about my charity work because I didn't want to have people in my business, but I know now that I was looking at it the wrong way.

Maybe having someone like Jennifer on my team for that sort of thing would be helpful.

"What about you?" she asks me as we approach an overpass that has a few tents under it.

"What about me?" I ask, hearing the bite that comes with my words.

She doesn't seem affected by it.

"What brings you to San Francisco?" The question comes out with a curiosity to it that I think I like.

Do I tell her that I'm a drug addict baseball player that just got traded here from his hometown and away from his mom because of his bad behavior?

Or do I lie? It's not like I will see her after tonight anyway.

"Work," I tell her, not lying.

She nods her head as if she was expecting that answer.

"Let me guess, you're a tech extraordinaire?" The question comes out as we make our way across another street and head toward a few tents on the sidewalk.

I shake my head. "Not tech. Sports actually," I say, giving her something but not everything.

"That's cool." Jen gives me a smile before she reaches for the bag of food I'm holding.

Without a word, I hand it to her. She rewards me with another smile before she takes it and starts to walk toward the tents ready to hand out the hours-old pastries.

I follow behind her as she goes tent to tent, talking to each individual as she hands them something to eat.

Every single man and woman that she approaches greets her by her name and with a smile, giving her their thanks for their food.

My eyes never leave Jen as we walk to the end of the street.

Maybe it's for her protection and to make sure she doesn't get hurt.

Or maybe because the more I watch her, the more I'm

captivated by her. More so than what I was in the coffee shop.

I don't know what it is that makes me keep my eyes on her, on how her body moves as she walks, on her face as it lights up when someone tells her they appreciate her, but it's something.

When the bag is empty and we reach the other end of the street, Jen looks both happy about what she did but also heartbroken all in the same.

"You okay?" I ask her as we wait at the crosswalk.

She nods. "Yeah, it just sucks that I can't do more, you know?"

I give her a nod in return. "Yeah, I do. Maybe one day you will be able to."

Even though I don't know this woman all that well, I hope that I'm right because it seems like her heart is in the right place. A part of me wants to make it happen for her.

We continue to walk a few more blocks until we reach a building that looks like it has seen better days. If I had to guess, the building is at least one hundred years old.

"Well, this is me," she says, nodding toward the metal door. "Thank you for walking me home."

I give her a smile. "You're welcome. Thank you for letting me, and for the free coffee."

"If you're ever back in the city, come by the coffee shop and I'll repay you for the walk home."

"I'll take you up on that," I say, not telling her that I will be in the city a lot more than she thinks.

She gives me a smile and I give her one back as we just stand on the sidewalk with a few feet between us.

I didn't plan on what to do after we had reached her place, it's not like I was going to invite myself in and invade her space.

Guess it's time for me to finally leave the captivating coffee shop girl.

"Have a good rest of your night, Jennifer," I say, breaking the distance between us and placing a small kiss against her cheek.

She wasn't expecting the action and the small gasp she releases tells me as much.

When I pull away from her, the scent coming off her hair in my nose, I give her a smile before turning to walk away.

I'm not even five feet away from her when I hear my name being called.

"Maddox."

I turn and see that she is looking at me in a way I sure as hell didn't expect.

Hungry.

"Want to come upstairs?"

4

Jennifer

THE SECOND MY front door is open and my hands are free of all my belongings, I'm grabbing my phone and shooting off a text message.

ME: Hunty can have you tonight!! I made other plans!!!

SELENA MUST HAVE BEEN WAITING for me to text her because she's sending a message right as mine says delivered.

SELENA: A boy??

She knows me so well. I love my best friend.

ME: Yes ma'am!!!

SELENA: I don't even want to know how you found someone so fast.

NOT WANTING to spend the next hour or so telling her how it came that Maddox is now walking into my apartment, I ignore her message. After placing my phone face down on the nearest surface, I turn to face my guest, who just walked into my tiny apartment and is closing the door behind him.

When he told me that he wanted to walk me home, I was shocked, floored and every synonym of those two words, I thought for sure that I had heard him wrong or that he was just pulling my leg.

But the sincerity in his face told me otherwise.

He really wanted to walk me home and to make sure that I got back here safely.

Then he told me that he found me intriguing, and I tried so hard not to melt into a small puddle.

I don't know why, but his actions plus his words, made this man one hundred times hotter to me. Not just hot, sexy hot and enough to make me want to jump his bones right there on the street.

I didn't, of course, but I wanted to.

Now he's standing in the middle of my apartment, looking around like he doesn't know what to do with himself.

He is sexy, hot and adorable.

"You can say it, I live in a shoe box," I say, breaking the tension that is floating around us.

Do I make it a mission to invite strange men that walk me home into my place?

No.

I actually don't remember when the last time was that I had a man in here that wasn't my dad or Selena's boyfriend, Hunter.

Usually when it comes to me and my activities with men, it's either their place, a car, a bathroom somewhere, or a hotel room.

Never here. I do have boundaries after all.

But for some reason, I wanted Maddox in my space, and I don't know why.

"I wouldn't say that you live in a shoe box," he tells me, looking around at the crowded area.

"I would. It's a shoebox that costs over two thousand dollars."

The way he kept his eyes from going a bit wide at how much I pay for rent is definitely not how I reacted when hearing the same information for the first time.

I'm pretty sure that my reaction had a few expletives thrown at the building manager before agreeing to the lease.

Of course, I agreed to a lease for a closet sized apartment. It's San Francisco, where you either live in a shoe box or in your car.

"It suits you," he states, giving me a small smile that causes little butterflies to flutter in my stomach.

Have I mentioned that this man is sexy as hell?

And he's in my apartment. There are so many possibilities with this scenario.

"I'm suited for a shoe box?" I tease, walking over to him and gently hitting him on the shoulder.

"I didn't say that. I meant the space, it suits you. It's like an extension of you."

This man has known me for no more than two hours, has been in my apartment for less than two minutes and already knows that I've made this place genuinely mine.

It may be the size of a closet, but I made it feel like home in every way that I could, and this man saw that the second that he walked in.

"I tried," I say, my voice barely a whisper.

Maddox looks down at me, a smile playing at his lips, his eyes bright even in the dim light of my apartment.

We look at each other for what feels like an eternity but in reality, it couldn't have been more than a minute or two.

I get so lost in Maddox's gaze that I'm not aware of the fact that I step even closer to him, only leaving a few inches between our bodies.

"You said I wasn't going to end up in your bed," he states, his face only inches from mine.

He's a listener, this one.

"I did," I breathe out, wanting to close the distance and feel his body against mine.

"Then why am I up here?"

I can feel his words against my lips, and I don't know how much more I can handle before I break.

The truth comes out of my mouth. "Because I wanted to see."

"What did you want to see, Jennifer?" Maddox asks, a

seductive tone coming through as he closes the last remaining inches between us.

I can feel the heat of his body through my clothes.

"I wanted to see if the attraction I felt for you was real," I say, my mouth so close to his.

"And is it?"

His hands are now on my body, on my waist, bringing us closer together so that you wouldn't be able to slide a piece of paper between us.

Our breaths are mingling together, and our eyes are searching for answers on each other's faces.

I don't have to speak for him to know the answer to his question, but I let the words flow out, nevertheless.

"Yes. It's very real," I let out, thinking he's going to kiss me right then, but he doesn't.

Maddox solely leans in and places his forehead against mine.

With his eyes closed and his breathing coming out a bit heavy, he stands like that for a long minute.

It's as if he's collecting himself and all I can do is let my hands wander over his body like his are doing to mine.

After a minute, he speaks. "I shouldn't be doing this."

I want to let out a gasp at his statement, but I'm able to keep it in. "Why? Are you married?"

Please, don't let this man be married.

I've done a lot of things in my short life, but I draw the line at sleeping with a married person.

His eyes open and if his hands weren't on my body, I would have fallen at the intensity that was coming out of them.

They're hazel but it is as if it's the ocean staring back at me right before sunset. The blues, the greens and the browns are all coming together to make the perfect combination of Maddox's eyes.

"I'm not married." He states, his mouth dancing around the three words.

"Then why shouldn't you be doing this?" I ask, my hands going up to his hair and sliding their way through his long strands.

"Because I just got out of something where they tell you that you shouldn't jump into anything until at least a year has passed."

I'm guessing he just got out of a long-term relationship. It must have just ended, otherwise he wouldn't be debating being here with me.

"It's just one night," I say, giving his hair a slight tug. "One night and that's it. Tomorrow we can forget about it."

His eyes grow more intense, and his fingertips dig deeper into my skin.

"And if I don't want to forget about it?" he asks, his voice almost a growl.

"Then you don't, and I get to live in your mind for however long you want me there."

Forever, have me there forever.

Heavy words for a one-night stand.

Maddox continues to look down at me as if he's trying to figure me out.

"Are you sure? One night with a complete stranger?"

I want more than one night with this man, but no way am I going to tell him that.

"I'm absolutely, one hundred percent, sure."

The last word barely leaves my lips before they are encapsulated with his.

His mouth is hungry, and I can't help but to fall deeper into his hold and fall in lust with the feeling of his face stubble against my skin.

Our mouths dance together and when I feel his tongue slide against the skin of my lower lip, a whimper escapes.

It might have been from me or him, I don't know. I don't know where he starts, and I end.

We're just kissing, and I already have a feeling that this is going to be an unforgettable night.

"Bed or couch?" Maddox mutters against my lips, not pulling back in the slightest.

As much as I want him to do delicious things to my body right here, my bed would be the better option. Especially given the height difference between us.

I can only be on my tiptoes for so long.

"Bed," I say, moving my mouth off his and gliding it down to his jaw and to his neck.

Maddox's hands move to settle against my hips, and he lifts me up until my legs are wrapped around his waist before he starts walking.

I don't have to tell him where to go. My apartment is so small that you can see the bedroom door from the entryway.

With just a few steps, I hear the creak of my bedroom door opening before feeling the softness of my comforter.

Once we are on my bed, we don't separate. My legs stay around his waist, his hands stay in my hair, against my hip, and our mouths stay fused together as if they have always been one.

"I didn't come up here to sleep with you," Maddox mumbles as his mouth moves off mine and down my neck.

"I know," I say through a pant.

We're just kissing but feeling his weight on me and having his lips on my skin is working me up to the point that I feel like I'm going to combust.

"Maddox." His name is like a moan as I try to pry his face off me.

Instantly, he separates our connection and looks down at me with a tinge of worry.

He thinks something is wrong.

Giving him a seductive smile, I put his worries at ease.

"Please take off my clothes. I need to feel you everywhere."

The smirk I saw back at the coffee shop is back and this time I do what I wanted to do when I first saw it. Kiss it off.

My tongue is just about to swipe along his bottom lip when he pulls away, his smirk now a full-on grin.

"I think you asked for me to undress you," he says, throwing a wink at me.

In one swift move, Maddox is off me, going straight to unbutton my jeans and pulling them off.

Not even a minute passes by when I'm completely naked with a man that I met not even two hours ago staring down at me like I was a slice of chocolate cake.

"So damn gorgeous." Maddox voices, all the while stroking himself through his jeans.

I can see the outline of his shaft through the material.

At the sight, my mouth waters and my legs open involuntarily so he can see what seeing him stroke himself does to me.

What's not involuntary is me leaning up onto my elbows and reaching for Maddox, replacing his hand with mine.

He lets out a groan as I give] him a few heavy-handed strokes and I'm about to lean forward and undress him like he undressed me, when he stops me.

"Not yet," he says, that smirk of his coming back to play.

"What do you mean, not yet? I'm horny as fuck and I need you to fuck me, like right now."

"You'll get what you need. I just need to get something first." He pulls off his shirt as he says the words.

For a few seconds I'm distracted by his glorious upper half that I forget how to speak.

This man is a legit god. I haven't seen a body this good since my college days during my athlete phase, and still Maddox is on a different level than those guys.

"And what exactly do you need? Because my needs seem like top priority at the moment," I say, able to find my voice again.

My hand continues to stroke him through his jeans and with every passing stroke, I feel him getting bigger and harder.

I'll be feeling him for days, that's for sure.

"To give you something to remember me by," Maddox says, seductively, before falling to his knees in front of me causing my hand to fall.

My legs are spread and the look of hunger in his eyes becoming even more intense, I'm sure that my wetness has reached the comforter.

I forget all the words that I want to say seeing him in this position.

And I forget him even more when his hands land on my thighs, opening them even more for him, and seeing his smirk disappear into my pussy.

A moan escapes me at the first lap of his tongue.

Then he does it.

Maddox, the forearm god that walked into my coffee shop a few hours ago, gives me something to remember him by.

With licks, kisses and sweet thrust from his cock all damn night.

When I wake up the next morning, to an empty bed and a note, I realize something. A one-night stand may have ruined me for all future men, and I'm okay with that.

As for his note, well, if I hadn't slept with him last night, I would have this morning.

You will be embedded in my mind for a very long time.
See you next time I'm in San Francisco.
Maddox.

5

MADDOX

I LOOK out the floor to ceiling window of my apartment that has a direct line of sight to the park and let out a sigh.

"Are you sure?" I say into my phone, hoping that the answer is different than it was when I asked the same question five minutes ago.

I hear rustling on the other end and without a word I already know her answer.

"I'm sure, my baby boy. Chicago is home, all my doctors are here, my friends, it wouldn't make sense moving out there."

Never have I wanted to throw a tantrum like I was three years old more in my life than I want to do now.

I need my mom and I want her here with me, no matter how fucking old I may be.

"There are some awesome doctors out here too, I'm sure it wouldn't take very long to find one that could take your case. Especially with Stanford a few towns away."

Hopefully she can hear my desperation in my voice.

"And where would I live, Mad? I can't very well live with my professional athlete of a son. I love you but I don't feel like catering to all the one-night stands you bring home."

Jesus.

Do I tell her that the last one-night stand that I had was over a month ago and before that I don't even remember how long it had been?

"I'd get you your own place. I'm here for the remainder of my contract, so it might be good to buy a house or something."

I wouldn't mind having a house in California, maybe by the beach or a lake or somewhere secluded. No doubt mom would love it.

Only if she would agree.

"You already have a house here, on top of you paying off mine. There's no need for any more houses."

"Their investments, Ma."

"Nope, there's no need to buy a house. At least not right now."

"You mean, you will move here eventually?" I ask, feeling a small smile on my face starting to form.

Maybe my plan of moving my mom here is working.

"Me? No. I mean, when you meet a nice girl and give me a grandkid or two, then you will need a house."

"Ma," I whine. We have this conversation at least a few times a year. "That's not going to happen anytime soon."

"And why the hell not? I may not be here in a few years. I have a right to see my baby happy, married and with a damn family before this horrible disease takes me away!"

It's the crack of her voice as she says that last sentence that makes me hate being in San Francisco.

My whole life, my mom has been the most important aspect of my life right next to baseball

Nora Bauer has been raising me on her own since my father walked out on us when I was not even one. For as long as I can remember, my mom has done everything to give me a good life. Everything included taking on two, sometimes three jobs to be able to pay for any activities that I wanted to do.

Baseball was supposed to be something that I did to keep me occupied and off the Chicago streets that tend to swallow people whole. I ended up loving it the second I learned how to properly throw a ball.

Every year, I would beg my mom to let me play and every year she would give me a smile and say three little words, "Anything for you."

I was good. So good that I was offered a place on a travel team, which spurred the multiple jobs my mom took on. That was something I didn't know about until I was around thirteen.

When I found out, I told my mom I was quitting baseball and that I would pick up a paper run or something. She sat me down that night and told me no. She told me that she saw how much I loved the sport, and I wasn't going to give it up just because she was working a little more. I was going to play and that was that.

That was the day that I decided that not only was I

going to play, but that I was going to play for my mom. I was going to play so that one day I could give her the life that she deserved. The life that she would have had if my dad wasn't an asshole, and walked out.

A comfortable one.

I've been able to do that.

I was able to give my mother, my best friend, the life that she deserves, but only in the material sense.

I'm not able to give her the most comfortable life she needs, not with brain tumors standing in the way.

Thinking of my mom's prognosis is making my hands shake and wanting to reach into my pockets for something that I know isn't there.

A shaky breath in my ear, takes me away from my urges and back to my mother.

"You will see it, ma. When it happens, you will be here to see it. I promise."

I know that it's not a promise that I should be making, but I have to have hope. I have to have faith that this isn't going to be what takes my ma away from me.

"Hopefully you're right," she says, and if we were on FaceTime, I'd be able to see the tears rolling down her cheeks.

Since the mood is already somber, I ask her about her appointment.

"What did the doctor say?"

She had her monthly check up this morning to see if there are any changes with the tumors.

"That's actually why I called you," she says, causing my

stomach to do a few flips. Instantly my mind goes to the worst possible scenario.

She's getting worse. I can just feel it.

"Is everything okay?" I try to keep my voice even but as I ask the question, all my emotions are trying to seep out.

"There was no growth. The tumors haven't grown for the third month in a row."

For the first time in over a year, a wave of relief flows through my body. An organic feeling that I haven't been able to get without the help of a white powder.

"Really?" I ask through the lump in my throat.

This is news that I've been waiting for since that fateful day last year.

"Yes, really. The doctors want to check for a few more months before they want to say anything final, but they are optimistic. I just don't know if I should be too." My mom has always been the hopeful one out of the two of us, and not hearing hope in her voice now, terrifies me.

And she has every right not to have a little faith right now. For over a year, she has been fighting this disease and at first, she was always hopeful. Especially because the doctors found the tumors when there were only at a stage two and had very little possibility of not being cancerous.

But of course, that all faded when the tumor did grow, and Ma went from stage two to stage three. The light that held on to that hope, faded right away when the news came.

I try to collect myself as best as I can before I give her a response.

"I get it, Ma. I do, but you've gotten so far. It's okay to have a little hope in this. I have it."

"Do you, now?" she asks, teasing me a bit, because once again she's the hopeful one in this family, not me.

"I do. You will get out of this, Ma, I know it. You'll get out of this and in a few years, you'll be having dinner with my new wife, who will be pregnant with my kid."

I try my hardest not to let out a groan at the scenario, but anything to please this woman.

"You know, I would be a lot happier if that happened now." I guess I opened that door back up for myself. "Especially now that you're in a new city all by yourself."

"I can take care of myself, Ma."

"Didn't say you couldn't. All I'm saying is that it would be nice to be able to sleep at night knowing that there is someone out there that cares about you and watches out for you if you ever decide to sink down again."

Sink down.

That's what she calls my spiral after finding out her diagnosis. A sinking ship she called it when she found out that I had developed a friendly relationship with the hateful nose candy.

It took me a lot to realize just how much I was hurting her watching me spiral like that, and I vowed when I got out of rehab that I will never put her through that again.

"Not making any promises, but I will see what I can do about finding that person you are requesting," I say, lying straight through my teeth.

Sure, I'll look for someone, but not right now. Right

now, I need to concentrate on getting back to my game and to the level I once was.

"If you find her, I want to meet her right away."

I roll my eyes. "Whatever you say, Ma."

She lets out a laugh knowing I'm full of shit, but not calling me out on it. "Alright my sweet boy. I will let you go so you can get to the game. I just wanted to wish you a good opening day. I know you won't be playing but I'll still be watchin' it."

"Thanks, Ma. I love you. Be optimistic."

"Love you too, baby. I will try. Have a great day and go find that girl."

Maybe if I find a random one, she'll be happy.

—

6

MADDOX

OPENING DAY, a random day at the beginning of April that brings joy to millions of baseball fans every time it comes along

Growing up, opening day was always my favorite. It was like Christmas morning when you'd wake up and run to the tree to open gifts.

It's the start of a new season. A fresh start that has you forgetting about everything that might have gone wrong the previous season. Because on opening day, it doesn't matter what your batting average is or how many shutout innings you pitched, all that matters is that you are ready to play.

Every season since I was called up to the majors, opening day has always made me giddy like a kid at the toy store. Filled with so many possibilities.

This year, this year there is no giddiness, not a single drop.

What is there?

Anxiety. So much fucking anxiety.

Why? I have no idea.

It's not like it's my first day in a new school and I'm terrified of meeting new people. I'm not.

Last month after coming to San Francisco, signing my contract and taking my drug test, which came back clean, I flew straight to Scottsdale to report for spring training. I arrived a week late, but that didn't matter. Every single person I met, whether it had been a teammate or a coach, they all accepted me with open arms. They were glad that I was there.

Everyone being accepting made the nerves I was feeling ease up a little bit. They eased up more when I was able to pitch a spring training game and heard fans cheering for me.

But now as I park in the player designated parking lot, the nerves, the anxiousness is back in full swing.

Maybe because this is a whole different ball game than spring training.

Maybe it's because my mom is missing my first opening day at home.

Maybe because I won't even be able to step foot on the field, or the dugout for that matter for another month.

Maybe it's all of those things.

Whatever it is, it's hitting me hard and making me sweat like crazy as I get out of the car and walk into the park.

It's early, and given that the team photographers are just setting up as I walk through the gate, I'm the first player in.

"Can't wait to see you back on the mound, Maddox," one of the photographers yells out, a smile on his face.

I give him a smile back. "Thank you. Hopefully you won't be disappointed."

"Never, man. Never." He gives me a smile before giving me a nod before getting the picture that he needs and letting me go on my way.

This is only the second time since I signed my contract that I've been here. The place is a lot more complicated to get through than the park back in Chicago. Thankfully there are guides everywhere that are more than happy to show me where to go.

After a good five minutes, I make it to the clubhouse, and the second I step through the double doors, the anxiousness from earlier grows.

I should be ecstatic to be here, but yet I'm not fully there just yet.

Maybe in May.

Walking deeper into the extravagant locker room, I see that I was right earlier, I'm the first player here.

I look around the place, seeing the familiar aspects of a baseball clubhouse and trying to take it all in.

Then I come to the cubbyhole that holds my name over it.

Bauer, thirteen.

It looks strange seeing my name in orange in black when I've spent my professional career seeing it in blue and white.

At least they let me keep my number.

Trying to control my nerves as best I can, I place my

backpack in the cubby and take a seat in the chair in front of it.

I guess this is home for the next couple of years.

Unless you mess up and get traded again.

Not going to happen, I will make sure of that.

For what feels like a very long hour, I sit in the chair, taking in every single inch of my surroundings. I sit there unmoving long enough for someone to walk in.

There's no surprise at all that Ben Kipper is the first from his team to arrive at the clubhouse on opening day.

"Maddox," he says, giving me a nod when he sees me. "I wasn't expecting to see you today."

I don't think anyone was.

When a player gets suspended by the MLB there are a few rules that they have to follow, all depending on the severity of their suspension.

My case is considered a level nine on a ten-point scale. So there are a number of things that I can't do.

With my type of suspension, I was allowed to participate in spring training, even pitch a few games and work out with the team. I'm also allowed to participate in batting practice, but that's where it stops. I'm not allowed to be in the clubhouse, the dugout, the bullpen, anywhere but the stands during the game. I can't even dress out. I can be in the stadium during it, but as a fan and nothing else.

I can't even take part in today's opening day activities.

So why am I here?

Because I needed to be surrounded by baseball so I can make sure my new team knows their investment in me is worth it. And even with the fact that I wasn't even going to wear my new jersey today, I'm still anxious as fuck.

"I wanted to see what opening day is like here," I state, standing up from my seat.

"It's a special one, I'll tell you that," Ben says, closing the distance between us and offering me his hand to shake. "I'm glad you decided to come today."

"Hopefully I feel the same way later on," I say as I shake his hand.

He smirks at my statement, but completely ignores it. "You want to stay for batting practice?"

I nod. "If it's okay with you, I would like to. I know my suspension isn't over yet, but I want to do my part as much as I can."

Ben looks at me questioningly. I know being here and wanting to take part in something so minimal as batting practice is new to him. No doubt that there are guys out there that would take every advantage they can with their suspension and be halfway around the world.

Not me.

I want to play.

I *need* to play.

"Fine by me. I think everyone will be happy to see you here."

"Hopefully you're right," I answer.

I may have spent the better part of the last month with my new teammates, and they seem okay with having me here, but it can all be a farce.

Ben doesn't say anything, he just nods at me to follow him to his office.

Once we're in his office with the door closed, Ben waves for me to take a seat in the chair that's in front of his desk.

At least it's not a foldable chair like I've seen in most visiting clubhouses.

"How is San Francisco treating you so far?" he asks, giving me a smile that I'm sure puts everyone at ease.

"Good, but it's only been a few days. Not long enough to draw a good opinion." That is if I don't talk about a certain dirty blonde barista that has been occupying my mind since I left her bed a little over a month ago.

If I do talk about Jen, then San Francisco is the best place in the world.

"At times, the city can be a very interesting place. Other times, it can be a little dark and gloomy. You just have to be sure that you take in the city in a way that's best for you," Ben says, giving me a nod.

What the actual fuck does that even mean?

"Um, okay?" Is he telling me not to go look for my next hit? "I will make sure to do that."

Ben nods and looks down at something at his desk before looking back up at me, his face more stoic than it was a few seconds ago.

It does"t take much for me to realize that the reason he invited me into his office was to give me a lecture.

Gotta love a grown man getting a lecture from another grown man.

But my actions have me deserving this.

"Whatever you have to say, sir, I can take it," I say,

leaning forward, placing my elbows on my knees, bracing for impact.

"Do you know why you're here, Maddox?" Ben starts, leaning back in his chair, looking me straight in the eye.

"Because my agent advocated for me as a player and the Miners wanted to see if it was true." At least that's what I was told when I came to sign my contract.

Ben gives me a nod. "For the most part, that's what happened, but there's more to it..." He pauses before sitting up and leaning forward on his desk. "I've known that you'd be a great player even before you were drafted. I've been following you since your third year at Notre Dame. You did amazing things in South Bend, and I knew you would do the same when you got called up. I tried to fight for us to draft you, but you being a Chicago boy, I knew that wasn't a possibility. So, when rumors started to flow around about Chicago possibly releasing you early, I fought. I fought for you to be here because this team needs someone like you. We need someone that will put in the work and help us win a title again after ten years. I didn't give a shit about the drugs because I knew from years of watching you that you would never get there on your own. You needed something to make you want to destroy everything you worked so hard for. The team was on the fence when I brought it up to them. They didn't want that type of image to define who the Miners are, but they still decided to take my gut feeling for what it was and agreed to sign you."

If I was younger, my ego would have been inflated knowing that an MLB manager was keeping an eye on me.

I'd be telling everyone I knew that I had caught the eye of someone big.

Now, I just feel honored that this man even looked into me.

"Thank you, for fighting to get me here," I say, eternally grateful that this man did everything possible to have me sitting in his office right now.

Because of my actions, I could be sitting back in my house in Chicago because no team wanted to sign me.

Ben gives me a nod. "There are some stipulations, though. Some that aren't a part of your contract. These stipulations are coming from me and me only."

Well, this is new.

I feel my eyebrows raise in question. "What kind of stipulations?"

If he wants to test my pee every day, I'll do it.

"I know for a fact that the man that I saw all over the news and social media last year, isn't the man that is sitting in front of me right now. I know that, some of the players know it, some of the fans, but not everyone. There are people out there that will not believe that you going to rehab helped. They will think, if they don't already, that you're not worth it. You need to show them that you are. Show them that rehab did help you and that who you were during those months doesn't define you."

Those months don't define you.

He's the first person that has told me that since I left Utah.

"And how do I do that?"

"Show up to games, like you did today. Give them a

small peek into your personal life, your struggles, anything you can on social media and in person. Open up about your mom. Hell, get yourself a girl and show them that you've settled down and that the drugs are behind you."

I can't help but snort a bit at the last statement. "My mom would side with you on the whole finding a girl thing."

"So do it," Ben urges.

I'm already shaking my head. "I can't. One rule of sobriety, no romantic relationships for the first year."

No romantic relationships. No sex.

The no sex rule is not a real rule, but it was one I made for myself. One I broke my first night out.

"Then hire a fake one."

I let out a laugh but when I see his stoic face, it dies down. "You're serious?"

Is hiring someone to be your girlfriend a real thing?

Ben nods. "Whatever helps to show people that you are worthy of being here."

"And you think that getting a fake girlfriend will help with that?"

Another nod. Motherfucker. "I do. People love relationships. They eat that shit up, why not play it a bit? Besides, you just said your mom told you to find a girl, why not make her happy too?"

Never, and I mean never did I think I was going to walk into the park today and get told by my club manager to get a fake girlfriend and lie to basically everyone. Including my mom.

I never would have considered getting into a fake relationship just to please people and make them see me in any kind of light. Like I would give two shits about what people think about me, but my mom wants to see it, and this is my career.

So why am I sitting here, looking at Ben, actually considering this shit?

Because it might actually be a good idea.

Fucking hell.

"From the look on your face, I know you're considering it, but don't decide right now if you're going to go through with it. Look at other things you can do, but in the meantime, go get dressed. We have batting practice."

Ben gets up from his chair but I stay in my seat trying to digest this whole thing.

Yes, there are other things that I can do to convince people that I'm worth having here. A number of them in fact, but this idea, may be the largest steppingstone to get me closer to that.

Ben might have told me not to decide right this minute, but my mind is already made up.

I'm doing it.

But how do I find a fake girlfriend? Especially in a new city. Is there a site for that?

"Or maybe you can find someone to help you with your social media. That would be somewhat better than a fake girlfriend." Ben voices before he leaves the room completely.

Social media.

It's as if a light bulb turned on in my head.

I might know someone who can help me with my social media and be my girlfriend.

My *fake* girlfriend.

I just have to hope that she still works at the coffee shop because I didn't get her number after our one night together.

7

Jennifer

IT'S OFFICIALLY my last day working at the coffee shop.

For years, I've been dreaming about this day and it's finally here. I'm both excited and scared about leaving, but it was time. No way in hell would I have been able to make it another year of coffee making, especially with the coffee Karens I deal with every day.

What made me finally put in my two weeks?

I don't know. The morning after my unforgettable night with Maddox, I got up from bed and dreaded just thinking about how I had to work a few hours later.

Dread was always something I felt when it came to my job, especially in the last few years, but it was never this strong. It was as if the thought of even getting dressed was going to make me cry.

It was crazy, nevertheless I still went to work that day. I thought that feeling was a fluke, but I continued to feel it the next day and the day after that. I felt it for over a week and after finally talking to Selena over dinner one day, and her telling me it wasn't a healthy feeling, I put in my two weeks.

Of course it took me another week to talk to the owner, but hey I did it and now it's my last day.

"Would you come visit when you can?" Annaleigh asks as she hands me a cup for an order she just took.

"Just because I'm leaving doesn't mean you won't see me. I'll be in here so much you won't even believe I'm gone," I say, giving her a smile.

Am I fibbing a little? Maybe. But hey, it might be the truth. I've been working here since I was in college, it's going to feel weird not coming in every other day.

"Do you have a job lined up and everything?" she asks as I lather the inside of the cup with caramel.

I shake my head. "As of right now, no job but I'm working on it."

And by working on it, I mean I am trying to convince Hunter, Selena's boyfriend, that he needs a social media manager in his corner.

What quarterback that just won his first super bowl doesn't need a social media manager?

If I took over his accounts, he would have a whole lot more time to fuck my best friend. I see that as a win.

Jacobi does not apparently because in the two weeks since I started to bug him for the job, he hasn't budged. I've even tried to get Selena to withhold sucking him off to see if that would work, and guess what? It didn't. So now I have to figure out a new tactic to make him see that I'm the perfect person to handle all his socials.

Maybe I'll get the job if I stop calling him Hunty?

I think about it for about a second before I laugh at myself at the ridiculousness of that.

"So, what are you going to do while you find one?" Annaleigh asks, concern coating her voice.

I love her for being concerned about me.

"I have a few freelance gigs lined up, so those should hold me down until at least next month. My plan is to find something more permanent during them, so fingers crossed."

I'm giving Jacobi one more month to hire me, and if he still says no then I will find someone else that would love my social media skills.

"You seem overly calm about this," she states, a small smile on her face.

Do I? Because on the inside I'm freaking out.

What if Hunter doesn't hire me?

What happens then?

Do I give up my apartment and move back to Seaside to live with my parents?

I love living in the city and even though my apartment is the size of a shoebox, it's my sanctuary and I don't want to give it up.

"Because everything will work out," I tell her, trying to give her my best smile.

I sure hope that I'm right because sure as hell don't want to come back here asking for my job again.

The rest of my shift moves slowly but thankfully with not very many customers. I'm guessing it's because it's opening day over at the baseball stadium and everyone in the city has a ticket.

I only know about the game because Selena told me that Hunter had gotten them tickets. She had invited me, but I declined her offer, what with it being my last day in all.

Because of the game though, my boss decided to close the shop early, just in case any of us had tickets to the sporting event. Some of the girls did.

As for me, I'm planning on taking a shower and spending the rest of my day in my bed, watching something random on Netflix.

A nap is definitely on the schedule.

Annaleigh, me and Courtney, the other barista, finish our shifts and go through all the closing duties together and are able to walk out the door five minutes after closing.

"Please don't forget about us," Annaleigh says as she gives me the tightest hug known to man.

She's so little but she gives the biggest hugs ever.

"I'm not moving across the country. I'm just leaving the shop," I remind her, returning the hug.

"We know but it still doesn't mean that we won't miss seeing your face every single shift," Courtney throws out as she replaces Annaleigh with herself.

"You guys will see me, I promise," I say, letting them both go, definitely starting to feel tears form in the back of my eyes.

I didn't think I would cry today, but I'm saying bye to a chapter in my life. That's reason enough to let a few tears spill.

"We better. You're like an older sister that neither of us had," Annaleigh says through a pout.

Given that I'm an only child, I know how they feel.

"I'll come back next week, how about that?" I offer.

Visiting them during store hours is the least I can do and if they are swamped it's not like I can't jump behind the counter and lend a hand.

"We like that idea," Courtney answers.

With one final hug and a few more tears seeping through, we say goodbye and head our separate ways.

I may have hated the coffee smell and dealing with customers, but I will definitely miss working with the girls.

As I make my way to my place, no food to give out this time, I pull out my phone and dial up Selena.

My best friend answers on the fourth ring.

"How did your last day go?" she asks, her voice muffled a bit by background noise. They must be on the Caltrain making their way into the city.

Hunter and Selena live about twenty miles outside of San Francisco, so anytime they come into the city they take the train. It's way better than looking for parking and paying fifty bucks for it.

"Surprisingly not as bad as I thought. I just said bye to the girls and cried while doing it," I answer.

"Well yeah, you were there for years. I would be concerned if you didn't feel sad leaving one last time."

"Yeah, but I definitely won't miss the customers, that's for sure."

Selena lets out a laugh. "I bet. Are you sure you don't

want to come to the game? Jacobi was able to get a box and there's plenty of room."

I snort a bit at hearing her call Hunter, Jacobi. I know how much he dislikes her using that nickname for him.

"I'm sure. There's a pillow calling my name," I state as I turn onto my street.

"Whatever you say."

"While you're in that fancy box, you should convince your fiancé that it would be a great idea for him to hire your best friend." I say a little too loud hoping that Hunter is right next to her and is able to hear my words.

"Not happening." Hunter's voice comes through the line all deep and shit. No wonder Selena fell for him.

"Oh common, Hunty. Why the hell not? You know that I will do an amazing job," I say. Well, more like I whine.

I seriously don't understand why this man won't hire me.

"Look, Jen. As much as I want to hire you, I can't. I already have a digital content manager and I signed a contract with her for another year. If you still want the job when my contract with her is up, you can have it."

I think I'm rendered speechless.

In a year I can be the social media manager for one of the most well-known quarterbacks in the NFL.

Sure, it's in a year, but I'll take it.

"So, you weren't hiring me because I call you Hunty?" I ask.

A growl sounds through the other end and I just know he's infuriated with my use of the name.

He can't blame me. It's not my fault his ex-girlfriend gave him a stupid nickname and Selena told me about it.

"As much as I wish it was, no."

"You know you could have told me this sooner, right? I wasted a lot of groveling these last few weeks. I could have used that for something else."

A laugh sounds in my ear. "But it was fun watching you sweat a little."

"I don't like you."

"Tough shit, your best friend does."

I hear some commotion on the other side and within seconds I'm no longer talking to Hunter but Selena.

"Behave." She says, I'm just not sure if it's to me or her new fiancé.

I'm about to say something childish to her but as I approach my building and look up, I'm at a loss for words.

My mind goes completely blank and all I can concentrate on isn't Selena's words but at the figure standing in front of my building.

No freaking way.

"No freaking way what?" Selena asks, telling me that I said the words out loud.

Not taking my eyes off the figure, the very same one that has noticed me walking up and is now looking me straight in the eye, I end the call with Selena.

"Selena, have fun at the game. I'll see you after, for dinner."

I don't even give her a chance to respond. No, I just hang up and continue to close the distance between me and the forearm god that I thought I was never going to see again.

Yet here he is.

"Hi," I say, a little too shocked to say anything else.

"Hi," Maddox answers, sounding a little shocked himself.

"You made it back to San Francisco," I say, trying to ease the tension between us.

He gives me a nod. "I did."

Maddox doesn't say anything else, so it looks like it's going to be me that has to get the words out of him.

"Did you come back here to get a repeat of your last visit?" I meant for it to come out as a joke but instead it comes out with a bit of a bite.

I'm all for one-night stands, but that's not all I am. If this guy thinks that, then he is barking up the wrong tree.

"Actually, no," he answers, shifting on his feet and reaching up to run a hand nervously through his hair. "I'm actually here for a proposition."

"A proposition?" I ask.

A proposition doesn't sound any better than a booty call.

"Yep. One that I hope benefits us both."

Oh, this should be fun.

8

MADDOX

I HAVE no idea how it's possible, but Jen looks even more beautiful than she did on our fateful night a month ago.

Maybe it's the sunlight shining down on her and making not only her skin glow but also her hair. As I look at her, it's as if she has this golden halo around her and I can't seem to look away.

And if I can't look away or can't stop thinking about how good her ass looks in those jeans, then maybe asking Jen to do this is the wrong idea.

"So, what's this proposition that brought you to my apartment building today?" Jen asks as she crosses her legs, getting more comfortable in the metal chair.

Right, the proposition.

After two hours of batting practice, I made up my mind about the conversation I had with Ben.

I was going to find a fake girlfriend, one that can take care of my social media presence at that, and I knew would be perfect for the job.

Was it a stupid idea asking a woman that I had a one-night stand with, that I knew nothing about, to be my fake girlfriend? Probably.

But she would be a better choice than some stranger off the street that I never talked to.

That's why I decided to leave batting practice and skip out on opening ceremonies and the game, and went to Jen's apartment.

I could have gone to the coffee shop but according to an Instagram post I saw few hours ago, they were closing early. So, I went to her apartment to wait for her outside. I figured it would be a safe bet and I had hoped that she didn't have plans after work.

Thankfully, she got there about forty minutes after I had shown up.

Now we are currently at a pizza place that has an outside patio overlooking some of the high rises San Francisco has to offer.

And Jen's looking at me as if she is trying to figure me out.

Squaring my shoulders, I answer her question.

"Look at it as a job offer more than a proposition," I start, and right away her eyebrows shoot up.

"I'm listening."

Here goes nothing.

"You told me that you went into digital marketing to be able to do something great, does that still stand?"

She nodded. "It does."

"Would that include possibly running social media

accounts for a professional athlete to show people of the impact he is making off the field?"

Now not only are her eyebrows raising but her eyes are going wide, and her back is straight.

"Did you put a wiretap on my phone?"

"What? No." Why the actual fuck would she even ask me that?

"Are you sure?" She looks like she wants to strangle me.

"I'm sure. Why would I do that? *How* would I do that?"

"I don't know, but you're the one that knows that I've been trying to convince an athlete to give me a job as their social media manager."

Now I'm the one that is having their back go straight.

"Seriously?" My mind's going crazy right now. I don't believe in coincidences, but this is too crazy to ignore.

"Yes." Jen nods and by the look of her face she's thinking this is crazy too.

"What athlete?" I ask out of curiosity.

"Hunter Jacobi." she answers.

Damn. "Like quarterback to the San Francisco Gold, Hunter Jacobi?"

"The very one," she says through a sigh.

Double damn, that would have been great for her, but that doesn't matter now.

"I didn't wiretap your phone," I say, getting back to the topic at hand. "The fact that I need a social media manager and you trying to convince another athlete to take you on, is just a huge coincidence."

A trippy one at that.

"Apparently," Jen says, shaking her head a bit before

giving me her full attention. "So, are you an agent or something? Who's this athlete you are trying to hire me for?"

Is she serious?

I had an inclination that she didn't know who I was when we first met, but a lot has happened since then. Like my face being all over the city and the ballpark and every local sports station talking about me and how spring training went.

Hell, I even got a text from Cole a little bit ago about how I was all over the team's Twitter page with my batting practice appearance.

But does she seriously not know?

"I'm the player," I say, a bit of confusion in my tone.

"You're a professional athlete?" she asks, bewildered as if she can't believe it.

"I am. Do you not know who I am?"

Jen shakes her head. "Should I?"

This is new to me. I'm so used to people knowing who I am everywhere I go. Back in Chicago, every time I went to a restaurant, the grocery store or took the train somewhere, I was always stopped for a picture or an autograph.

It's happened a few times here in San Francisco these last few days and I'm sure it will happen more and more when I get back on the mound. Hearing that someone doesn't know me, it's a little mind boggling.

"Not unless you're a baseball fan."

Jen gives me a shrug, her ponytail swinging in the process. "Baseball is more of Selena's thing. I'm more of a football girl."

I don't even know if I should ask who this Selena person is.

I let out a sigh and start from the very beginning.

"I'm Maddox Bauer and I'm a pitcher for the San Francisco Miners. Up until a few months ago, I was playing for Chicago but when I decided to drown my issues in cocaine, I got suspended, let go from my team and now I'm here. Given another chance at my career after spending six weeks in rehab."

A small gasp leaves Jen's pouty mouth when I say the word cocaine all the while her eyes going a bit wider than what they already were.

"Was it just for fun or was it to forget about something? The cocaine," she asks.

"Something happened with my mom, this time last year and I didn't take it well. I wanted to forget the possibility of losing her, so I drowned my pain in the coke, all while she was drowning in the pain of her illness."

I look into Jen's eyes as I speak, and a part of me thought that I would see disgust looking back at me, but no.

This woman isn't looking at me as if she is disgusted by the fact that I decided to hide behind a drug all the while my mom was suffering. No, she's looking at me with empathy, like she understands my struggles and will never judge me for them.

"What finally made you go to rehab?"

I know we're having a serious conversation, but I can't help but actually let out a snort at her question.

"Would you believe me if I told you that a strip club

owner that also happens to be the head of the Mafia back in Chicago was the one that set me straight?"

Jen is silent for a bit, her mouth opening and closing as if she can't find the words to say to my crazy scenario.

"That cannot be true," she says, shaking her head not wanting to believe it.

"It's true. I became a member of his elite club and one day I had a little too much blow while I was there, nearly overdosing, which made one of his dancers call him. I broke down in the middle of a strip club and he offered to help get me clean, so I took him up on it."

Again, she gives me a look that tells me that she thinks I'm talking out of my ass.

After staring at me for a long minute or two with her mouth wide open, she finally speaks.

"Holy shit. You would think that would be all over social media or something."

I give her a shrug. "One good thing about my breakdown happening where it did, is the fact that what happens in there, doesn't make it out. Dante protects his clients."

This information must still be making Jen's mind explode because instead of saying anything else, she takes a piece of pizza and shoves it in her mouth.

I watch her eat the slice as if it were my job to watch her.

Never thought that I would find a woman eating a pizza so damn sexy.

Never thought that I would be about to ask a woman to be my fake girlfriend either, but here I am.

"So," she starts as soon as she's done chewing. Ignoring everything that I just told her. "I'm going to guess that the reason you need a social media manager is because you need to show the world, show your loyal fans that you've rebuilt yourself after rehab. Is that right?"

She's right on the money.

"Right. My skipper thinks that I need to show people that I'm worth being here. To let people see that I'm not the man that I was before I went to rehab."

"Your skipper?"

Right, a football girl. "Sorry. My team manager. You know, the captain of the ship, the skipper."

A blank stare, all I get is a blank stare.

"What I call the team manager is not important," I say, grabbing a slice of pizza.

If you can even call it a piece of pizza, it barely has any crust. Which makes me wonder if I can find Chicago style pizza somewhere in the city.

"How soon will I be able to start?" Jen asks, my thoughts of deep-dish pizza fading away. "That is if I even want the job."

"I would say it whenever you wanted. The sooner the better, but I wouldn't want to mess with your job at the coffee shop." I have to be considerate here.

"Today was actually my last day there. So, I'm as free as a butterfly."

"Why did you quit?"

Now she's the one shrugging. "It was time. I couldn't handle another Karen telling me to remake their coffee eight times."

She gives me a smile as I'm taken back to the day that we met and she talked about the one customer that had her do just that.

"Well, I guess that means that you're open."

A nod for confirmation. "I'm open, but what's in it for you?"

I swallow down the last bit of my slice and look her straight on. "What do you mean?"

I know exactly what she means. I told her back at her building that this was something that would benefit the both of us. As of right now, besides building my image back up, what I'm proposing is only benefiting her.

"I know you want to rebuild your image, but there has to be something else. No way you would seek out a random one-night stand to take care of your socials. There has to be more to it."

This is only the second time that we're meeting, and I swear this beautiful, sexy woman can already see right through me.

My time has come. I have to tell her the real proposition.

Sitting up and squaring my shoulders, I look her right in the eyes and ask her a question I never thought would leave my mouth.

"Will you be my fake girlfriend?"

9

Jennifer

"Excuse ME?!"

I know I asked the question a little loudly, especially when I get a dirty look from the lady a few tables away, but right now loudness is excusable.

Did I hear Maddox correctly? No way I did. The pizza we're eating has mushrooms, maybe they're laced with something and I'm high as a kite right now.

Because no way in hell did this professional baseball player that has seen me naked and has had his mouth on my pussy, asked me to be his fake girlfriend.

Right?

"Will you be my fake girlfriend?" Maddox asks again, a little quieter now that we have some unwanted attention.

I guess I'm not high and I did hear him correctly.

Somehow, I'm able to get out of my stupor and finally find words to give him a response.

"You're a professional athlete, right?" Maybe he's faking being one and that's why he needs a fake girlfriend.

"I am."

"And I'm sure that you had your fair share of women crawling to your feet begging you to be with them, right?"

He looks at me like he is trying to figure out where I'm going with this, eventually giving me a nod.

"That scenario may have happened once or twice in my career."

Of course it has, because this man is sex on a stick and knows how to work a woman's body so damn perfectly. Let's not forget to mention he's hot as fuck and he knows it.

"Okay so essentially you can have any woman you want, why the hell do you need a fake girlfriend? And why me?"

Seriously, why? Out of all the women he probably has access to, why would he choose me? We've met once before, that doesn't make a fake relationship.

Maddox takes a long minute to think about his answer.

Eventually he lets out a sigh and answers me. "You're right, getting a woman to become my girlfriend wouldn't be a hard feat. It would be easy, I guess, but not something I'm allowed to do right now."

"What does that mean?" He's a grown man and he can do anything he wants.

"It means that even though I'm not in rehab anymore there are certain rules that I need to follow to stay sober. One of those rules is to stay out of a relationship for at least 6 months to a year. And no sex."

My eyes are wide. "No sex?" I ask, trying to remember how long it's been since I saw him. Definitely hasn't been

85

six weeks, let alone six months. "When did you get out of rehab?"

Maddox cringes a bit. "The day I walked into the coffee shop last month."

"So you broke the 'no sex' rule within twenty-four hours?"

He nods. "Yup."

I almost want to apologize for that night. Hell, I even remember him saying that we shouldn't have been doing what we were. But we're both adults here, we both made that decision.

It's not like I have a hypnotizing pussy and coerced him into it.

Trying to take my mind away from our one night together, I move the conversation back to the topic at hand.

"But that still doesn't answer the question as to why you need a fake girlfriend?"

Does it matter why he needs one? It's not like I will actually consider it.

Will I?

"There are two reasons," he starts, pausing a bit before he continues. "One of them being the same reason I need someone to run my social media, to show people that I'm worth playing in San Francisco. To show my team and its fans that I'm not a man defined by my drug use. According to Ben, my skipper, people like the fact when someone is in a relationship."

Makes sense, I guess. As much as the bachelor athlete garners attention, the athlete in a committed relationship is what keeps it there. Fans will concentrate more on the individual's athletic ability than their relationship status if they know he's taken.

"Okay, and the second reason?" I ask.

I swear if he says so we can repeat our night together whenever we want, I will get the remainder of the pizza and slap it across his face.

"My mom," he says and the second he does, all the pizza slaps go out the window.

"Your mom wants you to get a fake girlfriend?" I ask, trying to lighten up the mood a bit.

I know it's the wrong thing to do because his facial expression shifts. It was light a bit ago, but now it's as if he was hit by a dump truck.

"No, she wants me to get a real one," he says before pausing for a beat and then continuing. "She wants to see me with someone and have the whole package. The marriage. The kids. The house, all of it."

"So give it to her. I'm sure in a few years you will have all that." Without a doubt he would have that.

"She may not be here in a few years," he says, and I know he quickly regrets letting the words out.

"What do you mean?"

Maddox sits up in the metal chair that is a little too small for his body and gives me a look of defeat.

"What I'm about to tell you, isn't me trying to play any sort of game with you. It is the honest truth. This isn't something that I would take lightly. Ever."

His voice is deeper, more determined, holds more pain and I try to not get up from my own seat and go to him. All so that I can comfort him.

"Okay," I tell him. Giving him a curt nod for him to continue.

"My troubles with cocaine started when doctors told me that my mom had tumors in her brain. I took it a little hard and I took it even harder when the tumor started to grow, and she went from a stage two to a stage three. It was as if I was going through the mourning stages for someone that was still alive. I spiraled into the deepest hole imaginable. The doctors very recently told her that the tumors haven't grown in three months, and they are waiting to see if they stay that way. I was talking to her earlier today and for the first time in my life, I heard all hope in her disappear. The doctors may be optimistic, but she is not. She almost broke down when she told me that she wanted to see me happy and with a wife and kids before that is taken away from her."

The pain has really come out and coated his voice now. I can hear it with every single word that he says just how much his mom's sickness is affecting him.

"That's horrible," I say, because what else do I say? 'I'm sorry' don't seem like strong enough words.

He nods. "It is and I hate it. That's why I want to do this. To make her happy. All the rebranding shit can take a back seat for all I care. Nora Bauer wants to see her baby boy happy, and I want to give her that. Especially if the doctors end up being wrong and she really won't be here in a few years. My mind isn't in a good headspace to get into a real relationship. Not with me just leaving rehab, with her sickness and having to concentrate on being the baseball player my team is paying me to be. If I have to pretend for her, then I will. I just need someone to help me pretend and I think you would be perfect."

I want to say yes. I want to tell him that yes, I will be his pretend girlfriend just so that his mom will be happy. I want to, I really do, but I know that I have to think about it before I say anything concrete.

"So, you will hire me to run your social media and in return I just have to pretend to be your girlfriend?"

A small smile forms on his face. "I will pay you for running my socials, but yes, that's the gist of it. Like I said, it's something that benefits both of us."

I get the job that I wanted, and he gets to see his mom happy.

"Why me, though?" I ask.

I'm sure there are a plethora of women and the baseball stadium right now that would be willing to be Maddox's fake anything.

"Because you're the only woman I know in the city?" he states, making it sound like a question and when I just raise an eyebrow at him, he adds to the comment. "We may have only been together for one night, but there was a real connection happening between us. I would rather do this with someone that I have a connection with than with a complete stranger."

He's right there was a real connection between us, there still is.

A connection that I hoped to find with someone else because a part of me knew that I wasn't going to see Maddox again.

Yet, here he is sitting across from me, wanting me to be his fake girlfriend.

"Can I think about it for a few days?" My mind feels like it's about to explode and if I'm going to make a decision, I need to do it when he's not around.

Maddox nods. "Of course. Take all the time you need. I'll be in town for the rest of the month since I can't travel with the team. If you make up your mind. Just text me."

I nod, sliding my phone over to him so that he could put his number in.

It takes all of one minute for us to exchange numbers and get up from our seats, the pizza we shared nothing but crumbs.

"I'll text you or call you if I have an answer," I say as we make our way to the street.

"Yeah, of course," he says, a tight smile on his face.

Once we make it out of the restaurant and onto the street, there is nothing more we can do but look at each other awkwardly. So, with tight smiles and small waves we go our separate ways.

Instead of getting an Uber or Lyft back to my place, I decide to walk and think about this whole thing.

The job that I was urging Hunter to give me was just handed to me. I didn't think that I would have to be a professional athlete's fake girlfriend to get it.

But is that how I want to go about making a name for myself as a professional? Getting a job because I slept with a guy once and now he needs someone to play pretend with?

You were trying to get a job through your best friend's fiancé.

Fuck, I was. Me asking Hunter and Maddox offering it to me is not that much different.

But am I even capable of being a fake girlfriend?

I barely know how to be a real one, how am I supposed to know what to do a fake one?

Maybe I should shadow Selena and learn how to be a girlfriend from her.

Maybe I should call Selena and see what she thinks about all of this.

Without thinking, I take out my phone and start to pull up her contact when I see the time.

The game is still going on and knowing how big of a Miner fan she is, she won't pay attention to a word that I would say.

I could call my mom, but she will just hear girlfriend and freak out and start planning a dinner to get to know my new man.

God, it's times like these that I wish I had siblings.

Pocketing my phone, I continue my walk and my contemplation.

Taking away all the fake relationships stuff out of the equation, the job is a great opportunity. I'd be able to get the experience I want and find out the inner workings of having a high-profile client. Maybe I can even travel with the team and get another client or two.

What's holding me back, I think, is the whole relationship thing.

Can I do it?

Can I play pretend with someone I don't even know?

Can I play pretend and keep my feelings out of it?

I've never had trouble keeping feelings out of things but that night with Maddox, felt different. I don't know what it was, but I know it's not something I've experienced before.

And if we do this, if I pretend to be his fake girlfriend and I develop feelings, what happens then?

I don't know.

If I do this, if I agree to be Maddox's fake girlfriend, there needs to be some ground rules. Some very strict ground rules.

Don't think about it, just do it. What harm can it do?

Fuck it.

I pull out my phone again and text my new contact.

JEN: Okay, I'll do it, but we need rules.

MADDOX

"I THOUGHT you said you played for the Miners." Jen's voice comes through all the chatter of the park.

"I do."

"Then why are you sitting up here in this fancy box instead of being down in the dugout?" she asks, waving one of her garlic fries all over the place.

I should have gotten some of those.

After getting the text message from Jen a week ago where she told me that she will pretend to be my fake girlfriend, we decided it would be best to set ground rules in person.

She suggested her place, I suggested a baseball game. My suggestion obviously won.

Jen looked at me like I was crazy. But given that I jumped her bones the last time we were in her apartment, I thought it would be better to have this conversation in a somewhat public setting.

Do I still want to jump her bones? Absolutely, especially since she is wearing shorts that are currently rolled up her thighs and a white tank top that makes it hard not to look at her chest.

If we had gone to her apartment, she would be without a doubt naked the second I walked in.

This is safer. Somewhat.

As to why I suggested a baseball game, it all boiled down to the fact that I wanted to see the game.

Baseball has been a huge part of my life that not being in a stadium while there's a game currently going feels wrong.

It's also a public enough place that someone might see us together and start talking about who I may be seeing. It also gives me a better control of people hearing our conversation especially being in the suite, something that can't be done at a restaurant or a coffee shop for example.

After taking a bite from my huge ass corndog, I answer her question. "Because I'm suspended."

"Didn't you just sign with the team?" she says, dipping a fry in ketchup. Who eats garlic fries with ketchup?

"I did."

"And didn't the season just start?"

"It did."

"Then how are you already suspended?"

I look over at her but she's paying more attention to her fries than she is to me or the game. I'm making it my mission to make this girl a baseball fan by the end of the season.

"You didn't look me up, did you?" I ask. After we agreed

to meet at the park, I told her that she should look me up so that she knows what she is getting herself into.

Jen shrugs, finally meeting my gaze. "I figured if I were to learn about you, I'd rather you tell me than Google."

I think I like this girl more and more.

"I've been suspended since August because of a dirty drug test. Ninety games in total since it was my second offense. The suspension rolls over no matter what team I'm on."

Her eyes get a slight bit of concern in them. "Second offense? You've failed more than one drug test before?"

I've told her about eighty percent of what I've been through, will she still want to do this when I tell her everything else?

With a nod, I tell her. "My mom's diagnosis came in April, and it didn't take long for me to spiral. A couple of days tops and being a professional athlete in your hometown opens doors so it wasn't hard for me to get my hands on drugs. Failed my first test in June, got suspended for ten games. I was told not to do it again, and I didn't listen. Then in August I had another test, and of course that one came back dirty, so I got a fine and 90 games."

Jen looks as if she is taking everything in and really thinking about her words before saying anything.

"What happens if you test positive again?"

I won't, I want to say. I want to tell her that I will never touch another drug in my life, that I will never fail another drug test. But what if something happens that pushes me over the edge?

A drug addict is always a drug addict, right?

"Full season suspension, no spring training or post season and a major fine on top of it. If it happens a fourth time, well, it's bye-bye baseball. A fourth time is a complete MLB ban."

Getting a lifetime ban in this game is a rare feat but it has happened. From what I can remember the most recent one came about six years ago with a player in New York.

Jen goes quiet and after a few seconds of watching me, she turns back to giving her full attention to her fries before moving to the game.

As she watches the game, though, I take a few seconds to watch her. I take in every single inch of her profile as if she were an art piece I'm seeing for the first time.

Her hair is in a high ponytail, with small pieces of hair falling from it, framing her face perfectly. Her eyelashes are long and her nose is peppered with freckles that you can only see if you get a good look at her.

She may be wearing a simple white tank and shorts, but she looks like she's in her element. Like she belongs here. Belongs in a baseball stadium, eating garlic fries, cheering on her favorite team, her favorite player.

Cheering me on.

"Was it only cocaine that was your kryptonite?" Jen asks, moving my concentration away from her profile and thoughts of possibilities.

"Does it matter?"

She shrugs, not looking up at me. "If we're going to do this, I need to know what might trigger a relapse. I take edibles every now and then, so I need to know if that has to stop too."

She's looking out for me. She's willing to stop something that she does in her own time, because of me.

"It started with marijuana, then opioids. Quickly moved to ecstasy and then finally ended with cocaine. It's the one that made me forget the most."

I get a nod from her, and she goes back to watching the game.

At this moment in time, it doesn't seem like we're getting anywhere. So instead of waiting for her to ask a question, I ask one of my own.

"How often is 'every now and then'?" Is it a vice that she has? Something she does when she feels anxious? Nervous? Scared? Just because?

Jen turns, giving me an easy smile not only with her lips but also her brown eyes.

"Maybe once a month, if that. Usually when I'm over thinking something or just bored, not something I use to get by. Which is why I will be throwing away whatever stash I have when I get home. If you're drug free, so am I."

"Thank you," I say, because what else do I say?

She's giving up something just because I asked her to be in my life for a short period of time and because of my history. Saying thanks seems inadequate but that's all I can come up with.

"You're welcome," another smile, except this time it's warm and caring. "So should we start setting these ground rules we desperately need?"

Right, the very reason why we're here.

"What kind of rules do you have in mind?"

I don't know what it entails to have a fake girlfriend,

hell or even a real one at that, how would I know what rules are needed?

Jen turns in her chair and faces me straight on. "Well, no PDA unless there are people around, for one. We don't need our lines to be blurred."

"So, no repeat of the night we had last month?" I'm joking, mostly.

Would I love to repeat that night with her, right this second? Fuck, yes. I'm dying to get between those thighs again, especially seeing her in those shorts.

My comment earns me a smack on the arm. "As much as I want to, no. No repeat of that night. That would blur lines beyond repair."

She does have a point.

"Okay, so PDA where there are people around and no repeat. Anything else?"

"We only tell the people that really need to know. We can't have people spilling our secrets to the world." She says, her head shaking in the process.

Another good point.

"I'm only planning on telling Ben, my manager, since this was his idea. He might help spread the word about our new 'relationship.'"

He had asked me a few days ago how it was going with the whole rebuilding my brand for the people and I almost told him, but I wanted to run it by Jen first. So, I kept it minimal.

"That's fine. I was thinking about telling Selena, my best friend. No way would I be able to keep this from her. That girl may be quiet, but she is perceptive as hell when it comes to me, and she will call me out."

"That's fine by me." Who am I to get in between a girl and her best friend? "Another rule is you have to come to as many games as you can, both home and away."

This makes her eyebrows shoot up in confusion.

"You want me to travel with you?" she asks, surprised.

I nod. "It will make things more believable. Besides, you're also taking care of my socials, you need to travel with me to get content to post."

Her traveling with me was a fleeting thought that I had a few days ago. It made sense at the time, but now that I brought it up and seeing the look on her face, it might be a bad idea.

"Will I get my own room?" she asks, her voice getting a little high.

I shake my head. "I can't have my girlfriend sleeping in a separate room as me."

Actually, I can but that would just raise more questions.

Jen narrows her eyes at me, as if she is trying to see if I'm playing a joke on her.

She must see that I'm not because eventually she lets out a sigh.

"Fine, but I need my own bed."

"Deal."

Something happens on the field and we both turn to see that one of my new teammates just hit a triple, causing the players that were on first and second to score. Bringing the Miners to a three point lead.

"We also have to actually go on dates, do random things. We just can't be seen together at a game or when I have an event. We have to make this as real as possible," I say to her once all the commotion from the field has died down.

"I doubt people will care if they see you at the grocery store with a girl," she says through a snort.

I'm about to prove her wrong. "Pull out your phone."

"What?"

"Pull out your phone, I want to show you something."

With a roll of her eyes, she does what I say. "What now?"

I give her a smirk. "Open up Instagram and look up my name."

My hunch may be total bullshit but my gut is telling me that I'm right about this.

Jen once again does what she is told and when I see her type in my name in the search bar and hit enter, my smirk grows even more when the first picture pops up.

A picture of the two of us as we sit at this very game.

A small gasp leaves her mouth. "The game started not even two hours ago. How did someone already get a picture of us?"

"People are always on the lookout for something. Add in a suspended player to the mix that was slated to be the best of the best, cameras will always be ready."

I don't tell her that I had seen a few fans point their phones over to our box in the fourth inning. Which is how I knew there was going to be a picture of us online already.

"So I guess we can add dates to the list of rules then,"

Jen says, disgruntled as she closes out the app before looking at her phone and putting it away again.

"Don't sound too excited about it," I tease.

"I just didn't think that people would be all in our business so quickly," she states.

If I wasn't who I was, they wouldn't be. But I am and they are, and I can't fault her for wanting out because of it.

"You can still say no to this, you know? If you aren't comfortable with having your picture out there, you can walk. No hard feelings on my side."

Please don't walk.

Jen shakes her head. "No, we're doing this. It will just take some getting used to. Hopefully controlling your accounts will help with what we put out there."

I nod. "Do what you have to."

Another hit rings out through the park that takes our attention away from the topic at hand. This time a fly ball into right field closing out the inning.

"How long will we do this for?" Jen asks as the teams switch positions.

That's a question that I hadn't really thought about. I should have but two questions always stopped me from coming up with an end date.

How long does it take for someone to rebuild their brand?

And if I tell my mom that I'm seeing someone, what will she say after we end it?

Instead of thinking it through, I say the first thing that comes to mind. "Until the end of the season."

That should be enough time, right?

I'll ride out the rest of my suspension and then I have a few months to show people that I'm worth having here.

And it may be just enough time for my mom to see me happy.

Jen gives me a nod, agreeing. "Are we both okay with these rules, then?"

I nod. "I am, are you?"

A nod in return. "There may be a few added as we go along, but for now I'm okay with what we have."

"Should we shake on it then?" I hold out my hand to her and instead of taking it right away, she hesitates.

For a long minute, I'm thinking she's going to back away from all of this and leave me to find someone else to be my fake girlfriend.

But eventually, she takes my hand and seals our deal.

"Don't make me regret this, Bauer."

I'm going to try really hard not to.

11

Jennifer

THIS MAY BE the craziest thing that I have ever done, but hey at least I'm getting paid, right?

Right. It's a job and that's how I'm going to look at it because if I look at it any other way, I may not survive. If one night with Maddox possibly ruined me for other individuals, what would being in a relationship with him do?

So, a job. This is a job and I'm going to look at it that way until the season is over and we both move on with our lives.

And that's just how I explained it to Selena just a few minutes ago, which is why she is looking at me like I have two heads.

"A fly is going to get in your mouth if you keep it open like that," I say to her, taking a bite of the eggs she prepared for our breakfast this morning.

Once a month, Selena and I get together and spend a day together. Even though we live within twenty miles of each other, we don't see each other much with work, her going to grad school and whatever her and Hunter have planned.

We talk all the time, but once a month we make it our mission to actually see each other.

It just so happens that our monthly date came only a few days after me and Maddox set our ground rules.

I had to tell Selena, but I didn't think this would be her reaction.

Wanting to get her out of her confused trance, I lean forward and close her mouth for her, earning me a hand slap when she finally comes back to earth.

"I'm trying to digest what you just told me," she says, taking a drink from her coffee. "So you're going to be working with a professional athlete as his content manager and as his fake girlfriend?"

I nod. "Yup, that's about it."

"And does being his fake girlfriend mean you have to sleep with the man?" she asks.

Her question causes me to choke on my food and go into a coughing fit.

"No. I'm definitely not sleeping with him again." I'm able to get out through the coughs.

"Again?" she asks.

Right, I never told her about my night with the lovely forearm god.

Might as well tell her now.

"Do you remember a little over a month ago, I said I was coming over and I texted and canceled later that night?"

"You ditched me for a professional athlete?"

"Hey to be fair, you ditch me for one all the time. Can you blame a girl? Those forearms are something else and his tongue, magical."

Thinking about how his tongue felt against me that night and everything I felt when he slid into me, makes me want to rethink the whole not wanting to sleep with Maddox again.

Maybe it would be good for the two of us.

That is if feelings aren't involved.

"I can't believe this is the first I'm hearing about this," Selena lets out, a little shocked.

Honestly, I am too. I tell Selena everything, and I would have told her about this when it first happened but for some reason I didn't.

Maybe I wanted to keep what happened between Maddox and me that night for myself.

"First time hearing what?" A male voice sounds through the dining room, telling me that Hunter is officially infiltrating our girls' day.

"That Jennifer here, slept with a professional athlete that she is now working for."

I roll my eyes and stick out my tongue at her.

"What professional athlete?" Hunter asks, looking over his shoulder at me as he pours himself a cup of coffee.

I shrug. "Some baseball player from the Miners. Maddox Bauer."

My coughing fit from earlier has nothing on the one that Selena is currently experiencing as I say Maddox's name. I hand her a napkin to clean up the coffee that she spit out, but she just slaps my hand away.

"You slept with Maddox Bauer?!" she exclaims as if she's never met someone famous before.

"You've heard of him?" I ask.

Up until a few weeks ago, I didn't even know who this guy was. Given my best friend's reaction and the amount of pictures going around Instagram of the two of us at the game, the guy is a bigger deal than I thought.

Hunter lets out a snort as he takes a seat at the table. "Know him? She almost ruptured my eardrum when she found out that he was traded to San Francisco."

Selena throws a napkin at her fiancé. "It wasn't that loud and you're fine. You'd be excited too if you got a future Hall of Famer on your team."

"Lennie, baby, I am a future Hall of Famer. That's the only thing you should care about." He throws a wink at Selena, and I can tell she isn't impressed.

Frankly, neither am I. "Hunty, let's not get corny right now."

Hunter narrows his eyes at me when I call him Hunty. I just throw a shrug at him.

"Back to the topic at hand," Selena says. "Do you really think it's a good idea to work with someone that you already slept with?"

I don't even have to think about it. No, it's not a good idea, especially if I'm going to pretend to be his fake girlfriend, but I'm not going to tell her that.

"It's a good job, Sel. One that I've wanted for a long time. I can help him build his image back up and show people who he really is outside of baseball. It would be good exposure. Yes, I slept with the man and it might have been a great night, but I can forget about it and get the job done."

I will never be able to forget about it and I don't want Maddox to forget about it either, but things have to be done to get what we both want.

"Is it even possible to forget when you will be reminded every time you have to put on the fake girlfriend mask on?"

That's the question of the year, isn't it?

"Fake girlfriend?" Hunter asks, looking between me and Selena.

Selena doesn't take her eyes off me as she answers him. "Jen not only is working with Maddox, she is also pretending to be his girlfriend until the end of the season."

"Seriously?" Hunter asks, a bit dumbfounded.

I give him a nod. "He asked and I told him I would do it, but apart from what we show the public, nothing is going to happen between us."

"Are you sure about that?" Selena throws out.

"Yes, I'm sure. We've set rules. We will follow them and when the end of the season comes, we will go our separate ways. Hey, we might even be friends."

By the looks on Selena's and Hunter's faces, they both think that I'm full of bullshit.

And maybe I am, but I think this can really work. Maddox and I can fool the public and come out of this with our feelings unattached.

I just have to stop thinking about our night together and ignore this undeniable draw that we have toward each other, and we will be golden.

"You really think that both of you are capable of keeping your feelings out of this?" Selena asks.

I'm nodding before she is even able to finish the question. "I do."

I look at my best friend, the one that has been in my life since we were kids and continue to be friends now that we're adults. She looks hesitant about this, and she has every right to feel that way, but she has to trust me on this. Everything will work out.

"It's just going to be for a couple months, Sel. I promise you that that isn't enough time for cold hearted me to start developing feelings for the man. It will be fine."

"Hopefully you're right."

Yeah, hopefully.

12

Jennifer

AFTER SPENDING the day watching movies and eating junk food on Selena's and Hunter's couch, I decided to go home and sleep for a solid eight hours.

When I woke up the next morning, I woke up with a text from Maddox asking me to be ready by eleven.

I didn't even have to ask, I already knew that it was going to be one of two things. My first official day as his content manager or one of our 'dates'.

Given that it was a Tuesday, I was aiming for the former so I dressed in a professional manner. But as soon as I opened my front door to let Maddox in, I knew I was clearly overdressed.

"Why are you wearing slacks and a button down?" he asks, one of his dark eyebrows raising in question.

I look down and notice that he's dressed in sweatpants, a white T-shirt and a baseball hat, looking like he's about to head to the gym. All the while I look like I'm about to head to my job at the library.

"I didn't know what we were doing. So given I'm your new content manager, I thought professional would be a good choice."

Maddox lets out a throaty laugh that makes my insides swim a bit.

"Just because you work for me doesn't mean you need to dress like a school principal, you can be comfortable."

"Oh, well, you didn't say that in your text."

"No, I didn't. I thought it was implied. Go change if you want, we have time to spare," he says, coming into my apartment and closing the door behind him as if he's done it a million times before.

"Time to spare for what?" I ask, not moving.

"You'll see. Go change."

I do what he says and fifteen minutes later, and three outfit changes under my belt, we take an Uber down to the piers.

"Are we going to Alcatraz?" I ask, spotting the sign as soon as we get out of the car.

"As much as I would like to, not today, but that's definitely something we need to do before the season is over," he says, taking my hand and guiding me down the sidewalk.

I try really hard not to over think the fact that my hand is in his. We're in public, of course he's going to hold my hand.

"Then where are we going?" I ask, matching my strides with his.

"You'll see." He throws a wink at me and continues to guide me down the path.

By the time we reach Pier 39 and I see where he's guiding us, I instantly know where we're going.

"The aquarium?" I ask as we approach the ticket booth.

"Sort of," he says, throwing me a wink before talking to the person behind the glass in the booth. "I have tickets under Bauer. For the special event."

You can have special events at the aquarium?

I guess so because the employee nods at Maddox and hands him a piece of paper before telling him where to go.

With a thank you, Maddox grabs my hand and follows the guy's direction. Within minutes we are inside, making our way through the aquarium.

Growing up where I did, a little over two hours from San Francisco, I would go to the aquarium all the time. It was one of my favorite places to go to when I was a kid and even as a teenager. It was an escape of sorts for me.

When I moved here, I came to this very aquarium a few times, but it never felt the same way it did when I was home, so I stopped coming.

In the handful of times that I've talked to Maddox, I never mentioned anything about the aquarium. So, him bringing us here is making me scratch my head.

I'm about to ask him why we're here and where we're going when we stop at one of the exhibits that is filled with people.

From the looks of it, this must be the special event Maddox mentioned and given the amount of Miners' logos there are displayed, it's a team event.

"Is this a Miners' event?" I ask, when a group of kids run past us, yelling about seeing jellyfish.

Maddox nods. "A low-key charity event to help raise money for one of the exhibits. It gets put on by one of the outfielder's wife. He told me about it yesterday, and I thought it would be cool to stop by."

That explains why he's wearing a team hat.

"And here I thought you did some digging on me," I say, not thinking about the words that are coming out as I take in all the different tanks around me.

"What do you mean?" he asks, pulling my attention back to him.

"The aquarium is one of my safe places. Especially the one back home," I tell him and the smile that he gives me is one I have to return.

"Really?"

"Yes, really. Not only is this a good content opportunity but also a good 'date'," I say with air quotes around the word. Given that we're in public and I'm already feeling eyes on me, I lean up on my tiptoes and place a small kiss on his cheek. "Thank you for bringing me."

Maddox is a little surprised by the small kiss, but he is able to compose himself a bit when someone calls out his name.

"Maddox, glad you can make it." A set of big muscular arms comes into view and for a solid minute all I can do is stare at them.

"Aaron, thank you for the invite. This is a cool thing your wife is doing here," Maddox says, greeting muscle arms.

"Yeah, it's a real passion of hers. I'm just glad that the team can help in some way." Aaron pauses and I'm so enthralled with his arms that I don't notice that his attention moves over to me until he speaks again. "And who's this?"

I'm finally able to look up at his face and give him a warm smile before holding out my hand.

"I'm Jen. It's nice to meet you."

Muscle man shakes my hand. "It's nice to meet you, Jen. I'm Aaron, this bastard's teammate."

"Yeah, Maddox said that you were the one that told him about this. I'm happy that we were able to come and help out. The aquarium is one of my favorite places."

As I talk, I can't help but to hear just how put together I sound. Is that how a girlfriend is supposed to sound? Am I laying it on too thick?

"Well, I'm glad that Maddox was able to bring you along. I didn't know he knew someone here in the city outside of the team." I don't miss the smirk that Aaron throws in Maddox's direction. One that says that he knows who I might be to his teammate.

Maddox throws him a smirk back before dropping my hand and wrapping his arm around my shoulders.

"We met last month when I came to sign my contract, and we kind of reconnected a few weeks ago."

It's not a lie at least.

"That's great," Aaron says, and he's about to say something else, before a woman, who I assume is his wife, calls him over. "Looks like I'm needed. I'll catch up with you guys later."

After Aaron leaves us, Maddox drops his arm from my shoulders. A sadness rolls through me when he does that but the second he takes my hand in his again, the sadness disappears.

With my hand in his, we walk around the exhibit, looking into all the tanks and even stopping to interact with a few more players and their wives and some kids.

It's when Maddox is with the kids and listening to them tell him all about their favorite animals, that I take out my phone and take pictures.

I take pictures of Maddox with the kids as they point to something in the tanks. I take pictures of him with his teammates as they talk about something mundane. I take pictures as he talks to some of the aquarium employees and learns more about what they are raising money for.

The more and more pictures I take, the more I come to know who Maddox is. He's a caring person that is passionate about learning new things and helping in any way that he can. As I take the pictures, he's not just standing there waiting for me to take pictures, he's actually listening to what the person he's talking to is saying. He's not looking for the camera, he's just being himself.

That's the side of him that he wants to show people and now that I've gotten a glimpse of it, I want people to see it too. I want people to really see him for who he is, and not for who he was last year.

Toward the end of the event, a little boy comes over to me and Maddox as we stand by one of the octopus' tanks. The little boy asks Maddox if he can help him find an octopus because he's been trying to find one all day but can't seem to.

Maddox, with a big smile on his face, says yes to the boy and lifts him up so that they can look for one together.

Seeing this, makes me take out my phone again, but this time not because I need it to post on Maddox's Instagram. No, this time it's for me because right now my ovaries are exploding at the sight and I'm not the only one.

A few of the women around the exhibit stop and watch the two boys search for the octopus.

After five minutes of looking, the mission is accomplished, and an octopus is found.

The smile on both the little boy's face and Maddox is one that is contagious.

When we leave the event, I can't help but walk out with a huge smile on my face. One that I know Maddox notices and can't help but smile back at.

"What's with the huge smile?" he asks as we step out of the aquarium and out to the San Francisco breeze.

"Just really happy you invited me today. It was an awesome event, and I got some great pictures of you to post. But the icing on the cake was definitely the search for the octopus."

Maddox lets out a laugh. "Was it now? Was it because I was acting like a kid?"

We walk toward the edge of the pier where the sea lions are and I notice that he has yet to drop my hand.

"Yes, actually. You let your guard down with that little boy. You weren't a baseball player. You were just a regular guy having fun," I say, giving him another smile.

Maddox just looks at me. He was probably waiting for me to give him a basic answer instead of the one I gave.

"I'm happy I invited you today, too," he says after collecting himself.

"So what now?" I ask, not really wanting our day together to end.

"Now, we get something to eat and I try to convince you to go to Sacramento with me."

"Sacramento? Why?" I ask, a bit confused.

"My suspension is up in a few weeks. To get ready, I'm getting sent down to San Jose for a few days and then Sacramento for however long it takes for the team to call me up."

That explanation doesn't help with the confusion. "Called up?"

Maddox nods. "Right now, the team has a full roster. I will be playing in Sacramento until they need a new player even if my suspension is over. Either because someone got hurt or because they are moving someone down."

"So you don't know when exactly you will be playing for San Francisco?"

He shakes his head, not looking as defeated as I expected him to be. "No, it's all up to the front office, but I don't care. As long as I get to play."

By the sound of his voice and the expression on his face, this is a good thing.

So I give him a smile. "Then feed me, because I really want to see you try to convince me to head to Sacramento. San Jose, I can do. Sacramento may take some work."

He smiles all the while shaking his head. "Okay, let's go feed you, then."

I'm sure if he wanted to, he would have made that statement a lot dirtier than intended, but he doesn't.

Later that night after eating and Maddox trying to convince me to go to Sacramento, I go through all the pictures I took of the day.

I sift through them until I find the perfect ones to post.

The world is about to see Maddox Bauer in a different light that they weren't expecting.

My light and hopefully they can use it to see that he is very much worth rooting for.

13

MAY 7, 2022

MADDOX

THE STADIUM IS PACKED with fans, which is what I expected to happen since it's a Saturday night, but I didn't expect it to be this packed.

Every seat in the stadium is sold out and taken by a body, waiting patiently for the game to begin.

Waiting for the starting pitcher to come out and show them what he's got.

The starting pitcher tonight. Me.

I'm pitching tonight and every single person in this stadium, in the stands, is here to see me.

At the start of last season, that statement right there would have made my head three times bigger. My ego would have inflated to the point of almost explosion knowing that a whole stadium was here to see me pitch.

Now I'm nowhere near that.

I had a fear of being traded, but now I have a fear of messing up and messing up big. Because if this outing doesn't go well, I won't be seeing the mound in San Francisco anytime soon.

I was able to pitch in San Jose but it was only a few late innings but never a full game. Same thing goes for here in Sacramento. My first week here, I pitched in a few games but only an inning or two. That changed two days ago, though, when the Sacramento manager came up to me and said I was starting on Saturday.

Was I expecting it? A little. I knew I was going to have to pitch a few games so that the front office in San Francisco could take note. I just didn't think that it would be this soon.

Two days a few years ago would have been enough to get me going and get my head in the right place. Now my head feels all jumbled up and it's a minor league game.

What will happen when I pitch in the majors again? What will my head feel like then?

The worst part of all of this, my support system isn't here. My mom isn't here because it was so last minute and she didn't want to fly, which I understand. But Jen isn't here either, and for some reason knowing that she would be in the stands would have been somewhat relaxing.

After the aquarium, I tried my hardest to convince her to come to Sacramento with me. Mostly for appearances and so people could question who I had in the stands. Partly because a part of me really wanted her there. Why? I have no idea.

For the most part, she agreed.

She went to all of the San Jose games but she has yet to come to one in Sacramento. It doesn't bother me that she hasn't, mostly because she is visiting her parents a few hours away.

Not having her here today though is hitting me hard and I don't know why. It's not like she has seen me play outside of these past two weeks.

It has to be my first full game that I'm pitching in nine months that has me all over the place.

I look at the clock above my locker and see that I only have a few more minutes before I have to head to the field.

Cranking up the volume on my headphones, I try to lose myself in the music. I concentrate on every single note and word that is said and forget about every little thing that I'm about to do.

I forget about the game.

I forget about the sport.

Everything that is messing with my mind, I try to silence it and just concentrate on the task at hand.

Getting in the zone.

It works. I get so lost in the music that I don't realize that it's time to head to the field until the pitching coach comes and taps me on the shoulder.

With a nod, I grab my glove and throw my phone and headphones into my bag and follow him out of the clubhouse and into the dugout.

Even with it being May, the wind has a bit of heat to it, nothing like the wind back in Chicago or San Francisco for that matter.

I get a few pats on the back when I walk through the dugout and place my stuff down. I can already feel the crowd and I know that as soon as I get on the field, I'll be able to feel it more.

"Think you're ready to throw a whole game?" one if the infielders, whose last name is Brown, asks.

By the smirk on his face, he's trying to taunt me.

For the few days that I've been here, I've come to know that Brown's only mission is to get called up. He doesn't care much about his teammates, as long as he looks good, that's all that matters. From what I heard, he was almost called up last year, but the team went with another infielder.

I try to ignore him as best as I can, especially tonight, but I play nice.

"I'm ready," I tell him.

And it's not a lie, I feel ready.

"Are you sure? You look a little green, but don't worry, I have your back out there." With a smirk on his face, he gives me a salute and walks away.

I watch his retreating figure and vow that I will pitch a game where I won't need him to have my back.

The pre-game ceremony starts and after the first pitch is thrown and the national anthem is sung, it's time for the players to be called onto the field.

With me at the helm of it all.

"Tonight's starting pitcher, Maddox Bauer!"

The second that my name is called, and I step foot on the grass, the stadium roars with cheers and boos of ten thousand people.

Some are here to see me succeed, others are here to see me fail. Much like I have to Brown, I vow to throw a game that will have those here to see me fail change their mind.

I take a few practice throws and the ball glides out of my hand just like I want it to. It hits the catcher's glove where I want it to.

It might actually be a good night, but a few practice pitches don't make a game.

The cheers and the booing from the stands quiet down a few minutes before the game starts.

As I throw a few more practice pitches, I take in my surroundings, take in the fans since it's not something that you can do at bigger stadiums.

A few kids see me looking around, so they throw me a wave and they smile when I throw them one back.

A benefit of playing in a field this size is more fan interaction.

I look around for a few more seconds, sending a few more waves and nods toward a few more kids. I'm about to get back in the pitching head space when a sign captures my attention.

#13 I drove 3 hours to see you play! Better not suck!

NORMALLY THOSE TYPES of signs would piss me off, but when I see who's holding it, instead of getting pissed, a smile spreads across my face.

Her blonde hair is in a ponytail and mostly covered by

a Miners baseball hat, but I can still see it's her.

Jen.

She's here to watch me pitch a full game.

The second her eyes meet mine, it's as if all the nerves disappear.

She sends me a wave and bright smile just before the umpire calls the start of the game.

As I take my position on the mound and take one last look into the stands, I have a feeling deep in my gut that it's going to be a good game.

All because of a blonde with a beautiful smile.

———

Jennifer

"WHAT DO THE K'S MEAN?" I ask sometime in the fourth inning.

At least I think it's the fourth inning if I'm reading the scoreboard correctly.

"What?" Selena asks, her attention shifting from the game to me.

I point to the Ks next to Maddox's picture on the score-board. "Those Ks, what do they mean?"

Selena looks over like she doesn't know what I'm talking about. "Oh, they're the number of strikeouts he's thrown in the game."

"Why are some of them backward?"

"It means that the batter didn't swing at the last strike," she answers before narrowing her eyes at me. "How do you not know this already?"

"Because you're the baseball fan out of the two of us?" I say, taking a bite of my hot dog. I would kill for some garlic fries right about now.

"Yes, but I've dragged you to enough games for you to know at least the basics."

"True, but you know that I only went to those games for the food and to fawn over the baseball pants," I say with a shrug, taking another bite of my food.

"And what is your motive for coming to games now?" I don't even have to turn to face her to know that she has a smirk on her face.

"We made a deal. I would come to his games," I tell her, finishing up my food.

"So because you made a deal with each other, you abruptly decided to drive three hours from Seaside to here and drag me along?"

My decision to come to the game *was* spontaneous.

After I had quit the coffee shop, I made plans to go visit my parents this weekend since it's Mother's Day tomorrow and all. The plan was to drive down Thursday and head back to San Francisco on Monday. I had even told Maddox this and he was okay with it.

But for some reason, as I was sitting in my parents' living room earlier today, I felt the need to look up Maddox.

I told myself that I wanted to check if people were

liking the picture of Maddox at a charity event last week or even falling for our supposed relationship, especially since I had gone to most of his games in San Jose.

Instead of finding pictures of me at the games or seeing them talk about the charity event, I only saw posts talking about how Maddox was about to pitch his first full game in months.

There were so many comments on every single post I saw. Some were nasty, and a handful were encouraging.

Something about the mean comments didn't sit right with me and all I kept thinking about was what if Maddox read them before the game.

Would that cause him to relapse?

I didn't know.

So I texted Selena because I knew she was also in town, and an hour later we were on the road. It's going to be a short trip since we both have plans tomorrow but hey, we're here.

"Yes, because we made a deal," I say to her before giving her the whole truth. "Also, because I saw a few nasty comments online about him, okay? I wanted to be here just in case he read them."

My eyes find Maddox on the pitcher's mound just in time for him to throw his next pitch and when the umpire calls an out, I can't help but to cheer.

Another K added to the scoreboard.

"You care about him," Selena says when the next batter comes up. One more out to end the inning.

Hey, I'm learning.

"I've only known the guy for two months," I say defensively like it's the craziest thing in the world to care about someone after only two months.

"So? It took me and Hunter less than a semester to grow feelings for each other. You can care about someone after a few weeks."

I can go about this in two ways. One, agree with her and admit that I do in fact care about the man. Or two, I can deny it some more. I have a feeling if I go with option two, Selena will see right through me.

So, I give her the truth.

"Okay, fine. Yes, I care about the man, but only because he's my boss."

"He's also your boyfriend," Selena says in a loud voice.

It takes me a second to realize why she did, and when a few girls in front of us turn, looking at me through narrowed eyes, I know they heard her. Given the sign I was holding earlier, there is no doubt that they know who Selena is talking about.

Selena gives me a smirk because we both know that her comment will cause them to talk, and that's exactly what we want for Maddox.

For the rest of the game, Selena and I cheer for the Sacramento team every chance we get, and when Maddox adds another three Ks to the scoreboard, we're the loudest.

I might have even thrown in a few "That's my man" exclamations out there just to let everyone know that Maddox is taken. Twitter will no doubt be filled with posts about Maddox Bauer having a girl at one of his games.

Maybe I should post one myself.

The idea makes me pull out my phone during the last

inning and make Selena take a picture of me with my sign as my back faces the field.

I make sure that Maddox can be seen in the background and to tag him and post it right there and there. Of course, I had to add a cheeky caption that will for sure make people talk.

When the game ends, Selena and I wait in our seats until Maddox comes back onto the field dressed in street clothes. We make eye contact, and he gives me a bright smile before he waves us over.

Since there are still people in the stands, I decide, against my better judgment, to run to him as soon as the groundskeeper lets me onto the field.

Also, against my better judgment, I jump into his arms and kiss him as if I'm a starving woman.

Our first real kiss as a "couple".

My lips mold to his as does my body, and every inch of me lights up when he opens his mouth and lets me in. I light up even more when he drops his bag and wraps both arms around me, bringing me closer to him.

I don't know how long we kiss for in the middle of the field, it could have been an hour for all I care, but when we pull apart, I want more. I want so much more of this man.

It's fake, you can't have more.

It's at that thought that I'm detaching myself from him and letting my feet fall back to the ground.

"Hi," I say, sounding way more breathless than I intended to sound.

Maddox gives my ponytail a small tug. "I wasn't expecting you to be here."

"I know, it was a last-minute decision. One that has us driving back tonight."

Maddox nods. "Either way, I'm glad you came."

I can't help but smile at him. "I'm happy I came too. That game was amazing," I say, wanting to kiss him one more time, but I don't. Instead, I changed the subject. "I hope you don't mind, but I posted a selfie of me and it had you in the background. If you want to repost it or something."

He gives me another nod. "I will do that."

After staring at each other for a good minute, we put some space between us, and I introduce him to Selena.

My best friend tries her hardest not to freak out that she's meeting one of her favorite players, but I can see right through her.

Once introductions are done, Maddox walks us out of the field and to the parking lot. Once we get to Selena's car we talk for a good minute before we say goodbye.

A goodbye that includes another kiss. It might not have been like the one back on the field but it's still one that makes me want more.

An hour into our drive back to Seaside, a notification pops up on my phone.

Maddox Bauer has reposted my post onto his story.

The caption...

My girl cheering me on.

I guess I'm officially Maddox Bauer's girl.

His fake girl but the world doesn't know that.

14

SAN FRANCISCO MINERS ROSTER MOVES

MAY 16, 2022

LEFT-HANDED Pitcher Wesley Jones placed on the sixty-day injured list.

RIGHT-HANDED PITCHER MADDOX BAUER called up from Triple-A Sacramento.

15

MADDOX

No way in hell will I be sleeping tonight.

This morning, I was in Sacramento getting ready to head to the field for an early afternoon game. Now I'm back in my apartment in San Francisco as an official part of the San Francisco Miners.

I was buttoning up my jersey when the Sacramento skipper called me into his office and told me I was being called up. I guess one of the starting pitchers got placed on the sixty-day disabled list with an elbow injury and the team chose me to call up as his replacement.

I thought that it would have taken a lot longer than it did to get called up. I had only pitched two whole games in Sacramento, I was sure that wasn't enough.

But I guess it was.

After he told me, I went back to my locker, got redressed in my street clothes and gathered my things. As I was getting ready to leave, a few of the guys patted me on the back and congratulated me on being called up.

Almost everyone.

All but one.

Brown.

He gave me a snarl as I walked out of the clubhouse.

I wanted to tell him to fuck off, but I didn't. Instead, I just acted like an asshole and shot him a wink before walking out of there.

Sacramento was good to me, but I hope that I never make it back in that capacity.

After leaving the park, I sat in my rental for a good five minutes trying to wrap my head around the whole thing.

My suspension was officially over. Ninety games have come and gone and now I get to play in the majors once more.

Last year at this time, I had just started to let my demons control me. I was standing in the brightest place imaginable and let my demons encase it with darkness until I could no longer see. I was starting to spiral, and I thought that nothing was able to touch me.

Yet it did. Those demons destroyed me and now a year later, I was about to scratch the surface of who I was once.

It was a lot to take in, but eventually I was settled and started to make the one and half hour trek back to San Francisco.

On any normal day, I would have gone straight to the park and joined the team for a game, but since it was one of the rare Mondays off, I went to my apartment.

I spent the rest of the afternoon, talking to Cole and Ben and coordinating everything for tomorrow. Now it's close to midnight and instead of finding sleep, I'm pacing the length of my living room.

Tomorrow is my official day back in the majors and I feel like I'm going to puke.

There is no guarantee that I will even see the mound tomorrow, but the nerves are at an all-time high.

So, what do I do to calm my nerves?

I call my mom.

Call me a mama's boy all you want, a twenty-eight-year-old man still needs his mom every now and then.

The time doesn't register in my brain until she answers the phone with sleep in her voice.

"Maddox, why the hell are you calling me so damn late?" she says through the phone, and I cringe a little.

"Sorry, I didn't mean to wake you. I didn't think. My nerves are just messing with my head a little, thought it would be nice to hear your voice."

"You use that line on all the girls that you're trying to get with?"

"Ma! No. I just figured I'd call since I haven't talked to you in a few days."

Jesus. I guess having a young mom means that she takes shots at me every chance she gets.

"A few days? Maddox, I talked to you yesterday."

I mean yeah, I did talk to her yesterday.

"That call was justified. I was calling to see what the doctor said."

Mom had her latest checkup a few days ago, so I called to see what they told her.

Another month of no growth. Doctors are optimistic

that if she continues, they can get her into surgery and remove the tumors.

She sounded a lot happier than she did after her appointment last month, so hopefully that means that she is gaining her faith back that it will all work out.

My mom lets out a sigh. "That is true," she says, before taking a pause and coming back sounding a lot more awake. "So, tell me what's going on. Why are you pacing in the middle of the night, overthinking things?"

How the fuck did she know I was pacing?

I guess it's true what they say that a mother knows her child best.

I stop the pacing and throw myself on the couch before answering her.

"What if my games in Sacramento were just a fluke? What if I'm not mentally ready to get back on the mound at this level?"

Nora doesn't even pause to take in my words. She goes right for it.

"Maybe they were. Maybe they were a fluke, and you will never pitch like that again. Maybe your mind isn't ready to be on a mound pitching to players that have home run records that beat Babe Ruth's and have more Silver Sluggers awards than you will ever get. Maybe you being nervous is your mind's way of telling you not to go out there and to just go back to Sacramento where you can pitch like a champ. You have all these maybes, Maddox, but what if those maybes are wrong? You don't know if it was a fluke or if you really aren't mentally ready. You won't know until you get out there and throw the damn ball."

This is why I called the woman. I needed someone to whoop me out of my headspace and get myself out of all the maybes and what ifs.

"You sure know how to give a motivational speech at two in the morning," I say to her, letting her words sink in.

Ma lets out a yawn before she answers. "Yeah, well, when your almost thirty-year-old son calls you so late, you have to pull out all the stops to get him out of his head and lets you go back to sleep."

"Well I appreciate you whipping my mind into shape."

"Uh-huh, and I would appreciate it if you told me about that girl I've been seeing with you all over social media." She says and I can't tell if she is mad that I have yet to tell her about Jen or happy about the whole thing.

Ever since I reposted the picture of Jen at the Sacramento game and someone took a picture of us kissing on the field, the pictures have made their rounds. So much so, that even some of the major sport sites have been posted then. People are talking about me and Jen and wanting to know more and it's only been a week.

I knew my mom was going to see them at some point since she keeps up with everything that has to do with me. I just was expecting her to call me out a whole lot sooner than right now.

I let out a sigh. "Her name is Jen and it's relatively new, I guess. I was going to tell you if and when we crossed the line to official."

The lies roll off better than expected. I knew I was going to be able to lie to the Miners and to the fans, but my mom had me nervous. Hopefully she doesn't see right through me.

"From the pictures I've seen of her, she looks like a sweet girl. I have one question though," she states.

I nod even if she can't see. "What question?"

"Does she make you smile?"

Her question should have stumped me. It should have made me think about how to answer it, but instead I just blurt out the answer.

"Yes, she does."

It's not a lie. Out of what I just told my mom about what is going on with me and Jen, that is not a lie. Jen does make me smile and it's in the best fucking way, there's no denying that.

Every time she comes to mind, a smile forms and it's been happening more and more ever since my first Sacramento game.

Maybe it was knowing that she had made the trip just to see me play.

Maybe it was the kiss that happened on the field or the one in the parking lot.

I don't know, but something in me shifted and given our current situation, that shift is a very, very bad thing.

"I can hear it in your voice," my mom says, getting me out of the Jen bubble I am. "I can't wait to meet her."

"When we head to Chicago this summer, maybe I'll bring her along so you can."

"I can't wait," she says through a yawn.

I've taken enough of my mom's time. "Go to sleep, Ma. I'll talk to you in a few days."

"Good night, my baby boy. I love you. I'll be watching tomorrow hoping to catch a glimpse."

I smile a bit. "Okay. I love you too. Good night, Ma."

Ending the call, I feel a bit better about what tomorrow might bring, but I'm still a little wired.

I pick up my phone again from where I just placed it a few seconds ago and start scrolling through social media.

In the three weeks or so since Jen took over my accounts, I've been getting an influx of notifications. New followers, likes, mentions, everything has grown. Definitely not how it was this time last year when I was losing followers and getting hate messages every hour.

To think all it took was her posting a picture of me and a kid at a charity event for people to start seeing me in a different light.

Since then, she's posted a few pictures and videos of me pitching these last couple of weeks and those have kept people interested. But the one thing that people want more of, is pictures of her.

I guess Ben was right, people love seeing others in relationships and me posting a picture of Jen drove them crazy.

As I scroll through the videos and pictures on my screen, my mind never leaves Jen.

And much like when I was talking to my mom, a smile forms on my face at the thought of her.

Fuck, I may actually have feelings for this girl and probably in deeper than I thought.

But apparently, I don't give a shit how deep I am and

where my feelings lay, because as I continue to think about her, I decide to call her.

It's late and I'm about to hang up the phone after the fourth ring when she picks up.

"Hello?" Her voice comes through sounding a bit confused.

"Everything okay?" I say instead of a greeting.

"Um, yeah. Why?"

"You sound confused."

She's silent for a few seconds, finally responding after I had checked if the call was dropped.

"Sorry, um, I'm just surprised. We never talk on the phone. Or communicate so late."

"True," I say, trying to compose myself a bit. Maybe calling her was a bad idea. "I would have texted, but my head is a little wired at the moment," I say, telling her the same thing I told my mom.

"Are *you* okay?" she asks, and by the small squeaks in the background, she must be in bed already.

Like I did with my mom, I tell her the truth.

"I'm slightly freaking out about being called up," I admit.

"Why? It's not like you haven't been here before. Weren't you in this very position at the start of your career?"

My ears perk up a bit at her statement. I have yet to tell her that.

"You looked me up."

"What? No, I didn't."

"Yeah, you did, because I haven't told you anything

about the start of my career," I tease. We've touched a few things, but definitely not that.

"Nope, I definitely didn't look you up." Without a doubt, she is shaking her head and rolling her eyes at me.

"What school did I go to?"

"Notre Dame," she says all too quickly which causes her to let out a groan when I let out a laugh. "Okay, fine, I looked you up. But only because I needed to know all about my so-called fake boyfriend, okay?"

"You could have asked, and I would have told you."

"Yeah, well I was bored, and the internet was my best friend. So, bite me."

Gladly.

Fuck, control yourself, Bauer.

"You can be a pain in the ass, you know that right?" I deflect, trying to get my mind away from biting any inch of her.

"Yeah whatever, Skippy. Do you want me to help you to get you out of your head or not?"

"Skippy?" I ask through a snort.

"You said that your team manager is Skipper, wouldn't that make you Skippy?" She asks, a hint of teasing in her voice.

"No, it wouldn't."

"But don't all baseball players have nicknames?"

I shrug even though she can't see me. "Back in Chicago, I was called Kid, since I was twenty-two when I got called up. I haven't spent enough time with the guys here to warrant a nickname."

"Hmm, I think I like Skippy more than I like Kid. It's

definitely better than me calling you Mady or Doxy," Jen muses.

"Please never call me Doxy."

Jen lets out a laugh that is like a sweet tune in my ear. "I'm going to take a wild guess that you were called that a lot as a kid."

"All through junior high. Someone looked it up one day and found out what the word was slang for, and it became nonstop for three years."

"Wait, it's slang for something?" I bet if she was in front of me right now, her face would be in a full-on grin. "Let me look it up."

I let out a groan. "Please don't."

My plea is too late because the sound of her typing comes through and when she lets out a small gasp I know she's found it.

"Oh my god! Why are kids so mean? You were called floozy for three years?"

I pinch the bridge of my nose trying not to relive those memories. "Yup."

"When did it end?" Jen asks, shuffling something in the background. As if she sat up and the covers that surrounded her body moved.

"When I entered high school. I had bulked up that summer because of baseball, so they got scared I was going to hit them or something."

"Ah, poor baby. Who are they so I can go kick their asses?"

I let out a booming laugh. "I'll make a list and when we

go to Chicago later this summer, you can come along, and we'll hunt them down."

"You got yourself a deal. I can be very scary, you know?"

Another laugh escapes me. "I have no doubt about that."

We both laugh for a good minute before we quiet down and the only thing that is audible is our breathing coming together through the phone.

I look out the window and take in what I can see of the city, wishing that Jen was next to me and not a few miles away.

"Hey, Maddox?" Jen breaks the silence, her voice low and soft.

"Yeah?"

"Are you still freaking out about being called up?" she asks, and it takes me a second to understand her question.

Then it hits.

I had told her at the beginning of this call that I was freaking out. That I was still wired.

But now, a few minutes of joking around with her and bantering back and forth, I feel relaxed.

More relaxed than what I felt talking to my mom.

Heading to the field tomorrow will just be like any other day.

A small smile forms on my lips. "No, I guess I'm not."

"Good because the way I see it, you deserve to be on that field."

"Thanks, b..." I stop myself before the whole word makes it out.

I almost called her baby. All because at this moment, this all feels real. But it's not.

Nothing between us is real. Except maybe friendship.

"Thank you," I say, composing myself.

"You're welcome," she answers as if she didn't hear my slip up. "I'll see you tomorrow?"

I nod. "Yeah, I might not play though, but I'll still leave the tickets for you and Selena at the box office."

"You'll play. Good night, Maddox."

"Good night, Jennifer."

The call ends and it has me wishing there could be more between us, but there can't.

This is going to be a long season and not because of baseball.

Jennifer

"C'MON, Ump! Your zone is all over the place. That was a ball, and you know it!" Selena yells out, causing me to jump a bit.

I can't help but laugh a little before looking over at Hunter.

"Bet she doesn't get that worked up during one of your games, huh, Hunty?"

Hunter looks over at me with narrowed eyes. As much as he wants to, he won't call me out on it, because he knows I'm right.

In the years since they've been together, Selena has become a football fan to an extent. Mostly only being one when Hunter is on the field. She definitely cares a lot more about the sport than she did before they got together, but it's definitely not her favorite.

Her currently yelling at the umpire from our box seats informs everyone which sport is her number one.

"Maybe not, but she definitely gets work up after the game," he says, throwing me a wink at his innuendo.

"Gross." I gag a little bit.

I love these two, but I rather not hear about Hunter possibly having a magical dick. Thank God Selena hasn't talked about it either.

Someone who does have a magical dick just happens to be Maddox. If we weren't in this arrangement and he wasn't focusing on baseball and his recovery, maybe I'd be able to experience it again.

With thoughts of Maddox, my eyes instantly move down to find him in the dugout.

My eyes have been on him the majority of the game. Even with his hat on, sunglasses and dressed like everyone else, I was still able to distinguish him from the crowd.

From what I can see, he looks relaxed and in his element. He looks like this is where he belongs and if you asked me, he looks really good in cream with accents of orange and black.

Then again, I never saw him in Chicago colors.

I watch him for a little bit longer. I don't pay attention to anything happening on the field or in the stadium but instead, I watch him.

Even if he looks so small from where I stand, I watch him.

And I continue to watch when someone comes over and taps him on the shoulder and talks to him. After a minute, everything that I saw in Maddox a few seconds ago is gone.

Now he looks like he's gone into game mode and waiting for battle.

Maddox goes over to the dugout bench and when he picks something up, it takes me a second to put together that it's his glove. Then he leaves the dugout all together.

What is he doing?

"He's going to warm up," Selena says, answering my question.

I must have asked my question out loud.

"Warming up? You mean he's going in?" I ask excitedly, looking back to the field and seeing Maddox walk over to the bullpen.

"From the looks of things, he might," Hunter voices, before taking a drink of his beer.

I jump up excitedly.

I know he told me that he didn't think that he was going to play today. He told me last night and then again when I texted him to have a good game earlier today, but I had faith. I had faith that he be put in and at least pitch once.

Now it's happening.

Looking over at the scoreboard, I see we're at the bottom of the seventh inning with the Miners leading by one point. Meaning that he has two innings to possibly pitch.

And look at me knowing baseball stuff without Selena. By the end of the season, I'm going to be a pro.

The seventh inning ends and the eighth begins. Never in my life have I ever been so excited for an inning to start.

Why? Because Maddox is currently making his way to the mound.

"Oh my god, he's really going to pitch," I say, my voice low and filled with emotion as I see him take his place on the field.

Seeing him there, ready for anything, is affecting me in a way I never thought possible. I've known this man for two months, two months, and now I want to cry because he is going to pitch in a major league game.

A part of me wishes that his mom was here to watch him in person because I know that she would be proud of him. If she were standing next to me instead of being in Chicago, she would most definitely be proud that her son overcame his demos that came with her sickness and is back on the field. Back at this level.

Without a doubt she's probably watching back home with a smile on her.

I know there's a smile on my face.

The batter steps into the batter's box and I can't help but feel nervous.

Because the Miners are leading by one, the whole stadium is up on their feet, waiting with anticipation to see where the game goes.

I'm right there with them.

There are some people in the stands here today that think Maddox shouldn't have been called up.

That he doesn't deserve to play after two positive tests.

I heard it as we were walking to our seats earlier. I saw it in all the comments online yesterday when news broke that Maddox was called up.

Fans don't believe in him.

But right here, right now, I do. I believe in him; he just has to believe in himself.

First pitch gets thrown and I block out all noise and just listen to the TV in the suite and the announcers calling out the call.

A ball.

The ball gets thrown back to Maddox. He takes a second before he steps up once more to throw the next pitch.

Maddox whines up and lets the ball go and all you hear is the moment it hits the catcher's mitt.

Ball two the announcers call out.

It's okay, he can still get this batter out, no problem.

At least that's what I keep telling myself as I watch Maddox get ready to throw the third pitch.

My eyes close the second that the ball releases from his hand and they stay closed as I hear it hit the leather.

"Swing and a miss. One and two," the announcer calls out, but my eyes stay closed.

"That was a beautiful curveball," the second announcer voices and I would agree with him if I had seen it.

"It was. That curveball has become one of his staple pitches."

I continue to listen, still not opening my eyes and seeing what is happening on field. Instead, I let the announcers paint the picture.

"Here comes the wind up. Strike two."

"Bauer looks good in Miners colors. Definitely a change from the white and blue."

"There are just some guys that really know how to pull off the uniform, and he's one of them."

Oh my god, stop talking and just say what is happening on the field.

"And here's the pitch." There's a pause in the talking and if I was sitting, I would be at the edge of my seat. "Got him. That's the first strikeout for Maddox Bauer as a Miner."

My eyes fly open just as the clapping from the stands starts. He struck out the batter.

I look down at Maddox, wishing I can yell something at him but knowing that he won't hear me from up here.

The next batter is up and with four pitches, he's out just like his teammate before him.

When the third batter steps into the box, I don't look out at the field but at the TV screen and watch his concentration as he is getting ready to throw the ball.

He's in his element.

He's where he belongs.

And by the small smile on his lips and the concentration in his eyes, he knows it.

I watch him through the screen as he throws the first pitch. Every one of his movements is like a dance that you wouldn't think a man of his size could be capable of.

Strike one.

He's fluid and calculating with every one of his moves, and honestly, I'm a little turned on at the moment.

Now I know why Selena may be getting all worked up after one of Hunter's games.

Maddox throws another pitch, this time the batter making contact. The ball goes soaring into the air and I'm holding my breath watching it come down.

The breath doesn't leave my lungs until it falls into an infielder's glove.

He did it. Maddox got three batters out.

There's not much of a reaction from Maddox that is shown on the screen, everything about him is cool and collected. Just another day at the office type of way.

I have a feeling though while on the outside he's collected, on the inside, he isn't able to control his excitement.

The rest of the inning has the Miners scoring two more times, giving them a bigger lead.

When the start of the ninth inning comes along, my nerves start to get the best of me when I don't see Maddox walking to the mound. A new pitcher taking his place.

Selena calms me down when she explains that this new pitcher is the team's closer. I guess because of the Miner's lead, they thought it was best to have him close out the game instead of leaving Maddox in.

I guess it makes sense, but I'm still slightly disappointed by it.

When the game ends, the three of us make our way down to the field, where some of the players are interacting with fans while others are doing interviews.

Maddox just so happens to be one of the players being interviewed.

As we walk down the stairs, Hunter getting stopped a few times by fans, and we make it to the point where the field and the stands meet, my eyes never leave Maddox.

From the way he looks as he talks to the reporter, he looks happy, which is a good sign.

Between questions, Maddox looks up and meets my gaze, giving me a small smile and a wink before turning back to the reporter.

Something that catches the reporter's attention because she turns back and looks at me as Maddox answers her question.

The stink eye she throws in my direction is definitely not going unnoticed either.

Once Maddox finishes up the interview, he says his thank yous to the reporter and makes it over to where me and Selena are standing.

Hunter is still getting hounded by fans. Maybe bringing him down here while there were still people in the stadium was a bad idea.

As my fake boyfriend closes the distance between us, I notice that the reporter is conspicuously taking a phone call while keeping her eyes on Maddox.

She's watching his every move.

Might as well as give her something else to watch.

"How was the game?" Maddox asks when he's a few inches away from the wall.

Instead of answering, I reach my fingers through the netting, grabbing a small piece of his jersey and pulling him in until my lips meet his through the net.

There's not much you can do with rope digging into

your skin, but it's enough for the people left in the stadium to figure out that Maddox Bauer is taken.

Maybe until the end of the season but still taken, thank you very much.

"The game was great; I just wish that you were able to pitch more," I tell him as I pull away from him, giving him a smile.

"I'll get there, baby," he says, throwing me another wink.

I can't help but wonder if he called me baby because it slipped out or because we're in public. Either way, I'm not going to call him out on it.

"I know you will."

"I'll meet you guys outside? Then you can tell me how in the fuck you know Hunter Jacobi."

I shrug. "There's nothing to tell. This one,"—I nod toward Selena—"shares a bed with the man. But yeah, we'll meet you outside."

With a nod, Maddox leans in for another kiss before he makes his ways back into the dugout and disappears completely.

"If you ask me, there's nothing fake about the two of you," Selena says in a soft voice, only for me and her to hear.

It definitely hasn't felt fake in the last twenty-four hours.

MADDOX

I SCROLL through all the pictures in the file. I scroll until I find one that stands out to me.

It's a picture of me and Jen from two days ago after a game against San Diego. The picture was taken from the seats as we stand at the net. Her back is to the camera, her face isn't visible but anyone that has been keeping a close eye these last seven weeks will know it's her.

She's in cut off shorts and wearing my jersey number on her back and a Miner hat on her head. If the camera was on her face, everyone would see the bright smile she wore as an accessory.

We had just won, and I had pitched four full innings that night. So, we were doing what we've been doing after every single home game that I had pitched in for the past month.

Meeting at the net and kissing.

The picture may be mostly of Jen's back, but you can

see the smile on my face as I lean into her and going through our routine.

Except, it doesn't feel like just a routine to me.

"This one," I say, handing over the phone to Jen as we sit on my couch discussing my social media strategy for the next month.

"Are you sure?" she asks, raising an eyebrow at me.

I nod. "Why not? You said so yourself that I have to show people something other than baseball."

"But this still has baseball in it."

"Just post the damn picture, woman."

She gives me a smirk but gives me a nod, doing as I say.

"Okay, I think that might actually work. Gives a good mixture of work and personal," she says, sitting up from where she lays to show me my Instagram feed.

In the last few weeks, my posts have grown in numbers. Before Jen I may have had maybe one hundred pictures, now it's still not a huge amount but still significant for people to notice.

Which is why my following count on the platform has grown by thousands. I don't care, but Jen says it's a good push in the right direction.

"I just see pictures, but if you say it's good, then I agree."

She kicks my thigh with one of her feet. "It's more than just pictures. It's what the pictures say that people find captivating."

"I guess." I give her a shrug.

Jen just rolls her eyes and goes back to doing something on my phone.

"Okay, so I think we have everything set for next month. On days you pitch, we will post a game or action picture and in between will be personal," she says, giving me a smile. "Oh, and I saw on the Miners event calendar that the team is hosting an event to raise money for the school district for summer lunches for the kids. It's after this long stretch of away games you have. I think it would be perfect."

I nod. "Yeah, I already signed up for that. It's for a good cause so I figured why not give a few hours."

"Am I your plus one?" she asks, giving me a smirk.

"For the rest of the season, you will be." I don't know how I meant for the words to come out, but they sounded harsh, and Jen definitely caught it.

If my life wasn't where it currently is, three months out of rehab for drug use, trying to get back my baseball career to what it once was and worrying that tomorrow might be my mom's last day, I would make her my plus one for longer.

But it isn't.

And it sucks so fucking much and at times like right now, I hate it.

It's what it is, so I change the subject.

"Are you sure you don't want to travel with me and the team for two weeks?"

Every time I have a series of away games, I ask her to come along. You know since it's one of the rules that we have. She's been good about going to home games, going to almost every single one. Away games on the other hand have yet to happen, except for the series in San Diego, which was a quick three-day trip.

Girlfriends and wives travel with the team all the time, so having her travel with me might help convince a few more people that our relationship is legit. Not that anyone has questioned it so far.

"Where are you going again?" she asks, just like she does every single time.

It's not like she doesn't have the schedule memorized.

"Seattle for an interleague series, Denver, Houston and Arizona."

She makes a face at the last two. "The last two are going to be hot as hell."

She's right about that. "No doubt. I think I looked, and it was going to be over one hundred in Arizona when we're there."

Her distaste for the Arizona heat is prominent on her face. "How about I join you for Seattle and skip the other ones? No way would I be able to handle that type of heat."

"Too much for a San Francisco girl?" I tease.

A small snort comes out of her nose, and I can't help but smile at her. "Hardly. I grew up on the Central Coast and a few miles from the beach. The hottest it has ever gotten is the high eighties. Rest of the time was cold breezes."

"That sounds a whole lot better than one-hundred-degree weather." I say.

"Oh, it is. Maybe I should take you there sometime."

"I mean, I have a few days off in July for the All-Star break. I'm all for driving down if you are."

A smile takes over her face, telling me that my idea is a good one.

"I never turn down a chance to go home."

"Then you go to Seattle with me this week and I go home with you. Do we have a deal?" I hold out my hand for her to shake.

Jen sits up and gives me a look of contemplation, before she gives me a smirk and shakes my hand.

"You got yourself a deal, Skippy." Her hand slides into mine and it takes everything in me not to tighten my grip on her and pull her toward me.

I'm already having difficulty not leaning in and placing my mouth on hers.

Our eyes are locked on each other, and there's this electric current running through us that we both must be feeling.

Jen wets her lips as she looks at me.

I can taste her.

It would just be one small taste. We can break our rule of only kissing when people are around because the kisses she gives me at the games aren't enough.

I need more of this woman, I need her right this moment and if I'm not careful, I'm going to ruin everything.

So, I drop her hand.

I drop her hand and compose myself as best as I can, clearing my throat. I also try to clear my head because if I don't, I will have her naked on this couch screaming out my name.

Wanting to put distance between us, so I don't do

anything stupid, I get up and head to the kitchen. Is it to find food? Get a drink? I have no idea but I need to put some distance between us so I don't jump her.

"Do you want to order something to eat?" I call out as I walk away.

Jen doesn't answer and when I turn back to see if she heard me, I crash into her body.

She must have followed me when I got up.

Now the distance that I was trying to put between us is nonexistent because her body is plastered against mine. All the while my hands find a place on her hips.

"You okay?" I ask, not stepping back from her.

She nods. "Yeah, I'm fine."

Her eyes don't move from my mouth, and like a few minutes ago, she licks her lips.

My fingers flex against her hips as I watch the action, contemplating if I should say fuck it and kiss this woman the way I want.

"Do you want something to eat?" I ask, my voice coming out with a husk.

A husk that comes from the effect this woman has on me.

Jen shakes her head, not saying a word.

"Then why did you follow me?" I ask, the distance between our faces closing.

This time her eyes move from my lips to my eyes, her own hands moving up to my shoulders.

"Because I wanted to be near you."

Her words are a whisper, but they are loud enough to do things to me.

"Near me?" I say, my forehead landing against hers. Less distance between us.

"You didn't feel it on the couch?" she asks, her hands moving from my shoulders to my hair.

I close my eyes at the feeling of her nails sliding against my scalp, marveling at how damn good it feels.

"I did, but we have rules," I say, my eyes still closed.

"I know."

"We shouldn't break them," I tell her.

"I know."

"But I really want to."

"I do too."

My eyes fly open to meet her stare, letting her brown eyes pull me in and letting them hold me to her.

"What if we do? What if we break them? Just once. Would that be acceptable?"

For me, no, it wouldn't be acceptable and not because it would be wrong. Because I would want more. I've already had one night with this woman, and I know that wasn't enough. If I were to have her again, it could ruin me.

"Just once?" Her nails slide against my scalp again in circular motions.

No, I need more than just once.

"Just once."

"What would happen if we do?" Her voice is low, but it's strong, telling me she wants this just as much as I do.

"What do you want to happen?"

I'm leaving this up to her, because if it were up to me, I would lock her in this apartment until tomorrow. Only letting her come up for air to get water and food.

"I want to kiss you," she states.

My hands dig deeper into the fabric of her pants, holding her body tighter to mine.

"I want to kiss you too."

"I want to have sex with you, but we can't cross that line. Things are already blurred, that would blur it even more."

I nod. "What if something else happens?"

Her fingers wrap around my hair strands, holding me in place, her mouth an inch or two from mine.

"Like what?"

"There's a way that both of us can end up satisfied and getting what we both want with no sex," not being able to take it anymore, my hands move from her hips down to her ass.

She feels perfect in my hands.

"Stop talking in circles, Maddox." She starts to rub her body against mine, so I grip at her some more, stopping the motion.

If she continues to move against me, I will with no doubt embarrass myself.

"I'm suggesting mutual masturbation. We kiss and touch our own bodies, but we don't have sex with each other. The lines stay perfectly intact."

Her breath hitches and the seductive smile on her face tells me everything that I need to know.

"Let's do it."

I don't have time to respond before her lips are on mine and our mouths are devouring one another.

18

MADDOX

THE KISSES that happen between us after the games would never compare to what is currently going on between us.

Those kisses are child's play.

The way I'm kissing her right now are the type of kisses that make men like myself fall to their knees and devour their women

My hands are on her ass and my tongue is in her mouth and it's not fucking enough.

I want to rip every single piece of fabric that's between us all so I can feel her skin against mine. So I can feel her bare chest against mine, so I can feel her core slide against my cock and let out a release.

So many things that I want to do, but I have to be good. I have to give her what she wants.

Not breaking us apart, I lift her up and walk us back to the living room before setting her down on the couch.

If I'm going to watch her play with herself while I'm

not allowed to touch her, I'm going to do it while the moonlight comes down on her.

I break apart from her for a quick second to get rid of my shirt.

Her eyes never leave my body and when I look back down at her, I see her hand twitching as if she wants to reach out and touch me.

"The only body part we get to touch is our lips, nothing else." I state, solely for my own good.

No way would I be able to touch her tits just once and be able to pull away.

"Such a stupid rule, but I'll play," she says before she follows my lead and takes off her shirt.

Her breasts are being held up by a barely-there bra that I'm sure I can rip with my teeth.

It's sheer and her nipples are already in peeks asking for attention.

My mouth waters at the sight. "Fuck."

"No touching," she says with a smirk, pinching one of her nipples through the fabric of her bra.

"Just because I can't touch, doesn't mean I can't enjoy the view. You should take that bra off," I say, licking my lips at the visual.

"I will, when you take off those jeans," she says as she reaches around her back as if to toy with her bra clasp.

I follow orders like an obedient student and quickly rid myself of my jeans, leaving me in just my briefs.

With a smirk, Jen takes off her bra and flings it off somewhere. I don't even look where it lands because my eyes are on her chest.

The memories of our one night together don't do the visual I have in front of me justice.

"Good girl, now your pants. It's only fair. I can't be the only one with just my underwear on."

With a seductive glance, Jen stands up and turns around. I watch as she pushes the fabric covering her hips and thighs down. She bends in the process, causing my eyes to fall to her full ass.

It's a sensual move. One that makes me want to fuck her in that very position. If only I could touch her and make it happen.

Once her pants are discarded, Jen turns back around and starts her appraisal of me.

"I don't know what it is, but you look so much hotter tonight than you did back in March."

I'm taking that as a compliment. "It could be all the baseball that I've been playing."

"It could be." A smirk plays at her lips as the words leave her mouth, but it quickly turns to a grin when she starts to move her hands along her body.

Jen caresses her breast, giving each one of her nipples a tug. Her caresses quickly move to hard grips, her fingernails digging into her soft skin.

How badly I want to replace her hand with mine.

I grip myself through my briefs and give myself a few tugs at the visual.

"That's a hard grip you have on your tits there," I say, continuing with my strokes.

Her head rolls a bit as she continues with her movements. "I like my chest to be played with. Bites, tugs, hard grips, a few smacks, everything. The harder the better."

Fuck. I think I just leaked out some precum at her words.

I need to distract myself before I blow my load without even trying.

"Should we put something on? That way we can get comfortable on the couch and see where this adventure takes us?"

Jen gives me a nod before dropping her hands from her breast and taking a seat on the couch. I want to tell her to take her panties off so I can see if she's soaking wet, but I don't.

They will be on the ground eventually.

Grabbing my phone from where she left it on the couch earlier, I look up a porn video that we can watch together.

"Any preferences?"

"No anal," she says with no hesitation.

Nodding, I pick the very first video that I find that doesn't have anal and connect it to the TV.

With everything set, I take a seat next to Jen before pressing play.

We sit shoulder to shoulder as the video starts to play and the sex sounds fill the room. We watch as the guy kisses his way down the woman's body, as he licks her and finally makes his way to her pussy.

The woman opens her legs wider, showing us exactly what the guy is doing to her with his tongue and his fingers.

Does this turn me on? Sure. I'm feeling something down there, but I would be feeling a whole lot more if I were doing those things to Jen.

I look over at the girl in question and see that she is sitting ramrod straight, looking like she doesn't even want to move.

Maybe this was a bad idea.

Or maybe, we're going about it the wrong way.

Thinking of something, I shift a bit, throwing my arm across the back of the couch before I lean into her ear.

"Let's adjust the no touching rule a bit, shall we?" I say before placing a hand on her shoulder, shifting her so that her back is against my chest.

Once we're skin to skin like this, Jen relaxes a bit, her head settling on my chest as she watches the video.

Her attention may be on the video, but my attention is on her.

I keep my eyes on her hands. One slowly glides against her thigh, while the other glides against her breast again.

And when she shifts, I know she's getting turned on but not fully there yet.

So, let's get her there.

"Do you like your pussy eaten like that, Jennifer?" I ask in a low whisper, moving her hair away from her neck and ear. "Answer the question. Do you like your pussy eaten like that?"

Jen cradles herself deeper into my chest. "Yes."

"Do you like your clit being flicked by a tongue that knows what it's doing?"

Her breathing is starting to get more labored. "Yes."

Without touching her, I glide my nose along the edge of her neck, feeling her get more unsettled against me.

"Are you turned on, Jennifer?"

This time her answer comes instantly. "Yes."

"Then touch yourself. Touch that pretty pussy of yours while you imagine me doing to you what the guy in the video is doing to his partner."

I pull away from her to see if she does as I say, and she does. Her right hand moves down from her breast and moves down her body until it lands on her covered pussy.

She strokes herself through the fabric, every one of her movements methodical.

"Does it feel good, baby? Does my tongue feel good against your pussy? Does it make you want to pull at my hair like she's doing to him?"

She nods against me. "Yes, it feels so good."

"Do you want me to slide my tongue against your slit until I reach your entrance and fuck you with mine tongue?" I ask, my hand twitching to touch her but I keep it in place.

"I want that so much, Maddox."

"I know, baby. I know you want it. I want it too, but we can't. That's why you have to do as I say and fuck yourself just for me to see."

Jen shudders, her head getting thrown slightly back as she continues to slide her hand against the fabric.

Not being able to take it anymore, I push down my briefs and let my cock spring out. My shift must have been something that Jen notices because she shifts slightly so she can watch what I'm doing.

I grip myself tightly, moving my hand against the taut skin, getting harder by the second.

"If only it was my hand on that cock instead of yours," Jen says, her hips moving against my thigh.

"If only. Would you take it in your mouth?"

She nods, her blonde hair all over the place. "I would. I would take it until it reached the back of my throat."

Fuck, that picture. Why did we have to make such stupid rules?

"Are you wet just thinking about sucking me dry?" I say, looking down and watching her fingers move faster.

"I am. Do you want to see?" Her eyes are filled with lust that I find myself nodding as I look into them.

Jen shifts her panties to the side and runs her hand against her bare pussy. After she gives herself a few good passes, she brings her hand up for me to inspect.

"See?"

Her fingers are glistening. I would just have to move a few inches forward and her fingers would be in my mouth.

I could taste her right this second, but I think of something better for right now.

"Clean them off for me. Take your fingers in your mouth and taste yourself. Pretend it's me licking them clean."

She does as she's told, closing her eyes in the process and letting out a sweet moan.

I can't take it anymore. I have to taste some part of her.

"I like that you do what you're told. Dirty girl. Now play with yourself again and kiss me. I need to fucking taste you."

That's when her eyes pop up and with a sexy grin she does what she is told and places her mouth against mine.

My tongue wastes no time getting into her mouth and getting the last traces of her arousal off her own tongue.

I stroke myself faster when I get the small taste that I'm looking for. It's a small taste but it's enough to get me solid as a rock.

Jen must be feeling the same effects because she lets out moan after moan into my mouth as she continues to play with herself.

She bucks against me and even with the minimal contact that we have, I know that she's close.

"You're close, aren't you?" I ask, pulling away from her slightly. My lips ghosting on top of hers.

She takes her bottom lip between her teeth, giving me a nod.

"Why don't you come on those pretty fingers, then?"

Jen doesn't respond, she does what she is told.

Without taking her eyes off mine, she continues to play with her clit and then moves to insert a finger in herself.

I struggle between wanting to look into her eyes as she does it and watching her finger fuck herself, but I manage.

The whole time that she finishes herself off, I jack myself as if it's the last time my dick will ever get attention.

I match the rhythm of my strokes to the movements of her fingers.

Precum coats my hands, I want nothing more to shoot off, but even though we're not having sex, Jen needs to get there first.

"I remember just how tightly your pussy was wrapped

around my cock on the night we met. It was so fucking tight, I thought about being inside of you for weeks. All through spring training. I still think about it. The image of your pussy wrapped around me is what I jerk off too. It's such a glorious sight, if only we can get a repeat of it."

That's what does it. That's what causes Jen's body to shake uncontrollably as she continues to fuck herself with her fingers. It's what causes her to scream out my name as she explodes into a high.

"That's it, baby. Shout my name. I want to hear it."

"Maddox." It's a pant and I absolutely love it.

Watching her combust is what pushes me over the edge. After a few more fast, heavy handed strokes, I let go into my release, coating my stomach and chest completely.

The video all but forgotten.

"Holy shit," Jen pants out, sagging against me. "That was hot."

"It was," I agree. I've done a lot of things with a handful of women, but this, this with Jen tops every single one of them and it wasn't even sex.

"Can I make an amendment to the rules?" Jen asks, not moving from her spot.

"What's the amendment?"

"We say fuck you to this only being one time."

A small laugh escapes me. "I'm down with that."

Now, because I can, I kiss her again until she is completely breathless.

19

JUNE 26, 2022

Jennifer

HAS anyone ever gotten the feeling that a lot more time has passed than in actuality?

Because that's how I feel right now.

So much has happened in the last two weeks that it feels like it's been two months when it's only been fourteen days.

Maybe it's because I traveled with Maddox and the Miners for about a week instead of going for only one game. Maybe it's because when I got home last week, I spent the majority of three days trying to make sure everything was running smoothly on Maddox's social accounts. Maybe it's the fact that after I spent three days on Maddox's accounts, I spent the next two on mine, because people now care what I do.

I didn't think being a fake girlfriend to a baseball player was going to be this tiring, but these past two weeks have told me otherwise.

168 | JOCELYNE SOTO

I also didn't think that I was going to be so involved in baseball stuff, but yet I am.

Apart from going to home games and the week of away games that I went to; I'm now getting messages from a few of the team wives and girlfriends inviting me to stuff. Charity events, brunches, yoga classes, dinners, everything that you can think of I've been invited to since I got home from Denver.

I guess I wasn't the official fake girlfriend until I traveled with the team for longer than three days. Something that I was not prepared for.

Want to know what else I wasn't prepared for? Breaking the rules with Maddox.

Well, we really just broke one rule, but I still should have mentally prepared myself for it.

It would have been better than thinking that the rules will never change.

Ever since the night in his apartment before leaving for Seattle, there have been a lot more kisses between me and Maddox that weren't all that fake.

Especially when we were behind a closed door and away from peering eyes. Kisses that have as if they were a natural thing between us.

Was it a bad decision on my part to tell Maddox that I wanted him to kiss me that night? Yeah, it was.

Do I regret it? No, because me telling him gave me one of the hottest experiences of my life.

I also think that now that we threw away the PDA rule and are participating in activities behind closed doors, we are becoming a better fake couple.

Makes things more believable in a way.

At least, that's what I keep telling myself.

It has helped us become more affectionate toward each other in public, which is a good thing. It makes everything, from the outside at least, seem like a real relationship.

As for the no sex rule, that is still in place. The one night in his apartment has not been repeated, sure there has been some heavy petting through clothing but that is about it.

Again, I see that as a way to make our relationship more believable.

I'm all about making that possible, even if I like his kisses a little more than I should.

Shaking all thoughts away from Maddox, his kisses and our fake relationship, I go back to the task at hand.

Doing something with my hair so that it doesn't look like a bird's nest. It's days like these that I wish my hair had a natural curl to it because then I wouldn't have to deal with a curling iron.

I have my mom to thank for that.

I'm currently getting ready to meet up with Annaleigh and Courtney from the coffee shop to head to a street festival.

San Francisco is this eccentric city that always has something happening. Festivals, parades, celebrations, anything that you can think of, happens.

I was supposed to go to the Miners games but when the girls texted last night, I thought I would skip it. This will be the first home game that I won't be going to since Maddox got called up, but that's okay because I'm able to do things for me.

As much as I wanted to go to the game, I couldn't say no. I missed seeing the girls and besides this street festival means a whole lot of food, music and a good time.

So, I thought that I would dress up a bit, and get out of my regular jeans and T-shirt. I even pulled out a flowy skirt for the occasion.

I'm finishing up the last strand of hair when my phone starts to ring.

Grabbing it from where it lays next to the sink, I see that Maddox is trying to FaceTime me.

A smile forms on my face as I see his name across the screen and hurry to answer before I miss him.

"Hey," I say as I place my phone to rest against the mirror so that I can see him.

"Hey," he says as his face fills the screen. He's wearing sunglasses and seems to be in a car. Which means he's driving to the stadium.

"What's up?" I ask.

This has become some sort of a routine between us this past week. He's called every time he's been on his way to the stadium. I don't know why he does it, but I like it.

"Just checking to see if you needed a ride to wherever you're going to meet up with your friends," he states.

"That's kind of you, but totally out of your way, you'll be late for batting practice."

I see him shrug through the screen. "I don't think Ben would mind."

"Ben might not, but the rest of the people that run the

team will. I'm fine, I'm going to catch the MUNI to the Mission District."

"If you're sure," he says with a relaxed smile on his face.

I nod, but not like he can see what with him driving. "Yeah, I'm sure. I'm just going to finish up doing my makeup and head out. I should be out of here in the next ten minutes. We're just going to a street festival."

He gives me a nod. "If you ladies are finished before the game is over, you can head over there. I'll leave tickets at the box office for you."

A small snort escapes me. "Ah Bauer, you can just say you need me at your games to play better. There is no shame in admitting that."

"Funny. I played my best season without you there." He is right about that. "Should I remind you that I got named Rookie of the Year?"

"Eh, but have you won a ring?" I tease him, knowing that the answer is no.

"Have you?"

I grab my mascara and start to apply it. "No but I am Selena's best friend and Hunter won one back in February and I was there so that should count by association."

A hearty laugh escapes from Maddox and I can't help but laugh right there with him.

Once the laughs quiet down, he speaks.

"So do you want me to leave the tickets at the box office or not?"

I check the time quickly. It's just past eleven and I'm supposed to meet up with the girls at twelve with the game starting a little after one. Without a doubt we will be done with the street festival in two hours, so the game would still be going on.

If we don't make plans for after we can definitely go.

"Yeah, go ahead and leave them just in case. I don't know what the plans are for after the festival."

"Will do. If you don't end up going, call me after?"

I nod. "Will do."

"Have fun."

We end the call and as I swipe on my lip gloss, I realize something about the call.

It felt very much like a call that would happen between Hunter and Selena.

Normal and very much real.

Looking at myself in the mirror, I realize that I don't want the season to end. Because when the time comes, I will be broken without repair. While this between Maddox and me is fake, the feelings I'm experiencing right now are real.

Very much real.

THE MUSIC, all the food and all the little stands that make up the street festival make my heart and soul so damn happy.

It brings back memories of when my dad would take my mom and me to the flea markets down in Los Angeles and San Diego and buy us everything we wanted.

I wanted an *agua fresca*? He would buy the biggest cup that they had.

My mom wanted a *torta de jamon*? There he went to stand in the long line just for her.

And I can't forget about the huge bags of candy that we would buy to take back home. Not that they lasted long, I would finish a whole bag of *paletas de chile* in a week.

The second I stepped through the barrier of the festival I was in my happy place.

"*Hola, si me puede dar una libra de mango seco,*" I say to the lady at one of the stands asking for a pound of dried mango.

The lady gives me a smile and gives me a bag full.

"Sometimes I forget that you speak Spanish," Annaleigh says from next to me.

I give her a smile. "It's the hair, for sure."

I'm Mexican American, the half Mexican in me coming from my dad.

Growing up, I was always called *güera* since my mom's genes just so happen to be a lot stronger than my dad's, what with me getting her dirty blonde hair and her not so tan complexion.

People are always surprised when they hear me speak Spanish and they are even more surprised to find out that it was my first language, but it doesn't bother me. I always loved sharing that part of me with others and seeing their shocked faces might have been a little fun.

I'm both of my parents and love the fact that they came together and created me.

"It's definitely the hair." Annaleigh laughs and the three of us continue to walk the remainder of the street festival.

About two hours into the festival, we decide to grab some food here and find a place on the grass to eat and enjoy the atmosphere.

Everyone is laughing and dancing and having a good time, even more so because San Francisco decided to gift us a nice sunny day.

The day passes by so quickly that when I check my phone to check the time, I see that it's a little bit past four in the afternoon. We will not be able to catch the game, which will probably be over by the time that we make it to the park.

I make sure to shoot off a text to Maddox telling him that we are still at the festival. He won't see it until he gets back into the clubhouse but at least I let him know.

The girls and I continue to catch up and enjoy our afternoon. I ask them about the coffee shop, and they ask me about Maddox.

Apparently, they've been keeping up with our relationship since the first picture I posted. That was only two months ago but it seems like it has been forever.

I'm about to answer a question that Courtney asked when I turn and notice a few people running.

That's odd, especially since they're all coming from one direction.

"Why are they running?" I ask out loud, prompting both of the girls to turn to look in my direction of sight.

As the people running come closer to us, more people start to join them and it's not in a fun type of way. No, by the look on their faces it's from panic. Men and women are picking up kids and others are grabbing people by the arms and dragging them along.

A large group of people run by us, some falling to the ground, causing us to get up and grab our things and look at each with panic.

"Hey! What's going on? Why is everyone running?" I ask one of the guys that tripped a few feet from us. The panic clearly in my voice.

I make eye contact with Annaleigh and Courtney and they both look terrified as we slowly start walking.

"You have to run. Someone said that they heard gunshots go off and they saw people get shot," the guy yells out before he continues to run.

Every inch of me goes cold as I digest the guy's words.

Gunshots.

People shot.

The panic.

We have to get out of here.

I look back at the girls and they have tears in their eyes, looking at me for some sort of answers.

I don't have any, so I just tell them what the guy told me.

"Run!"

20

MADDOX

AFTER THROWING my wet towel in the bin, I go back to my looker, or cubby hole I should say and grab my stuff to head out.

With the game that we just had, where we lost eight to two, I feel like going home and crashing on the couch.

I pull out my phone and I'm about to text Jen back, when I hear my name being called out.

Turning, I see Ben at the threshold of his office, waving me over.

Pocketing my phone, I head to his office.

What could he be calling me in for?

For the past month and a half my game has been on point. My late game appearances have been coming more regularly and from what our pitching coach has been telling me, I may be in a starting position after our break.

All my weekly drug tests have come back clean.

My whole rebrand shit is going off perfectly. The fans

love what they are seeing and definitely love me and Jen together. And from what I can see, so does the team.

Maybe I've been traded again.

Trade deadline is at the end of July and until then a lot of movement will be happening.

Am I one of them? Is that what Ben wants to talk to me about?

There's only one way to find out.

I approach his office and knock on the door to announce myself.

"You wanted to talk to me?" I ask, not fully stepping into the room.

"Yeah, come on in. I have some news for you."

News and getting called into the skipper's office this time of year is not always great.

"What's up?" I ask, taking in a seat in the same chair I sat in back in April.

Ben leans back in his chair and looks at me straight on. "I was talking to Rossi, and he said that you may be ready to start soon."

I nod. "Yeah, he told me the same thing, but he said that he had to run it by you."

Ben nods. "He ran it by me and if you're ready for it, the first game back from the all-star break can be your first start of the season."

"The game in Chicago?" I ask, my voice going up a notch or two with excitement.

Ben gives me a grin. "Why not? Your mom is still there, right? I bet she would have your balls if she wasn't there to see you start your first game of the season."

I let out a laugh. "She will definitely be pissed if she missed it."

"Then it's settled then. You're getting your first start in July."

Fuck that feels so good to hear.

I stand up and extend my hand out for Ben. "Thank you, sir. You have no idea how much this means to me."

He shakes my hand. "You're working hard for it. You still have a lot of work to do, and a lot to prove. So, keep doing what you're doing."

"Of course." Anything to get my career back to what it once was.

"I also see that things are going good with that 'girl-friend' of yours. I'm glad you followed my advice."

I can't help but roll my eyes at the man as he says the word girlfriend as if it had quotations around it.

Yeah, it was his idea, but I'm not going to thank him for it. It will go to his head.

"Anything else you'd like to talk to me about?" I ask, standing up and grabbing my bag from the floor.

Ben looks at the time on his watch, his tattoos peeking out from under his dress shirt. It still trips me out that the guy has full sleeves and hand tattoos.

"No, that's it. I'll walk out with you."

I wait for him to grab his stuff and within a few minutes were walking out of the clubhouse.

We run into Aaron in the corridor and the three of us walk out of the stadium together.

Before I reach my car, the one I bought at the beginning of the month because I was tired of being driven around and returning rentals, I shoot off a text to Jen.

She had texted me right before the game ended that they wouldn't be making it, so I figure since they weren't able to make the game, I'd invite her and her friends to dinner.

Crashing on the couch can wait a few hours.

"Any plans, boys?" Ben asks as he slings his bag into the bed of his truck.

"I have a tea party with my daughter. You know for a fact that there will be a picture of me wearing a tiara and a feather boa on my wife's Instagram later."

"Oh, if she does, I'm definitely taking a screenshot of that and putting it up in the clubhouse," Ben roars out, hunching over just thinking about the visual.

It's moments like these that make me happy to be on the team that has a skipper that knows how to have fun.

"What about you, Maddox?" Ben asks once he calms down a bit.

"I don't yet, plans are still up in the air." I look down at my phone and see that I haven't gotten a reply from Jen yet.

Yeah, I just sent the text a minute ago, but she always texts me back right away.

"Just waiting for your girl to get back to you?" Aaron asks as if he knows the feeling.

"Yup." A notification goes off and I check my phone, but there is no notification in sight.

Must have come from someone else's phone.

Great, I'm turning into a teenage girl waiting for the boy that she likes to get in contact with her.

"Oh, shit," Aaron lets out, looking at something on his phone.

"What?" I ask, because the way his face looks right now means that whatever he's looking at has to be serious.

"My wife just texted me, I guess there was an active shooter alert over at the Mission District," he states, typing something out on his phone.

The hairs on the back of my neck and arms stand up when he says Mission District.

That's where Jen said she was going to go.

"It just happened?" I ask, going on high alert now.

Aaron shakes his head a bit. "It started about forty minutes ago."

Forty minutes. Jen texted me almost an hour ago.

I can already feel my heart start to beat faster. "Where in the Mission District?"

I'm trying to think of all the scenarios that he might say, but none of them are any good. I don't even know the city all that well yet, so I don't know if this is going on a few blocks away or miles away. Jen could be miles away from where the shooting happened, or it could have been where she was at.

Aaron is silent as he types away, possibly getting information from his wife. When another ping sounds out, he answers my question.

"At a street festival."

My bag drops to the floor, and I frantically start calling Jen's phone.

"What's wrong, Bauer?" Ben asks, concerned all over his face, probably seeing the frantic expression on my face.

"Jen told me this morning that she and a few friends were going to a street festival. I offered her a ride, but she said she was just going to take the MUNI to the Mission District." Her phone goes straight to voice mail, so I hang up and dial again. "Now she's not fucking answering."

My chest feels constricted, like I can't get enough air into my lungs.

Not only is my chest hurting, but my head feels like it's spinning.

Why the fuck won't she answer her phone?

"Get in the truck," Ben orders, causing my head to spin a bit more.

"What?"

"Get in the fucking truck, Bauer. We're going to drive over there and see if we can find Jen," he rounds the vehicle and I just continue to stand there completely still trying to find my bearings. "Now, Maddox."

I take a few breaths before I do what he says. I get in the passenger seat, Aaron getting in the back, all the while Ben raves up the truck and speeds out of the parking lot.

My phone is never far away from my ear as I dial Jen's number repeatedly. I call her close to twenty times in a span of five minutes and not one of those twenty calls gets picked up.

I'm about to chuck the phone out the window when I decided to call someone that might pick up and maybe heard from her.

Maybe Jen and her friends changed plans. Maybe they

left the festival a few minutes after Jen texted me and went to somewhere else. That's possible, right?

"Hello?" Selena answers the phone call after the second ring.

Jen had called me from her phone a few days ago while they were hanging out. So I saved the number in my contacts in case of emergencies.

Like today.

"Selena, it's Maddox. Is Jen with you?" I ask, my voice coming out uneven and full of panic.

"No, I thought that she was going to some festival with some friends."

"Fuck." I pinch the bridge of my nose.

"Why? What's going on?"

I don't know if it was Selena's question or the hopelessness that I'm feeling at the moment, but for the first time in months, I feel like taking a hit.

I feel like reaching for the little white powder that will make me forget about all my problems and make everything better.

My mind, my heart, they need a release and no matter how many times I pat at my pockets looking for it, the release is nowhere near sight.

"Maddox!" Selena yells out.

She's going to freak out. Once I tell her why I called, Selena is going to freak out but if something bad happened, then she has to know.

"There was an active shooting situation happening over at the Mission District. At a street festival and Jen is not fucking answering. I'm heading over there to see if I can find her."

I hear Selena gasp and for a long minute she doesn't say anything.

After a few beats, she finally speaks. "I think I have Annaleigh's number. I'll try to call her. If she answers, I'll call you back."

"Okay."

"Maddox," Selena says, her voice shaking in the process. "Please. If you find out anything, please call me."

"I will."

The call goes silent, and I go back to trying to get a hold of Jen as Ben continues to maneuver his way through the San Francisco streets.

Aaron is able to get the exact location of the street festival and once we get about a block away, we come up to a closed-up street. Police cars are everywhere.

My phone beeps and for a quick second I relax thinking that it's Jen finally getting back to me, but it's not.

A text from Selena appears on my screen telling me that Jen's friend Annaleigh doesn't answer.

"Fuck." I slam my phone against the dashboard, feeling frustrated and hopeless.

If only I had something that would take the hopelessness away. Even if I had a miniscule amount of coke, I would be fine.

I'm so focused on trying to find a way to get rid of this feeling inside of me that I don't notice that Ben has driven over to where the police are and started talking to them, until they are right in front of me.

"Someone we know was at the festival and we're looking for them," Ben tells the cop.

The man in uniform nods. "A lot of people were told to go to the park three blocks over. You might be able to find them there."

"Were there any victims?" I find myself asking, even though my throat feels as if it's being constricted.

The cop looks at me, as if he's debating telling me, but eventually he answers. "Two adult males. It was a targeted drive-by. From what we know there are a few people injured but from the panic not the shooting. If you're looking for someone, your best bet is the park. We tried to get people to go there to get a few questions answered, but some went home."

"Thank you," I tell him.

Ben doesn't wait for the police officer to walk away before he drives off in search of the park.

A part of me is relaxed at knowing that Jen wasn't a victim of such a heinous crime, but I won't fully relax until I see her with my own eyes.

Even though I know it wasn't her, I'm still tapping at my pockets waiting for the relief to magically appear.

"There." Aaron points out when a huge crowd of people comes into view.

There are kids, men and women everywhere, that my eyes are frantically moving left and right trying to see if I'm able to find Jen from my spot.

The answer is no.

Ben finds a spot to park and the second the truck stops

moving, I'm out of the vehicle and running, trying to see if I'm able to find her.

I pass so many people that look like they have been crying. There are some that are holding the people that they are with tightly as if they don't want to let them go.

The cop said that the shooting was a drive-by, but that still doesn't negate the fact that these people experienced real panic. They probably didn't know what was going on and they just ran for their lives.

I move through people as carefully as I can, looking all over the place trying to catch even a small glimpse of her.

Anything. I will take anything at this point.

A little boy bumps into me as he walks by with his mom and when I abruptly turn to look at him, that's when I catch a glimpse of blonde hair.

Turning fully in that direction, I notice that the blonde-haired person is wearing a black tank just like Jen was wearing when I called her earlier.

That's her.

She's with two other women, and they are all getting checked out by paramedics.

I catch sight of Ben and Aaron and nod to them in her direction before running to her.

With her back to me, she doesn't see me so as I close the distance between us, I yell out her name.

"Jennifer!"

She doesn't hear when I call out her name the first time, or even the second time, but it's the third time that has her turning around.

It's the third time that I yell out her name that has me

seeing her beautiful brown eyes bloodshot and her face red from all the crying that she has been doing.

She sees me and it takes her a second to comprehend that it's me before she abandons the people that she is with and runs to me.

My arms open for her and the second that I have her in my arms, all the hopelessness, the anxiety and the fear I was feeling earlier is gone.

Every single urge that was moving through my body disappears when my arms wrap around her body and the scent of her hair is in my nose.

A sob releases from her and I bring her body closer to mine.

"You're okay. You're okay," I tell her repeatedly, but I don't know if it's for her or for me.

"How did you know?" she says into my neck, not pulling away from me.

"Aaron's wife told him there was a shooting and where. We drove over here as fast as we could. You wouldn't answer your phone." My voice shakes the whole time I speak.

I'm trying my hardest to keep my emotions in check but I'm failing.

"I dropped my phone. I was so scared to go back for it." She lets out another sob, tightening the hold she has on me a bit more.

"I know. You're safe now. I got you, okay? I will always have you," I tell her.

And I will.

No matter where me and Jen end up at the end of this season, I will be there for her. No matter what.

I will be there.

I will hold her when she needs me most, because I know what it feels like to think that I've lost her.

And if I don't hold on to her tightly, the demons will take over and there will be no light in sight.

Losing her, like losing my mother, will be the end of me.

Completely.

21

Jennifer

I LET the hot water cascade down my body, not bothering to make it less scolding.

My whole body will probably be red and covered with welts when I get out of here, but I don't care. I need to wash everything I experienced today away.

Never did I think that I was going to experience that type of panic in my life. For a good chunk of time, I thought that I wasn't going to make it home.

People were running all over the place. There were screams coming from every single direction and every single person that I passed had tears in their eyes.

The panic didn't really hit me until I saw people hiding in doorways and police putting on their bulletproof vest and telling people to take cover or to continue running.

That's when I realized the severity of the situation and tried to make sure that me, my friends, and many others made it out of there.

Somewhere in all the commotion, I tripped scratching

up my arm and my cheek and dropping my phone in the process. As much as I wanted to go back for it, I didn't. It's probably shattered on the street somewhere, if someone didn't find it and took it for themselves.

Once we got to the park, everything got a little crazier. People were looking for their loved ones that they got separated from. There were people who were injured and people crying all around.

There were even different rumors floating around about what happened. Some people were saying that there was a person spraying mace around and people ran to get away from it. Others were saying that they saw someone with a machine gun, and they were gunning down everyone that they saw. Everyone had a different story about why the running started, but it was a police officer that finally cleared things up and said it was a drive-by.

Two people were targeted, and those two people are now dead.

No matter where you are, who you are, things like this can happen and now all I can do is hope that it never happens to me again.

Because those were the most terrifying moments of my life and just thinking about what could have been has tears seeping out.

The shower is able to mask the tears but even a few hours later, I'm struggling to relax and not let the panic take over.

I continue to stand under the scorching water until it starts to cool down a bit, telling me that I've almost used it all up.

I guess it's time to get out.

Stepping out of the shower, I grab a towel and wrap it around myself and walk out. I avoid the mirror because if I look at all I will see is my red eyes and the scratch, and the tears will start up again.

Walking into the bedroom, I see that Maddox put out some clothes for me.

After the paramedics checked me out and we talked to a few more cops about what happened at the festival, we were free to go.

The three of us weren't really in a good headspace so, Maddox, with the team manager and Aaron was able to get us in a car and take us home.

Annaleigh and Courtney both said that they were okay to be alone when I asked if they wanted to come back to my apartment. I was hesitant about it, but I didn't push them if they wanted to be alone.

I was going to get dropped off next, but Maddox said that he would take me home. So, Ben drove to the stadium and dropped off Maddox, Aaron and me.

Once Maddox and I were alone in his car, he asked me what I wanted to do.

Did I want to go to my apartment?

Did I want to go to his?

Or did I want to go somewhere else completely different?

All I said was that I didn't want to be alone, that I didn't care where he took me.

So, he brought me here, to his place.

When he got here, he asked what I wanted to do.

I didn't answer.

Instead, I just went to the couch and curled up into a little ball until I fell asleep. I woke up about forty minutes ago and right away wanted to shower to get rid of the day.

So, he walked me to his bedroom, and left me to have some time alone.

I've been here a few times, the last being our faithful rule breaking night, but in the times that I have been here, I never ventured past the living room. If it was any other night, I would venture out and take every inch of the place in, but right now I don't feel like it.

After getting dressed and putting my hair up, I leave the bedroom and head to the living room, where I find Maddox sitting on the couch watching TV.

When I walk in, he grabs the control and turns the volume off, giving me all his attention.

"How are you feeling?" he asks, his eyes filled with concern.

I shrug. "Tired."

There's nothing else to really explain the day. What happened, happened and there's not much I can do about it.

"Want to talk about it?" Maddox offers, patting the cushion next to him.

Taking a seat, I shake my head at him. "Not really. I just don't know why it's hitting as hard as it is."

Maddox scoots closer to me, wrapping an arm around my shoulders and bringing me into his body. "Because you didn't know what was going on, nobody really did. Your brain and body automatically went to the worst-case scenario, and that's completely fine."

I think that's what I hated the most, the not knowing. I didn't know if it was a prank just to cause mass hysteria or if it was something that would end up on the news all over the world.

Leaning into Maddox's hold a bit more, I position myself to see what he was watching.

The news of all things.

"Have they said anything?" I ask, nodding toward the TV mounted on the wall.

Maddox lets out a sigh. "Yeah. I guess someone caught the whole thing on their phone and posted it on Twitter. The video apparently got some of the license plate, so the police are investigating."

"And the men that died?" I ask.

It's horrible that someone had to die today, especially like this. I can't even imagine what their families must be going through tonight.

"No names have been released yet, but there were both in their late thirties."

So young.

Maddox and I sit like that, watching the silent tv for a few more minutes. I even start to doze off when a knock at the door scares me awake.

"I ordered something," Maddox says as to explain why someone would be knocking at his door on a Sunday night.

He gets up from next to me and heads over to go grab whatever it is he ordered.

I continue to watch the news on mute.

He must have ordered something heavy because I hear two sets of footsteps coming from the door.

When they get closer, I turn to see what was so important that he had to get it delivered at nine at night.

But I don't see a random delivery man with him. It's Selena, holding a white bag.

My best friend gives me a sad smile. "Maddox ordered you a new phone, so I thought I would pick it up and bring it over."

If my feelings for Maddox weren't conflicted already, they are going to be off the roof with this.

He saw I needed someone, and he called Selena. He called my best friend even when I didn't tell him I needed her.

I do need her and I'm so happy that she's here.

Patting the cushion next to me, silently asking her to come sit with me.

She does, and she wastes no time wrapping her arms around me, surrounding me with everything that is Selena.

Maddox must have told her what had happened because when she pulls away from me, I see tears in her eyes. They become more apparent when she sees the scrap on my cheek.

I give her a small smile to reassure her that I'm fine, that I'm okay, but I don't know how good I am at doing that because tears form in my eyes.

Maddox ends up turning off the news and putting on a movie. At some point I end up cuddled between him and

Selena, making me realize that I've never felt this safe in my adult life.

Growing up, I always felt this way when I was with my parents or around Selena and her family. I thought that the feeling had moved with me as I got older, but now I'm realizing that it hasn't, until now.

Sandwiched between my best friend and my fake boyfriend slash boss.

When the movie ends, Selena ends up going home soon after with the promise that she will see me tomorrow.

Once she's gone, it's just me and Maddox left to our own accord.

"I'll sleep on the couch, and you can take my bed. The guest room isn't set up yet," he tells me, looking awkward in his own living room.

We may continuously be breaking our no PDA rule, but we have yet to share a bed or actually sleep together.

Even during the week, I traveled with the team or went to San Diego, Maddox made sure that he got a room with two beds.

But right now, making him sleep on the couch seems wrong.

I shake my head. "Please don't sleep on the couch. Sleep in the bed with me."

Maddox looks at me as if he's trying to get a read of my mind and get a better understanding of what I'm thinking.

Eventually he gives me a nod and walks me to the bedroom.

We're awkward as we get ready to go to sleep, but eventually the lights get turned off and we're lying in bed.

Not being able to handle the distance between us, I turn over and cuddle into Maddox's side causing him to wrap an arm around me and bring me in closer.

We lay like that for a bit, no words just feeling each other's warmth, neither one of us falling asleep.

Eventually Maddox breaks the silence. "I called Selena when you didn't answer. I thought maybe that you might have been with her, so I called. I promised to tell her when I heard something, so when we got here, I called her and had her come over."

I can hear just how much me not answering his calls really put him through the wringer.

"Thank you for calling her. And thank you for getting me a new phone. You didn't need to."

With the little light that is flowing through the room, I can see him nod.

We go back to being silent, and this time my eyes start to droop with sleep.

But all sleep goes out the window when Maddox speaks again.

"Today was the first day since I got out of rehab that I felt a real urge to use." He pauses for a couple of seconds, taking a few deep breaths in the process. "Not knowing if you were okay made me feel helpless and all I wanted to do was forget and not feel a thing. The urge to find an escape was prominent until I had you in my arms."

Silent tears escape my eyes as I hear the pain in his voice.

Hearing what he felt for that short time, makes me want to hate this day even more.

"I'm sorry," I say, not knowing what other words would make this any better.

"You have nothing to be sorry about," he says, bringing me closer to him and placing a small kiss against my hair. "I didn't do it. I didn't go looking for something that would ruin all my progress. You're here, you're safe and that is all that matters."

All that matters.

We may have only known each other for a few months, but in those few months, we have grown to care about each other.

I care about him, and he cares about me.

He cares about me enough that not knowing if I was okay almost caused him to relapse and stop all the progress that he has made. Everything would have been for nothing. All because of me.

I don't say anything after that. I just continue to lie in his arms and let tears flow until sleep takes me.

I'm not under the cloud of sleep just yet when he speaks again.

"This may be fake, Jennifer, but losing you will destroy me. Just like losing my mom would."

In my dreams, I promise him that he will never lose me, not even when this arrangement ends.

MADDOX

WHEN SHE FIRST TOLD ME that the aquarium was a safe place for her, I didn't really understand it. I just thought it was a place where she made a lot of memories as a kid.

But as I watch her as she sits on the floor looking at the creatures in front of us, I see why she said it. I see why this is a safe place for her.

For the last two weeks, she's been on high alert. Every little thing makes her jump. One top of the fear, she also doesn't want to spend any time alone, not even for sleep.

She always has someone at her side.

Since the festival, she has either slept at my place or Selena's, only going to her own apartment to get clothes and to make sure her plants haven't died.

She won't say it, but that day and what happened really messed with her head and my confession of what it did to me, sure as hell didn't help.

Yet as she sits cross-legged on the floors, she's calmer, a lot more relaxed.

Maybe it's the environment she's in. Maybe it's the two individuals that are sitting next to me that are looking at her with love and adoration.

Whatever it might be, Jennifer Zaragoza is in her element. So much in her element that I'm finding myself taking pictures of her just so I can capture her being in the moment.

Capturing her as the person that I've come to know and care about but haven't seen much of in two weeks.

"That's a beautiful picture," Jen's mom, Dana, whispers as she looks over as I survey my handy work with the camera.

A small blush creeps up my face at the fact that I was caught taking pictures of her daughter.

All-star break officially started yesterday after our afternoon game against Los Angeles. After the Miners won three to two, Jen and I got in the car and drove down to her hometown of Seaside to visit her parents. A short trip since we are flying out to Chicago early, but one she was excited about it.

One she needed, no doubt.

Given the number of pictures of us together there are online, her parents were eager to meet me, so we thought that this would be a good opportunity.

It was close to a three-hour drive since we drove along the coast, but the smile on Jen's face when she opened the door to get out of the car made it worth it.

Her parents were so happy to see her, that they all hugged the second she walked into the house. The hugs lasting for a good five minutes before they remembered that there was someone else in the room.

Both Dana and her husband Javier, welcomed me with open arms. I guess their daughter had never brought a boy home and me being the first was a time to celebrate.

It was at dinner that I learned that Jen could speak fluent Spanish. It was the rapidness in how she spoke that left me in awe.

Without a doubt, no matter how long I known her for, I will continue to find out something new about her every single day. That something making her even more attractive to me.

I was a little hesitant to meet her parents at first, mostly because I didn't know if they knew about my past or better yet, if they would be able to see through our façade of this fake relationship we have going on. For the most part though, they seem to believe that we are a real couple.

As for them knowing about my past, that is still up in the air. They may know, but they have yet to say a word about it.

I smile over at Dana before closing my photo app. "Thank you. She's always taking pictures of me, it's nice to be the photographer for a change."

Dana gives me a nod. "She told me that she runs your social media, I hope you don't mind that I followed. I love seeing every picture she takes."

"Not at all, I think that she would be disappointed if you didn't."

Dana gives me a smile that is so much like her daughter's before she goes back to look at the sea creatures in front of us.

As the mother and daughter get lost in the movement of the water and the animals in the tank, I look over at Javier who is looking at his two girls with a smile.

He catches me looking at him and instead of ignoring me, he stands and nods his head for me to follow.

So, I do, leaving Jen and her mom to have a moment.

"Has she always liked the aquarium?" I ask Javier as soon as we're out of hearing distance.

A small smile spreads across his face as he answers. "Whenever her class had a field trip here, she would hardly sleep the night before because of how excited she was. Every birthday she always begged us to bring her."

Javier looks like a man of minimal words. Yet in the handful of hours that I've been around him, he is happy to talk about the people he loves. His wife and daughter being at the top of that list.

"That sounds like something Jen would do."

He gives me a curt nod. "I was actually surprised that she didn't go to school to work with marine animals. Given how much she loves coming here, it would have been a good place for her."

"She called this her safe space a few weeks ago. Maybe she chose not to work in a place like this so that her safe space wouldn't be taken away."

"Maybe," Javier states.

I can't help but notice that the man looks intimidating as fuck with not only the way he is standing but also the hard exterior that radiates from him.

He gives off don't fuck with me vibes.

His arms are crossed across his chest and his stance is wide as if he's ready to jump into any fight that might come up.

Why do I get the feeling that that fight might be with me, though?

"I've read about you, Maddox," he says, getting straight to it. Right away, all my defenses are up.

I guess I have my answer about them knowing about my past.

As much as I want to copy his stance and go into flight or fight mode, I don't. I keep my shoulders down and my hands in my pockets, ready for anything that might come my way.

I have nothing to hide.

"And what did you read?" I didn't mean for the words to come out condescending, but they do.

There are a lot of things about me out there that aren't pleasant. A handful of gossip sites have spewed so many lies that contain my name it's hard for people not to find them and believe every single word.

Hell, there was a point late last year where I would read the things people were saying about me and because I was high out of my mind, I even thought that they were true.

God only knows what Javier could have found.

For all I know, it could have been a picture of me butt-ass naked doing a line off a dirty toilet.

Is it even possible that that picture exists? I don't even know anymore.

"A number of things. Should I list them?" His face is stoic, and if I look hard enough, I can see the rage in his eyes. Rage directed at me. "That you can give two shits about your career. That you cared more about your next high than doing your job. That the only reason you are passing your drug tests now is because you're paying off the person administering said test."

That last one is one I have yet to hear. Good to know that people are still trash talking me.

I bow my head, trying to compose myself as best as I can, so that when I respond it's controlled and not filled with the anger brewing inside of me.

"And do you believe these things?" I ask, my voice not yet composed and my jaw ticcing in the process.

Javier is silent for a minute, a long one at that. When I look up again, I see that he's not looking at me but toward where Jen and Dana are.

"Can you blame me if I do? If you were any other man, I wouldn't give two shits about what you did with your life, but you're not. You are the man that my daughter brought home for us to meet. A man that is currently taking space in her life. I have to believe all the stuff I read and hear until I see with my own eyes that they are false. Right now, all that I see is someone undeserving of her. I will continue to see you that way until you prove to me that they are wrong."

Isn't that what I've been trying to do since Jen and I started this whole fake relationship?

Haven't I been trying to prove to baseball fans all over that I'm still the baseball player that I once was?

Haven't I been trying to prove to the team that picked me up when my old team gave up on me that their investment is well worth it?

Ever since I got out of rehab and left Utah, I've been trying my damn hardest to show people that the man that I was last year wasn't me. That the baseball player that cared more about his next hit instead of his game, isn't me.

But I guess everything that I've been doing hasn't been enough.

I shouldn't care that Javier, a man I just met, believes that I'm the man that tabloid and gossip sites say that I am. But I do.

Because of her.

Because he's Jen's dad and I care.

I care about his daughter more than he can comprehend.

I care about her so much that I'm at the point that I know that when we end things at the end of the season, I will be lost without her.

I care about her that I'm at a point where I want to say fuck it and jump into all the real things that she has to offer.

She's my constant and I'm already in too deep to give her up.

And I have to show him that.

Javier just moved to the top of the list of people that I have to show that I am worthy.

Worthy of being a baseball player.

Worthy to be a good asset to the team.

Worthy of being with Jen, even if it's for a limited time.

I meet his stare straight on, not backing down from anything. "Let me show you that the man you read about, isn't me. Yes, I did drugs and I let them drag me down for my own reasons, but that isn't me anymore. That isn't who I am with your daughter."

"And how do you plan on showing me?" Now it's Javier's turn to meet my stare straight on.

"I don't know," I answer him truthfully. "I don't know how I'm going to prove it, but I will. I will prove to you that I'm not that man, and I will never be that man when your daughter is concerned. When it comes to her, I will be better."

The stare down between us continues.

This is definitely not something that should be happening in the middle of an aquarium while there are strangers walking by every five seconds yet, here we are.

"*Bueno*, I look forward to seeing it. I hope for my daughter's sake that you are right."

I do too.

I really do because as Javier walks away to join Dana and Jen again, I realize that without many words, I told him what his daughter means to me. Something that I have yet to tell Jen.

Something that I'm *afraid* to tell Jen, all because of what our relationship really is.

I watch as he reaches the women and places a hand on each of their shoulders grabbing their attention.

Jen looks up at her dad, giving him a smile before looking around and meeting my gaze.

Her smile grows a bit more as she gets up from where she's sitting and walks over to me.

"Are you having fun?" she asks, her smile growing a little more.

Because her smile is contagious, I give her one of my own, putting the conversation I just had with her dad on the back burner.

"I can definitely see why this is your safe place. You can sit here for hours."

Jen looks around, waving at a little girl that passes by.

"You're right about that, I've done it before. Want to see my favorite part?"

Without even thinking, I take her hand in mine and bring her body closer to mine. Loving every single inch of proximity between us.

Loving it more than I'm allowed to.

"Show me," I say to her, giving her a grin.

Because while the aquarium may mean nothing to me, it does mean something to her.

And even if this is fake, I want her to be happy, protected and to feel safe in all aspects of life.

Including when she's with me.

But I can't help agreeing with Javier on one thing.

I am undeserving of his daughter. Very undeserving.

Being undeserving of this woman, still won't stop me from holding every moment I can get with her as tightly as I can.

23

JULY 12, 2022

Jennifer

I UNDERSTAND IT NOW.

I see why Maddox wanted to escape. Why he wanted the pain to go away, wanted to lose himself instead of being at his mom's side through her sickness and the possibility of losing her.

It was in the way that he hugged her when we walked into his childhood home. It was in the way that he helped her clean the kitchen even if there wasn't a thing out of place. I see it in the way he cares for her, in how he loves her.

Maddox didn't use drugs because he was trying to escape his mom's sickness. He used them to cope with her death even though she is still here.

Since I met the man, I wondered what caused him to get so deep into such a dark place. Why he would go through such lengths.

And now I know.

Maddox will be absolutely shattered if he loses his

mom. She's his everything and not having her in his life will be the end of him.

I know if it was my parents, I would be the same way.

Which is why when Maddox asked if it was okay if we stayed here for the night instead of going to his apartment, I said yes.

No way am I going to deny him time with his mom, especially when he doesn't get to see her as often now that he's in San Francisco.

"Please tell me that you are going to at least treat this woman to a good deep-dish pizza while you're here. You know, a real pizza and not that shit they have in California."

"Ma," Maddox says, a smile on his face as he reprimands her for cursing.

"What? Tell me I'm wrong," Nora challenges him.

Maddox tries to hide a smile but ultimately fails. "Some of the pizza is shit."

Nora nods as if she's met her point.

Wanting a small part of the conversation, I turn to Maddox, looking at him with narrowed eyes.

"Um, excuse me, in all the times we've eaten pizza, not once have you complained." Given the smile that is trying to come out, I know he can see right through my glare.

"Babe, I might not have complained with words, but I have definitely complained in my head. Especially with that pizza place we went to when I got back to the city."

I try to keep myself stable and not melt as he calls me babe. He's called me that before and I should be used to it, especially with people around, but it still does things to me.

"That was good pizza." I throw back at him.

He gives me a smirk that has me wishing I could jump his bones. "It was thin as hell, and it had avocado on it."

Okay he has a point. That pizza wasn't my brightest choice, and it wasn't even that good. I just picked it because in the picture it looked so good.

Either way, I concede. "Fine, you may have a point. So, you should do as your mother says and treat me to some good Chicago style pizza."

"Whenever you want," he says, throwing me a wink.

I can't help but smile and let out a giggle at this whole thing, but it quickly dies down when I turn to face Nora.

There's a small smile on her face and tears in her eyes as she looks at Maddox and I interact.

"Are you okay?" I ask her, taking her hand in mine.

Nora nods, giving me a tight smile and wiping away at the tears.

"I'm fine, sweetheart. This is just nice to see. When I told Maddox to find a girl to make him happy, I didn't think that it would happen so quickly."

My eyes go wide a bit at her last comment but I'm able to compose myself before she notices and give her a smile.

"Trust me, I wasn't expecting it to happen this quickly either, but I'm happy it did."

It's not a lie. I'm happy that I met Maddox. Do I wish we weren't in a fake relationship? Yes, but only because a huge part of me wishes it was real.

Maddox Bauer is the type of man I wish I could spend the rest of my life with.

I can really see him being the Hunter to my Selena.

Nora gives my hand a hard squeeze. "I am too. Very happy."

As I give her a squeeze back with a smile, a part of me, a large part hates that we are deceiving her. Her smile tells me that she is so happy that her son has found someone, and I hate the fact that once the season ends, that smile will be gone.

All because we're lying to her.

Maddox will find someone else, and she will smile like that again.

Even though that thought is true, I hate it. I don't want to think about Maddox with someone else.

What if that person doesn't see how much this man loves his mother and doesn't stand by his side if he loses her so young?

I don't want to think about it.

Maddox must have sensed that we might need to talk about something else, because he clears his throat and changes the subject.

"Ma, what time is your appointment tomorrow?" Maddox asks.

My stomach falls a bit at the subject he chose to talk about, but we can't avoid it.

I've seen pictures of Nora from before last year, how full of life she looked. In every single picture that I found of her online to the pictures that Maddox showed me, she looked like she could take on the world.

When we walked into her house that's how I expected to see her, but it wasn't.

Nora is stronger now that she looked in those pictures but in a different type of way. In the type of way that she needs to battle this cancer. Nora Bauer is gorgeous but the brain tumors are definitely taking a heavy toll on her.

"At nine," Nora answers her son with a tight smile.

I can tell just by that smile that she doesn't like talking about what is going on with her.

"I'll go with you," Maddox announces, which has Nora shaking her head.

"No need. I can handle a small doctor's appointment. Besides, Jen is here. Take her to see the city or something."

"Mom," Maddox throws back.

We've been here for half a day and the whole time Maddox has only called his mom Ma.

I may have only known him for a few short months, but even I know that when he uses the word mom, that he's trying to be serious.

"Don't 'mom' me, Maddox." I guess I was right about the word mom. "You have a guest. No way in hell am I going to let you leave her here all by herself while you take me to the doctor. That's not very nice." Nora throws back at her son.

My eyes move between the two of them as they stare each other down. After about thirty seconds, Maddox drops his mom stare and turns to look at me.

There is pain in his eyes with maybe a little hint of fear. Without saying a word, I know just how important it is for him to go to her appointment and with his eyes he is asking for help.

So I turn to Nora. "Nora, I can stay here. It's fine. I have work to do anyway, I won't even notice that I'm here alone."

She is already shaking her head before I even finish. "Nope, not happening. He can stay with you. I'm a big girl, I can go to a stupid doctor's appointment. Pretty sure all they will tell me is that the tumors aren't growing and that they will monitor me for another month. Doubt that they will even mention surgery."

Nora sounds angry and she has every right to be.

"Then me and Jen will both go with you. I don't give a shit if the doctors tell you that they are waiting until Christmas, I will be in that room."

Maddox's tone is affirmative and final, which causes the room to go completely still. Well, everything but Nora's tightening grip on my hand.

The mother and son stare each other down again and I'm just sitting here, my eyes flip-flopping back and forth.

I don't know if I should continue to sit here or if I should get up and let them handle this by themselves. This is definitely a family matter and I'm nowhere close to being family.

I'm about to get up from my seat when Nora finally drops my hands before clearing her throat.

"Fine but you're taking us to get pizza afterward." Nora gets up from her seat and starts to walk away before sticking out her tongue at her son.

I love that even with such a serious topic flowing

around, Nora is still able to find a way to bring a smile to her son's face.

It may be small, but Maddox is wearing a smile as his mom leaves the room.

The smile falls a bit as soon as it's the two of us, telling me that going to the doctor's appointment is going to be hard for him.

"I can stay here. I don't mind," I say to him, reaching out to place my hand over his.

When it comes to holding hands, we have done that plenty of times, but for some reason, touching him now feels more intimate than just our fingers intertwined.

Maddox looks down at where our hands connect and moves to slide his fingers through mine. He keeps his eyes on our hands until he finally lets out a sigh.

"No," he says, shaking his head. "I want you there. I *need* you there."

His eyes look like they are ready to release a few tears.

I've never seen this side of him. Right in this minute, it's as if he's a boy and not the man that I know that he is.

He's hurting and I want to do everything in my power to take that pain away.

"Then I will be there every step of the way."

24

JULY 14, 2022

MADDOX

"Well, Nora, it's a good thing that we watched those tumors for another month," the doctor started, causing every single ounce of blood flowing through my body to drop to my feet.

This is it.

This is where they tell her that the tumors have grown and there won't be any surgery to remove them.

It has to be, because no way in hell does a sentence that starts off with 'well' is good.

"The tumors haven't grown. That's the verification that I needed. I think we are good to go with that surgery."

My blood was still flowing at my feet as the doctor spoke and my mind tried to comprehend his words.

"She's in the clear?" I found myself asking out loud, the grip that I had on my mom's hand growing by the second.

The doctor's facial expression changed a bit as he looked at me, trying to figure out how to answer my question.

"For now. There is no cure for cancer, especially something as big as brain cancer. Things could be clear one month and come back *bigger and uglier the next. There is a possibility that the tumors may come back, but for right now I will answer your question with this. It looks like the treatment that Nora went through last year helped. The tumors have stopped growing and we hope that with the surgery, they will never come back, but that isn't a guarantee. We will still need to keep an eye out to see if they return later down the line," the doctor answered, but it wasn't good enough.*

So I asked my question again.

"Is she in the clear?"

The doctor looked at me and then to my mom. Whatever was in her expression must have told him that I would not stop until I heard him give me a definite answer.

The doctor let out a sigh before he spoke. "For now, yes. Nora is in the clear."

———

I DON'T KNOW why I had it in my head that once I heard the doctor say the word yes, everything would be okay. That it will all go back to how things were before the diagnosis came and changed everything.

Maybe it was my mom's wishfulness running through me. Maybe it was that hope and faith that I told her to have all those weeks ago.

Whatever it was, it came to bite me in the ass.

For now, yes.

Three words that should have been a cause of celebration, but the only thing that they are causing is my mind to over think.

Those three words can quickly change into something completely different, and my brain is telling me every chance it gets.

Which is why my leg is currently bouncing while I sit in the clubhouse waiting for the game to start so I can take my place on the mound.

Today is the day that I've been waiting for since my suspension last August. Today is the day that I'm the starting pitcher in a baseball game in the major leagues.

I should be relaxed and, in the zone, but instead my mind is working in overdrive and every inch of my body is on high alert.

And most definitely not in the fucking zone.

I knew the second I got up this morning that I was definitely not ready to pitch today. Once I knew I should have gone to Ben, to our pitching coach and told them to put someone else in, but of course I'm a glutton for punishment and now I'm here.

It's a good thing we're in Chicago because then if my game is off, they can say that getting rid of me was a good idea.

There will be boos being heard today, that is for sure.

At the very least, my mom and Jen are here to see me possibly pitch the worst game of my life.

Don't think that way, you will go out there and pitch a clean game.

Let's hope my mind is right about that.

I'm tying up my cleats when Aaron sits next to me, looking as relaxed as I should be feeling.

Yeah, he's relaxed, the stupid bastard doesn't have to pitch today.

"You ready?" he asks, a smile on his face.

I want to snarl at him, tell him to fuck off, but I don't. Just because I'm having an internal panic episode doesn't mean I can take it out on the man that has not only treated me like a teammate but as a friend these last few months.

So I give him a nod. "As ready as I will ever be."

"This is your old stomping grounds; you know that mound better than anyone. Don't think about the people in the stands and just think about how the ball leaves your hand. You pitch and the team will do the rest. We got your back."

A clap lands on my back as I take in Aaron's words.

I might have not told him about all the doubt I was feeling today, but in a way he knew.

He knew and came over to bring me down from the anxiety train that I was riding.

Maybe if Aaron was my teammate last year, I wouldn't have gone down the hole that I did.

"Thanks, man," I say to him, a part of me relaxing a bit knowing that he and the rest of the team have my back.

Aaron gives me a curt nod before standing up. "Let's go put some runs on the board for you. Maybe then you won't look like you're about to cry."

I try to trip the asshole as he walks by but he's like a ninja and is able to avoid it. He just laughs as he grabs his glove and makes his way out of the clubhouse.

A few seconds later, I'm following right behind him with the mind trick still at play but not as prominent.

The game starts off, and like Aaron promised, the Miners are able to get two runs on the board.

We were able to hold the lead through my first three innings.

Were they good innings? More or less. Runners were able to get on the bases and I threw more than twenty-five pitches in the second, but Chicago wasn't able to score.

That is until in the fifth, when Bobby Getz, a Chicago infielder that got called up earlier this year, was able to hit a home run off me.

After that, everything started to go to shit.

My fastballs aren't hitting where they are supposed to and my curveballs have started to lack speed. Every single one of my pitches is hitting outside of the box and not only is it pissing me off, it's showing. The fifth inning was shit and so was the sixth, the seventh might be the same.

It sure as hell doesn't help that I also have to bat in this game.

The current score? Four to three, with Chicago having the lead.

Alex, our catcher, is currently at the plate and after he hits a line drive past first, I'm up.

Cheers roll through the stadium as I walk to the plate, much like they did during my first two at bats. They feel nice but they still aren't enough to get me out of my head.

"I for sure thought that they would have taken you out of the game by now, kid," Troy, the Chicago catcher, says to me as I approach the batter's box.

Troy is the one with the big mouth on the team, always has something to say about something. While I was here, I didn't necessarily hate the guy but he sure as hell made me want to punch his face in a couple times.

All game though, he's been taunting me whichever way he can.

So far it hasn't been working but who knows what he will say now.

"I still have a good few pitches in me unlike your boy," I say as I get into position and wait for the ball to come my way.

I swing on the first pitch, barely tapping it and sending it into the stands.

Home runs may not be my thing, but I can sure as hell hit the ball.

"I heard you have a new girl," Troy starts as we get ready for the second pitch, but before I can even answer him, he continues. "Hopefully she's watching the game so she can see just how badly you suck."

The second pitch is released and I swing the bat, completely missing the ball.

Two strikes.

"Fuck," I say out of frustration.

"You just proved my point." Troy lets out as I adjust my batting glove.

I ignore him as the next two pitches come, both coming as balls.

It's when I'm setting up to get my fifth pitch, that Troy starts talking again.

"Think I can have your girl's number? That way I can show her what a real ball player is like. I've seen her pictures, definitely a beauty that I wouldn't mind seeing on her knees in front of me with her mouth wide open. I wonder if she has a gag reflex."

"Strike three!"

I didn't even notice when the pitcher released the ball. I don't even hear the crowd as they cheer at the second out of the inning.

No, the only thing that I notice is all the fucking anger that I have inside of me right now directed at my ex-teammate.

"Sorry, kid. Better luck next time," Troy says, his snarky laugh, digging under my skin.

There are two choices presented in front of me at the moment.

Walk away or engage.

The choice is made the second I throw down my bat.

25

Jennifer

"YOU WOULD THINK it was a damn baseball game and not a wrestling match. I swear if that boy wasn't over six feet tall, I would kick his ass for thinking that he could throw punches around."

Nora is pissed and I would be too if I wasn't so worried that Maddox was possibly hurt.

The game was going good, well at least to me it was going good. Maddox was pitching okay and at one point the Miners had the lead. Sure, there were a few rough innings, but I had faith that the Miners would pull through and win.

Hell, I was even letting my inner Selena out and yelling at the umpires about their calls.

I thought it was a good game until the seventh inning and all hell broke loose.

One second, Maddox was waiting for a pitch and the next he was out, his bat was on the floor, and he was coming face to face with the other team's catcher.

At first, I thought it was just going to be two of them spewing out words at each other and they would both walk away.

Nope.

Words were definitely exchanged but when the catcher threw a punch toward Maddox, it was like a wrestling match like Nora said.

Benches were cleared, the bullpen got involved and both Maddox and the catcher were taken out of the game.

After the fight, the stadium felt different. There was tension between the two teams even with Maddox and the catcher nowhere in sight.

I tried to call and text Maddox, but he didn't answer. He still hasn't answered as we make our way down to the visiting clubhouse with the rest of the players' families that are here.

"The catcher threw the first punch." I say in Maddox's defense. It's a weak one, but it's all I got.

"And my idiot son threw the second," she throws back.

I mean, she's not wrong.

We continue to walk through the tunnels of the stadium until we reach the meeting area of the clubhouse. Family members, kids, and news people are all over the place.

Some players have trickled out but not the one that me and Nora are looking for.

After about ten minutes of waiting, the crowd has dwindled down to the point that we are the only family members left with some reporters that are waiting for a picture.

Finally, after another five minutes, the doors open again, this time Maddox coming out with another man.

A man that has Nora adjusting her hair, that she says has grown out a lot since her last chemo session in December, and baseball hat.

"Damn. That man can bend me over and take me anytime that he wants," Nora says only for me to hear.

"Nora!" I say, through a laugh.

"What? I could have said he could fuck me any time he wants. Just because I have a grown man for a son, doesn't mean that I'm a prude. I'm only forty-six," she says, throwing me a smirk that is so much like the one her son wears.

As the men approach us, I can totally see why the man has Nora drooling.

The man is hot as hell, with bulging muscles, a thin beard and tattoos all over his arms and hands.

I know from my newfound baseball knowledge that this man is Ben Kipper, the Miners manager. Or Skipper, as Maddox calls him.

But my attention doesn't stay on him long because it's quickly taken by the bruise that is forming on Maddox's face.

It looks angry and like it will take a few weeks to go away.

Without thinking about it, I break the distance between Maddox and me and reach up to gently touch his cheek.

He flinches a bit at my touch but then leans into it.

"I'm fine," he voices, placing a hand on my mine and lowering it from his face, but he doesn't let go of me.

"Like hell you are," Nora exclaims, grabbing her son by the face to inspect it.

I want to laugh, because seeing them interact with each other this is really cute, but it's not the time or place to swoon over the mother-and-son relationship.

Maddox lets out a sigh and wiggles out of his mother's hold and turns to Ben, who is just watching the whole interaction with an amused look.

"Ben, this is my mom, Nora, and my girlfriend, Jen. Ladies, this is the team skipper, Ben."

I give Ben a smile and shake his hand.

When he turns to Nora, I watch them interact as if it were a movie.

"It's nice to meet you, Mrs. Bauer," Ben says, holding out his hand to her.

Nora giggles a bit before shaking the hand that is being offered to her. "Never was a Mrs. Bauer is actually my birth name. You can call me Nora."

Ben gives her a smile as if he is taken by her. "It's a pleasure to meet you, Nora."

"It's nice to meet you too, Ben. Now you want to tell me how long my son is suspended for?"

Instantly I forget about Nora and Ben's interaction and dive back into what caused that bruise on Maddox's face.

Ben looks over at Maddox and lets out a sigh before answering Nora. "It hasn't been officially announced, but if I had to guess, I would say a full game of play and a fine."

"I'm sorry, suspended? But you didn't throw the first punch," I argue.

My mind right away goes to what another suspension might do to Maddox.

"I was still involved in a fight. It's fine, it will be just one game, I can handle it," Maddox reassures me.

One game may not mean much to him but when he is trying to rebuild his brand and show people that he is worth supporting, one game is more than enough.

Without a doubt, people on social media are going to have a field day with this.

"What was the fight about anyway?" I ask, looking back up at his bruise.

At my question, Maddox's whole body goes rigid, which tells me that he doesn't want to talk about it.

And his answer tells me just that. "It doesn't matter. What's done is done and I will deal with the consequences when they come."

Ben looks over at him as if he wants to say something but when Maddox turns his hard stare over to him, he drops it. He just places a smile on his face and looks back at Nora and me as if nothing is wrong.

"Ladies, it was really nice to meet you. Hopefully we get to meet again. If you excuse me, I have a bus to catch."

Ben walks away and the second that he is out of hearing distance, Nora goes back to scold her son.

"You want to tell me why the fight even happened? You are better than that, Maddox."

Maddox just shrugs at her. "It just happened. So can we just drop it and go?"

Nora is already shaking her head and crossing her arms. She is going to get to the bottom of this whether Maddox likes or not.

She's a little scary, if I'm being honest.

"No, I want to know. So, tell me what the hell drove a man to punch you, or I will walk over to the other clubhouse and I will have Troy tell me."

"He said something about Jen, okay? The bastard had been taunting me all damn game and trying to get under my skin and the second he mentioned Jen, he fucking succeeded. That's why I charged at him. That's why I have a fucking bruise on my face and I'm going to be suspended."

Both me and Nora go silent.

Nora because she can't believe that Maddox actually told her.

And me because I'm trying to wrap my head around the fact Maddox got into a fight with someone, an old teammate at that, over me.

So many questions start forming in my head, but two questions stand out, why and how?

How did the catcher even know about me and why would he use me to get under Maddox's skin?

Nora is the first from the two of us that is able to compose herself enough to speak.

"Alright then. I guess Troy deserved it. Should we go get some pizza?"

I want to say no. I want to tell her that no we shouldn't get some pizza, not until Maddox tells me what exactly this Troy guy said, but I can't seem to find my voice.

That seems to be the case as we leave the stadium or get into Maddox's car, and that continues to be the case as we eat and head out.

Our late lunch itself was quiet, like there was this cloud hanging over us and none of us knew what to say. Maddox was still clipped from the fight, Nora would say the occasional small sentence, and well, I was too into my thoughts to say anything.

Even during the car ride back to Nora's, the cloud still hangs.

But once we get back to the house, it gets a little worse, especially when Maddox's brooding gets onto a whole different level.

Nora must feel the tension that is flowing between us because the second we walk into the house, she announces that she has to go to the store for something.

It must have been so important that she completely forgot about it in the car.

Once Nora is gone, Maddox heads upstairs and to the bedroom that we are staying in.

For the last couple of days, we've been staying in the same room and sharing a bed. Nothing has happened between us besides a few goodnight kisses and cuddles.

I was okay with that, because when Maddox was in the room, it felt warm and comforting. It especially felt that way since I'm still coming down from the scare of the street festival, but right now it feels a little cold.

After a good minute of watching him throw his clothes around, I've had enough.

"So are you going to tell me what the guy said about me, or are you just going to continue being pissed off at the world?" I ask, crossing my arms across my chest.

"I'm not pissed," Maddox throws out, not even turning to look at me.

"Really? Because the scowl that hasn't left your face since you walked out of the clubhouse, would say otherwise," I mutter.

Finally, Maddox turns to face me. "What do you want from me?"

"I want you to tell me what exactly that guy said and how it resulted in you getting a nasty ass bruise on your face."

"It doesn't matter," he lets out.

I can't help but roll my eyes. "Stop saying that. It may not matter to you, but it does to me. Especially if my name was somehow involved."

Maddox just stands there in the middle of the room, unmoving. His facial expression is still hard, and his shoulders are so ridged that he can probably plow through the door.

His jaw even starts ticking.

"Fine, you want to know?" His tone is clipped but I still give him a nod. "Troy has a big mouth, always has. He started spewing shit during my first at bat and I ignored him. I ignored him until he decided to say your name. I ignored him until he asked for your number. I ignored him until he said that he wanted to see your knees with your mouth wide open and if you had a gag reflex. I can take all the shit about my game and my past discretions but when they add you into the mix, I will fucking lose it every single time. As to why am I pissed, that has nothing to do with how my face looks and everything to do with your dad."

My eyes go wide. "How is my dad involved in this?"

"It's just an added thing that tells him just how undeserving I am of you. As if I didn't know that already. Now he has even more reason to tell you to leave me. All because of a stupid fight."

All of this is crazy. "What my dad thinks shouldn't matter. All of this is fake."

Maddox's shoulders drop. "How did that lie feel on your tongue? Because things between us haven't been fake for a while. I know that and I think you do too. Hell, every single time I think about you and the word fake in the same sentence, I want to punch something. So yes, what your dad thinks does fucking matter. It matters, because I care about you, because I want to fucking be with you." He pauses to pull at his hair before startling up again. "But I guess the question is, do you feel the same way?"

Never, I mean never, did I think that it would be Maddox that would be the one to say that he wanted to be with me. I thought I was going to be the one to say those words first and that he would just push me away.

Yet here he is, vulnerable, saying all the right words and making me want him even more.

I have so many things I want to tell him. I want to tell him that, yes, I feel the same way. That, yes, I was lying when I said things between us were fake. That yes, I want him and everything that he has to offer.

My dad may think that Maddox is undeserving of me but that's not how I see it.

Maddox is everything I need and want and I'm going to take it.

Instead of using my words, I use actions to give Maddox his answer.

26

MADDOX

If I wasn't watching her eyes, I would have thought that she was going to walk.

Was a part of me scared that it was going to happen? Yes, but the way her eyes spoke to me told me that I had nothing to fear.

My eyes stay on hers as she continues to stand there, not saying a word.

I can see it in her eyes what she wants to say, but she's holding back.

I'm about to step forward and show her just what I mean by my words when she takes a step toward me.

One step.

Two.

Three steps to close the space between us and the second she is within arm's reach of me, her arms go around my shoulders.

I expect her to say something but instead, she grabs me

by my hair and brings me down to her face, causing our lips to slam together.

It took me by surprise, but I quickly recover, letting my hands move down her body to bring her closer to mine.

My mouth, my tongue, my hands, all of me can't get enough of her.

Our mouths glide together, fighting for more. Our tongues dance together trying to get every last taste.

We've kissed, but we've never kissed like this.

Our kisses before this were out of want. This kiss is out of desperation, out of need.

I need this woman in every way she is willing to give.

"Fuck being fake," Jen mutters against my mouth, pulling away and letting her lips travel down my neck.

I can feel her almost everywhere and yet it isn't enough.

Lifting her up by the waist, I bring her face up to meet mine. I needed to see her face when I say the words.

"If we say fuck it to being fake, this thing between us will be one hundred percent real. I won't let you go. You will be mine for real and the word 'fake' will not exist in my vocabulary. So tell me right now, do you want this?"

Her eyes bore into mine like they have never done before. I'm able to see every single emotion running through them.

Fear.

Anxiety.

But best of all, excitement.

A bright smile takes over her face before she gives me a nod.

"I want this. Fake, real, I want everything that involves you." A feather-like kiss lands on my lips but before she takes it further, I pull back.

"I'm still in recovery. I may always be. Is that included in everything?"

I had intrusive thoughts already in the last few weeks, without a doubt something will happen that will cause those thoughts to come back.

When that happens, I want her at my side to bring me back out, at least to try, but she has to want to be there. I won't force her.

Jen doesn't even hesitate with her answer. "Everything, Maddox. Every single thing."

A smile forms on my face. "Then fuck being fake."

Our lips are back to being intertwined and our tongues trying to one up the other.

My fingers dig into the material of her leggings, wishing it was her bare skin that I was feeling and not the fleece material.

Jen wraps her legs around my waist and grinds herself against me as best she can.

I walk us over to my bed and take a seat with her on my lap, not putting any distance between us.

My mouth travels down the length of her neck while my hands move from her hips to under her shirt. The same shirt that has my name and number on the back.

Her soft skin feels so fucking good that I wish I could hold her forever.

A sweet purr leaves her mouth causing me to smirk against her skin.

"Have I mentioned just how much I love seeing you with my name on your back?" I say, drawing circles with my tongue against her pulse.

Jen shakes her head. "No."

"Since the first time you wore it. I've beat off the image of you in just my jersey too many times for me to count." I open my mouth slightly, letting my teeth graze her skin.

"Maybe you should show me just how you got yourself off," Jen pants, her hips drawing circles against me.

I move my mouth away from her neck and move it back up to her lips. "I will. Don't worry about that, sweetheart, but not tonight. There are other things that I want to show you tonight."

"Can't wait." Her mouth slams back onto mine and we stay like that for a few minutes.

We get so lost in the kissing that we don't notice that the front door has opened until my hands are on her chest pulling at her nipples and my mom is calling out our names.

I don't know who jumps up higher, me or Jen, but somehow, we both end up on the floor a few feet apart.

"Are you two having sex?" my mom asks.

If I were to ever wish for a black hole to appear and swallow me whole, right now would be a good moment.

"No," I say through a crack in my voice. I clear my throat before answering again. "No, we're not having sex."

Jen lets out a laugh, without a doubt at my humiliation.

"I guess 'other things' will have to wait," she says through a giggle.

My mom's voice cuts through her laugh, and I can't

help but let out a groan, and not the type of groan that would have left me if Jen continued her hip motions.

This whole thing is messed up.

Luckily, an idea pops into my head.

"Nope, 'other things' will happen. Grab your things."

———

I HAVEN'T BEEN BACK in my apartment since before I went to rehab.

The night at Perversa, after Dante Rossetti gave me a good mental kick in the ass and told me he would help me get clean, was the last night I stepped foot through my front door.

It was a mess back then. There were clothes everywhere with more than a few bits of trash scattered around. It felt unlivable and it was like I wasn't able to breathe when I walked in. Add that I had a few stashes of drugs calling my name, I couldn't stay there. I had to leave. So that night I packed a bag and stayed in a hotel.

In the days after that, Dante sent a couple of his men to come clean out the drugs. Once that was done, I hired someone to clean the place from top to bottom and to come in every few weeks to clear out the dust.

Now, walking in it feels strange. It's the same apartment, just cleaner and it doesn't make me feel like I'm going to suffocate.

Maybe it's because I know there isn't any coke waiting for me to take a snort. Or maybe it's the woman that's at my side that is making me feel calmer than I have ever felt.

"This is a really nice place, but I think I like your apartment back in San Francisco better," Jen muses, turning to give me a smile as she walks deeper into the living room.

"Yeah, I think I like that apartment better too," I mutter out, not really feeling the need to talk about real estate.

"Then why keep this place?" she asks, heading to the window that overlooks the river.

"Chicago is home, got to have a place to come back to in the off-season. Can't really live with my mom."

But given the history this place has, maybe I should get rid of it.

Her smile falls a bit at my comment about this being home.

Looking at her, I think it might be less about me calling Chicago my home and more about what we agreed would happen once the final pitch of the season was thrown.

Wanting her in my arms, I close the distance between us, molding her body to mine when we are only a few feet apart.

"Now that this is real, we don't have an expiration date. You know that, right?"

"I think I still have to wrap my head around that. It hasn't fully sunk in that we are together in an official capacity just yet."

"It's only been an hour or so. Give it a week and all you will be able to talk about to Selena is your professional baseball player boyfriend." I lean down and place a kiss right under her ear.

I fucking love that I can kiss her whenever I want now.

"Oh, I have to tell Selena!" she exclaims, wiggling out of my hold.

The relationship this girl has with her best friend is insane but for right now that's going to have to wait.

"You can call Selena later, I have something else in mind right now," I say as I bring her body back to mine.

When she comes back to me, her bottom lip sticks out to give me a sad face. "Calling Selena and your plans can be done simultaneously."

Speechless.

This woman has rendered me speechless, and my mind has to take a few seconds to even come up with something to say.

It takes me a few tries, but eventually I'm able to get the words out.

"I know you love your best friend but I'm pretty sure she doesn't want to hear you moaning out my name as I slide my tongue against your pussy. Better yet, when my cock is sliding into home base."

"Did you just use a baseball analogy to describe you fucking me?"

I give her a shrug. "My baseball analogy is better than you wanting to call your best friend while I screw the ever-living shit out of you."

Jen lets out a laugh. "Selena may look like a shy girl, but trust me, she's kinky. She would have been all for it."

The smile she is giving me is telling me that she's joking but she very much could be telling the truth. If it is the truth, it's not an image I wanted to have in my head.

What Hunter and Selena do in their own time is their business.

"Definitely did not need to know that. Now I won't be able to look her in the eye."

Another laugh comes out of Jen's mouth and I can't help but smile at it. The smile grows even more when she wraps her arms around my neck, bringing us closer together.

"You'll be fine. Now," she says as her lips hover over mine. "What are these other things that you had in mind?"

"Well," I lean my forehead against hers. "We were rudely interrupted."

Jen just gives me a shrug. "I mean, we were fooling around in your mom's house. What did you expect?"

"I expected to at least get you off before she came back." I lean forward and take her bottom lip between my teeth.

A sweet moan leaves her mouth.

"Then get me off now. Nothing is stopping you," she purrs.

I'm about to do what she says and rip every single article of clothing off her body when she pulls away fully.

So many fucking interruptions.

"What?" I ask, confusion in my voice.

"Your no sex rule," she says, her eyes going wide as she remembers the one rule I gave myself. "And the no relationship rule. You can't break those."

"It's fine," I argue, reaching for her. I'm really getting tired of starting and abruptly stopping.

"It's not fine, Maddox. These rules are there to help you

through your recovery. You can't break them," she says, worry in her tone.

I take her face in my hands and look into her eyes as I speak to her. "There was a point in all of this that I thought that I needed those rules, and maybe a part of me still needs them. But I need something more and that's you and I'm not talking about needing you in a sexual way. While I do need you in that way, I need you more as the person that stands by my side and is there for me to hold on to whenever I need her. Not having you in that capacity will be more catastrophic than breaking any rule I have in place."

She looks at me with glassy eyes. Without a doubt, she wasn't expecting me to tell her all of this. I understand that it might scare her, but I would rather break every single rule than to lose her.

"Okay." Her voice is small, but the word holds power behind it.

"Okay." I nod. "Can we stop with all the interruption now?" I ask, placing a chaste kiss on her lips.

She gives me a nod and a sweet smile. "No more interruptions."

"Thank fuck."

Within seconds we go back to kissing with the same intensity that we had back at my mom's house.

With all interruptions out the window, I have Jen completely naked, on her back with me between her legs minutes after our last words were spoken.

I lick every single inch of her, savoring every ounce of her taste that I can.

Our night of exploration last month was definitely not enough. I didn't realize just how much I wanted Jen until I had the taste of her release on my tongue and my cock begging to be inside of her.

"I'm so fucking happy I walked into that coffee shop back in March." I say with a growl as I rip the condom open with my teeth.

Jen lets out a giggle while her hand travels between us and gives me a few heavy-handed strokes. "I'm happy I finally get to feel you inside me again. You have no idea how much I wanted a repeat of that night."

I give her a smirk. "Now you get to experience it anytime you want."

I take my place between her open legs and when I slide into her tight entrance, moans and groans fill the room.

"We should have done this on the bed." I groan as I thrust into her.

Jen's eyes roll back, and her bottom lip gets trapped between her teeth.

"For round two." She is able to let out.

I thrust into her a few more times, loving the visual of her full tits bouncing with every single one of my moments.

"Fuck, your pussy feels better than I remember."

"Maddox?" Jen moans.

"Yeah, baby?" I pant.

"Shut up and fuck the living shit out of me."

"Gladly."

27

Jennifer

"THAT WAS A STRIKE! The whole damn park saw it! Get some glasses," I yell toward the field.

Got to love when the stadium quiets down and everyone is able to hear you yell obscenities to the field.

You also have to love being so close that even Maddox was able to hear me yell from where he's on the pitcher's mound. The smirk he's wearing makes me want to run onto the field and kiss it off.

"Never thought you would become a baseball fan, I'm actually surprised," the male voice next to me says.

I look over at my cousin, Lucas, and give him a little shove. "I'm a Maddox fan."

He lets out a laugh before taking a drink of his soda. "Sure, this coming from the girl that has been yelling at the umpire that his strike zone is complete shit."

"It is! Maddox would have a lot more strikeouts if his zone was a lot bigger," I argue.

And he would. Maddox is pitching a good game, but the umpire isn't doing him any favors.

Lucas gives me a look as if to prove a point.

I can't help but roll my eyes and accept defeat. "Fine. I like baseball now, okay? But it's all Maddox's fault. If he wasn't my boyfriend, I sure as hell wouldn't care."

"I still can't wrap my head around the fact that you are dating Maddox Bauer. Like how does that even happen?"

I give him a smile, because I can't wrap my head around it either.

I'm dating Maddox Bauer. For real.

Definitely not what I expected to happen after our one night together. But if I'm being honest, I like being Maddox's real girlfriend a lot more than being his fake one.

It's been close to a month since our fake relationship became real and an amazing month it has been.

Maddox and I have come together like two puzzle pieces, our lives intertwining a lot more than they did before.

I've even started traveling with the team a lot more. Which is why I am currently sitting in a stadium in Los Angeles wearing black and orange in a sea of blue and white.

Me coming on this trip though was less than being a baseball player's girlfriend and more because I wanted to see Lucas. We may be cousins, what with my dad and his mom being siblings but we don't get to spend a whole lot of time together. We see each other maybe once a year, if that.

242 | JOCELYNE SOTO

"Trust me, I have a hard time understanding it too, but enough of the baseball player," I say, giving him a dismissive hand wave. "Why didn't you bring Mia? I think she would have had fun."

"Her mom had this family thing in Arizona, and she wanted to take her. So, I switched my days for her to go."

At twenty-one, Lucas has a one-year-old daughter. He was nineteen when his then-girlfriend got pregnant, and from what I understand, they tried to make it work between them but things didn't work out.

"That was nice of you. Someone else would have told her no."

He gives me a shrug, his eyes on the game. "We may not be together, but just because we aren't doesn't mean I have to make things harder for her."

"So, you're friends?" I ask, wanting to know more about the dynamic he has with his baby mama.

"Yeah." He nods. "We were never good as anything more. Too much toxic shit and baggage between the two of us, but I'm glad that she's Mia's mom. That way, if anything happens, Mia is taken care of."

My stomach instantly churns at the last bit.

I should drop the subject, but I can't hold myself back.

"What do you mean if 'anything happens'?" I whisper and even through the loudness of the game, he's able to hear me.

Lucas turns to me, giving me a knowing look as if I should know what he is talking about. And in a way, I do.

I try my hardest to push down the lump that is starting to form in my throat.

"I thought you got out," I whisper to him, a slight hint of anger in my tone.

"I did, but just because I'm out, or at least think that I am, doesn't mean that something won't come knocking at my front door."

Something like what happened at the street festival? I want to ask but I don't. I do not want that image in my head. It would be a hard one to unsee.

I look over at Lucas, seeing a man instead of a boy that I've been used to seeing my whole life.

I guess that's what happens when you become friends the wrong people at a young age and get thrown into a world that a little boy has no business being in.

Lucas has become the man he is today not because of his upbringing but because of his decisions and the people he surrounded himself with.

People see the tattoos and the way he dresses and automatically think thug, but that's not who he is. There is more to this man than how he presents himself to the world. They don't see the little boy that I do, they don't see the father that he is to Mia.

Without a doubt, I honestly believe that if Mia didn't come into his life, he would still be a part of the world he didn't belong in.

Either still part of it or dead.

"How's my *Tia* doing?" I ask, changing the subject, something that he notices.

I can't continue thinking about something bad happening to him.

"Nice segway there. She's good, still working at the nursing home, but she's living life the best she can."

"My dad told me that he told her to move up north," I say, giving him a smirk.

Ever since I can remember, my dad has been trying to get his sister to move up to Seaside. For years, it was just playful banter between siblings but then after Lucas's dad died a few years back that banter became serious talk.

But no matter how hard my dad tries, she won't move.

"She'll never leave LA. As much as she says she hates it here, it's her home. No matter all the bad that happens, she'll still stay."

Makes sense given that she didn't leave after my *tío* died.

But I have to ask. "Will you ever leave?"

From the look on his face, I can tell that he is surprised by my question. I don't think anyone has ever asked him that before.

After watching Maddox pitch a few more times to get the batter out and to close out the inning, Lucas answers. "If I could have, I would have grabbed my mom and left a long time ago. If not the city but at least the neighborhood. I think about it now, especially with Mia. I don't want her growing up in the same environment I did."

This is the side that more people need to see of my cousin. The one that cares way too deeply about the people that he loves.

"Then do it," I urge.

Lucas lets out a laugh as Aaron walks up to the batter's box. "Not that easy."

"Why not?"

"Let me go back to school first and get a degree and then we can talk about moving to a different side of L.A. County."

Aaron hits a ball out to left field that gets him to first base. The whole stadium boos.

"You're going back to school?" I ask, a smile forming on my face.

Lucas is a smart guy, got A's all through high school, so when he graduated and decided not to go to school for anything, not even a trade, I was a little shocked.

He works as a mechanic and he's great at it, but I always thought he could do more than oil changes. Like maybe starting a business to restore old cars. He would be great at that.

Lucas gives me a nod. "I start in the spring. At USC for business."

"That's awesome, Lucas. I'm proud of you."

"Yeah, well, let's hope it works out. If not, I can see the dream of opening my own shop go down the drain."

I give his forearm a reassuring squeeze. "It will happen and when it does, I will be there to promote the shit out of it on social media. We can even get Hunter and Maddox to show up at your grand opening."

Lucas just shakes his head at my comment. He may think I'm crazy but if it ever happens, I will be pulling all the stops for him. Mark my words.

For the remainder of the game, we watch as the Miners beat Los Angeles three to two. The other team played a good game, but the Miners played a better one.

It's as we wait for Maddox by the net for our routine kiss that Lucas says something that I wasn't expecting.

"You look really happy, Jen."

I take in his words and for the first time I take a survey of what I'm feeling.

Happiness may radiate off me on the outside, but on the inside, I'm beyond happy.

I'm excited and I'm jumping up with glee every single change I get, and it's all because of Maddox.

Every single smile, every single laugh, every butterfly soaring through my body, every single inch of happiness is because of him.

And I wouldn't have it any other way.

28

AUGUST 18, 2022

MADDOX

AT TIMES, I have a love-hate relationship with baseball season.

One hundred and sixty-two games in a span of twenty-seven weeks is a lot. It's that type of schedule that can take a toll on a person. More so when they only have a full day off every two weeks or so.

It's a lot, especially for someone that has a family, or a significant other that they want to see more than just a few hours a day.

Add in traveling and it can be grueling.

But at the same time, I'm getting paid to play the game I love for one hundred and sixty-two games.

Right now, though, my relationship with the schedule is at a hate.

My game is at an all-time high, even after my suspension in Chicago, and the team is only a few weeks away from possibly clinching a spot in the playoffs.

But all that means less time with my girlfriend. Which

is why I'm currently pacing Jen's living room waiting for her to finish up getting ready.

During the season, time with someone is fucking precious and no matter how many times she travels with me to away games, time with her isn't enough. Something that I learned in the last month.

I look down at the time on my watch. If we leave in the next five minutes, we might make it.

"Babe, c'mon. We need to go," I yell in the direction of her room.

Jen usually is a puts on the first thing she finds type of girl. Tonight though, she has been getting ready for over an hour.

"I'm coming," she calls out, but no footsteps can be heard coming down the hallway.

"We're going to be late," I call out again, growing slightly impatient.

"Well, if you would have told me we were going some-where fancy, I would have been ready."

She has a point. When I told her to be ready by seven, I didn't really tell her how to dress. So, when I showed up wearing a black suit sans the tie, she went off.

She was wearing jeans and a T- shirt covered with a leather jacket and the second she saw what I was wearing, she started going off about communication and it being critical.

Like I said, she has a point.

"Maybe I didn't think about telling you because I was too busy thinking about seeing you and what I was going to do to you when that happened," I throw out, using my charm.

"I saw you yesterday," she yells out, still not coming out.

"Baby, that was a FaceTime call. I need the real thing," I say to her, checking my watch one more time.

Four minutes.

Jen says something but it sounds like a mumble so I ignore it and go back to impatiently waiting for her to be ready.

Finally with two whole minutes to spare, I hear high heels clicking against the floor.

The second she comes into view, I curse at our time constraint. If only we had ten more minutes and then I could hike up that piece of cloth she calls a dress and splay her on the kitchen counter.

I would make her my dinner.

"You look a little hungry, Bauer. Do you need a small snack before we go?" she asks, giving me a smirk, like she knows what I was thinking.

Not giving in to her satisfaction, I walk up to her and place a chaste kiss against her lips, barely grazing them.

"You look beautiful, baby. Now let's go." I place a hand on her hip and guide her over to the door.

"Seriously? Just a whisper of a kiss? I saw your eyes; they were filled with lust." She pouts as we walk out of the apartment, and I take her keys to lock up.

"Trust me, that lust is still there, but it will have to wait. We're going to be late," I say, pocketing her keys and waving for her to start walking.

She narrows her eyes at me before she does what I say and starts to walk in front of me.

The whole way to the car, I walk behind her just admiring the things that her dress does to her body.

It's form-fitting, causing each and every one of her curves to be on display. The material hits a few inches above her knee and every time she moves, the material rises bit by bit, showing the edge of her ass a bit.

I know she's not pulling down the material because she wants me to see. She wants me to suffer a bit for not doing more back in her apartment, and as long as nobody else walks by us, I will let her. I may be enjoying the show too much.

When we get to my car, I show her just as much by bringing her body to mine, her back to my chest as I open the door for her.

I lower my head so that my lips are right by her ear. "If you're the good girl that I know you can be, then maybe you won't have to wait until after dinner to know what I was envisioning back in your apartment."

She lets out a whimper and pushes herself more into my body.

I've come to learn in our month and a half together that Jen not only likes when I take control of her body, but also being praised.

One of her favorite phrases, good girl.

The shit that happens to her body when I say that.

"Promise?" she asks, her head landing on my shoulder and her turning to me giving me sex filled eyes.

Not being able to resist myself, I lean in and give her the kiss that she wanted back upstairs.

We stay connected like this for what feels like an eternity before I break us apart.

Jen opens her eyes and there is so much need in them that for a split second, I want to say fuck everything and take her back upstairs.

But I don't because I have plans.

Jen finally lets out a sigh when she realizes that the only thing that we are doing is getting in the car.

"Fine," she huffs, sliding into the passenger seat. "Take me wherever you're so damn determined to get to."

———

I MADE A GOOD CHOICE.

A spectacular one at that given the look on Jen's face right now.

With the help from Aaron and his wife, I was able to make a few calls and close the San Francisco aquarium down for a private event.

The event?

Me and Jen finally having our first real date as a couple.

We had our first fake date here. Why not have our real one? And because of the damn playing schedule, I was finally able to do it.

All the stops were pulled out for this. The surprise cruise, the caterer, the venue, everything down to the exhibit. I needed everything to be perfect.

And I would say that I achieved that.

First, we went on a boat cruise that had us under the Golden Gate Bridge, then we came back here to the aquarium. We ate the dinner I had catered from the highest rated Italian restaurant in the city in front of the Jellyfish. We had dessert in the coral reef exhibit. Now we are laying on a blanket on the floor of the deep-sea exhibit, watching all the sea creatures swim by.

Fuck, I'm a damn good boyfriend.

"I still can't believe that you rented out the whole place." She says, looking up at me from where her head lays on my shoulder.

The lights of the exhibit make her eyes sparkle.

Not only am I a good boyfriend, but now I'm using the word sparkle. I've become soft because of this woman, and I think I'm okay with that.

"Believe it. I would do anything to see you smile like you did when we walked in. That image is engraved in my head."

She was near tears when she figured out what I had done. She thought our night ended with the cruise. For a solid minute or two, she didn't say a word. She just took in every little detail.

When her trance finally broke, she jumped into my arms and if we didn't have the place to ourselves, we for sure would have been kicked out for our level of public display of affection.

"No one has ever done something this romantic for me. Thank you." Jen leans up and places a kiss on lips.

"You're welcome," I say, putting way more effort than necessary into the kiss.

When we come up for air, Jen starts to tell me about every animal that's in the tank.

The way she tells me about the sea creatures, I start thinking about where I would be right now if Ben hadn't pulled me into his office and told me I needed to show I'm worthy. If he hadn't suggested that I find someone to help with my social media or to find a fake girlfriend.

Would I still be here in an empty aquarium feeling to the need tell the woman in my arms how I feel about her?

Would I even have Jen in my life? If I left Ben's office that day, would I have gone back to the coffee shop or her apartment and sought her out?

Probably not.

I most likely would be sitting on my couch back in my apartment, waiting for something to happen. I probably would be trying my hardest not to let temptation take over and eventually throw my sobriety down the drain.

I should thank Ben one of these days for lecturing me about rebuilding myself, because without a doubt, I wouldn't be here with the woman I love.

And yes, I love Jen.

I think I loved her for a while now, but I started to realize it more after the events of the street festival. But we were still fake and as of right now, I don't think that she's ready to hear the words. And that's okay.

A finger stabs into my side.

"Are you listening to me, Bauer?"

I love the girl, but she is still a pain in my ass.

I take her stabby finger in my hand and bring it up to my mouth where I take it between my teeth.

She lets out a small yelp.

"I'm listening, just thinking about where I would be if Ben didn't tell me to find a fake girlfriend."

Jen leans up onto her elbow, digging herself into my chest. "Oh yeah, and where would you be?"

Instead of continuing the banter, I tell her the truth.

"Nowhere near where I currently am. Definitely stuck in my head and fighting urges left in right. I don't know if I've told you this, but from the very beginning, you've centered me, and I would be lost without you."

Jen's eyes shift from being playful to looking like that are filled with love. At least, I think that it's love.

I watch her as she watches me and for a few seconds, I think she might actually call what I said bullshit when she shifts.

She goes from laying at my side to straddling me in two seconds.

My hands instantly go to her hips, holding her in place. Her dress riding up past her thighs, giving me a glimpse at her black lace panties.

"What are you doing?" I ask, letting my hands draw circles along her hips.

"Thanking you," she says, her voice soft and barely a whisper but I still hold it close.

"Thanking me for what exactly?"

Jen moves until she is laying on me horizontally, her hands sliding into my hair.

"For coming to the coffee shop that day so that I could

meet you for the first time. For coming back a month later. For asking me to be your fake girlfriend and for making me your real one. Thank you for being you and letting me see you from every single angle. And thank you for giving me a night that I will never forget."

Her lips land on me in the gentlest way. Almost feather-like. A chaste kiss if she had ever given me one.

Our mouths are gentle until they aren't.

There's a shift and we become as hungry for each other as we did on our first night together. There is this pull between us that can't be explained and fuck me if I don't want more.

"Think we can get away with more than just kissing?" Jen asks, grinding herself against me.

If we were home right now, her dress would be in shreds on the floor, and she would be bouncing on my cock like there's no tomorrow.

Maybe I can make that dream a reality.

Pulling away from her and ignoring her questioning look, I look around the room.

It's dark, and the only light is coming from inside of the tank, but my eyes are adjusted enough to see where the cameras might be.

I find a blind spot and without thinking, I get up, taking Jen in my arms before grabbing the blanket and walking us over to the little nook area.

"What are you doing?" she asks as I set her on her feet and work to place the blanket back on the floor.

"You wanted to do more than kissing. There are no cameras over here," I tell her, giving her a smirk.

It takes her a few seconds of looking around and her giving me more confused looks before she puts two and two together.

"You do know we have a car, right?" she tells me.

"I do, but where's the fun in that?" I give her a shrug, standing to my full height.

"I can see a lot of fun in that. Definitely can suck you off in the back seat and nobody will be able to see." She gives me a nod.

I let out a small laugh and close the small distance between us.

"If you want to go to the car, we will go to the car." I lean down and start kissing her neck. It doesn't take long before she is melting in my hold.

As my tongue glides up the vein of her neck, she lets out a moan. "The car is too far."

Her hands move to my belt, where she starts to tug at it and unbuckling it.

"Okay then," I say, letting her slide my belt off and pop open my slacks. My suit jacket was discarded a while ago.

"You better be right about the cameras, Bauer. I don't need my bare ass to be on the internet."

Pulling away from her, I take her face in my hands and look into her eyes.

"Never, and I mean never, would I let you be exposed in any way if I thought someone was going to see you. You and your body are for my eyes only, no one else's."

I shift us, making sure that her back is to the corner of the nook and my back is to anything that might see.

"Now the only thing that they would see is my bare ass."

The grin she has on her face says it all. She is totally here for this little adventure.

"I'm about to make the aquarium your favorite place in the world," she says, leaning up and kissing my lips gently.

"And how are you going to do that?"

She doesn't answer. No, instead of using words, my girl gives me a devilish smirk and sinks down to her knees.

The smirk stays on her face as she slides a hand into my slacks and gives me a few tugs before taking me out.

The way she is licking her lips has me letting out a moan and her lips have yet to even touch me.

Before she takes me in her mouth, I look over my shoulder just to double-check that nobody has entered the exhibit without us knowing.

Seeing that nobody is there, I turn back and look down at Jen. I place a hand on her face, and she gives me a devilish smile before leaning in and taking me in her mouth.

As soon as I wrapped around the warmness of her mouth, it's as if I'm on a high I never want to come down from.

She works me in the best way possible, sucking, licking off any precum that is leaking out of me.

When her hand starts to cradle my balls and she gives my tip a good suck, I about lose it.

"Fuck, baby. This mouth of yours is perfect." My hand lands in her hair, giving her a good few tugs, asking for more.

Jen looks up at me, and I get lost in her eyes for a little bit. With this lighting, you can't see all the different tints come together to give her that brown eye color, but they are dark and enticing and make me want to give her everything that I fucking can.

"You look so beautiful with your eyes in this light and your mouth taking all of me. If only I can take a picture to keep this visual forever."

I may not have meant the words in a literal sense, but they still have Jen nodding yes at me.

"You want me to take a picture?" I tug at her hair, making her look up at me.

She gives me another nod right before she releases me with a pop, as she comes up for air. The mixture of her spit with my precum all over her lips.

"Yes, take the picture," she says, taking me in her soft hands before placing me in her mouth again.

As I take out my phone, I have to think of something other than her mouth on me. I'm on the verge of shooting out my release but I need to get myself in check.

Baseball plays spring to mind as I put in my passcode and bring up the camera. The image of Jen takes over the screen.

My cock in her mouth, her eyes wide with my hand in her hair is everything that I need to snap the perfect picture and get closer to the edge.

Getting tired of the Baseball plays and stats frantically running through my head, I pull at her hair for her to release me.

"Why did you do that?" she asks, running a finger under her eye to wipe away the tears that have escaped.

"I need my release another way. Stand up and turn around. I need to see you take me from behind," I say, dropping my phone to the floor.

With a flirty smile, she does what I say, standing up and turning around, placing her hands against the wall.

I take my time hiking up her dress to reveal her ass that is asking for a few teeth marks.

Leaning down, I palm her ass and give one of her cheeks a good bite, leaving an indentation before moving to the other.

Jen lets out a yelp that is quickly followed by a moan when I stand to full height and slap a hand against the bite mark.

"I'm going to take a wild guess and say that I'm being a good girl tonight." The playfulness in her tone has me giving her ass another slap.

"Very, now I think it's time for your reward."

I lower her panties just slightly, sliding my hand to her inner thigh and caressing the folds of her pussy.

She's wet and by the way her legs shake slightly when a finger glides along her clit, she's needy.

"It looks like you're ready."

"Hmm, I am," Jen purrs, arching her back more, grinding herself against me.

Palming her ass, I grab my wallet quickly and take out the one condom that I left and cover myself before positioning myself at her entrance.

"We fuck here and then we will go back to my place

where I will fuck you all night. Sound good?" I ask as I slide myself against her wet folds.

"Sounds perfect."

"Good," I say, thrusting into her.

Her moans fill the room and as I slide into her again and again, I forget where we are and how there is a possibility that someone might walk in on us.

I could give two shits.

All I can focus on is Jen, how she makes my heart pound and how her pussy wraps perfectly around my cock.

As I lose myself in my release, I tell Jen that she was right, the aquarium is now my favorite place.

29

SEPTEMBER 4, 2022

Jennifer

"I'M SORRY, can you repeat that? I think the high elevation is messing with your head., I say to Maddox, who's face so happens to be taking over my computer screen at the moment.

"It's not, and I said move in with me," he says, followed by an eye roll.

"Are you sure about the elevation thing? I mean, you are in Colorado. Or maybe it's the San Francisco fog finally affecting your mentality."

"My head is fine," Maddox argues.

"You just asked me to move in with you over a video call, you must be experiencing some sort of shock or something."

Maddox has been gone on an away series for the past two days and is due back on Tuesday. Because it was such a short trip, I decided to stay behind and concentrate on planning content for the next month for him and the new client I got last week.

The man has been gone for two days and now he is spewing out words like move in and I don't know whether I should laugh or frantically say yes.

"Babe, I'm fine. My head is fine, I don't see why you are freaking out about this."

"You just asked me to move in with you, Maddox! We've only been together for not even two months. How are you even thinking about that?"

"We've technically been together since April," he says, and the bastard has the audacity to shrug.

"It's only been official since July," I argue back.

"Years from now, if we're still together and people ask you what's your anniversary, what are you going to tell them? They can look it up online."

Shit, he's right.

If people look into us, they may know that I first started to pop into Maddox's life back in April while he was playing in San Jose and Sacramento. Hell, the picture he reposted of mine is still circulating with a damn time stamp.

Maybe I can tell people that we were just talking then, and it didn't become official until July, keep the truth alive.

But that may raise some questions.

Crap.

"Okay, fine. I would tell them that we got together around the time you were in Sacramento. Happy?"

He gives me another shrug. "Not until you answer my question."

"It wasn't really a question." I throw back.

I'm deflecting. I know it, he knows it, I'm pretty sure everyone within a mile radius of me knows it.

Maddox gives me a look, like he might be slightly annoyed with me.

"Jennifer, will you move in with me?" he says, annunciating each word.

I shake my head. "That sounds like a wannabe wedding proposal."

"Jesus," Maddox mutters, running a hand against his face. "You're making this harder than it has to be."

He's right again.

But are we even ready to move in together?

"You're the one that brought the subject up. I was ready to make this a sexy video call and flash you my chest, but you had to go and ask me to move in with you."

One of his perfectly sculpted eyebrows raises. "If you move in with me, then you can flash me anytime you want. You can also go topless anytime you want. Just move in with me."

"Why?" I ask.

Why is he asking me to move in with him now and not later down the line?

"Since we got back from Chicago, and when I'm in town, can you think of any time that you've slept at your place?" he answers.

I give him a questioning look, but he waves through the screen as if tell me to think about it.

Up until this point, I haven't seen anything wrong with our living arrangements. We do spend most nights at his place when he's in town, that's for sure, but we definitely spend time at my place too. Don't we?

I try to think back to the last time that Maddox spent the night here and I can't think of one besides the night we met.

He's been to my apartment plenty of times, but in the time that we've been a couple, he hasn't slept here.

Not only has he not slept here, but his place has always been the default.

I shake my head in defeat. "No, I can't."

Maddox nods. "Look around your room. Do you see anything of mine there?"

It sounds as if he's giving me riddles, but I do what he says.

Looking around, I try to find something that might be his.

There's one of his jerseys that he wore a few weeks ago during a game, but it's only here because I took it from his place.

There's a hat, but he gave that to me when he got called up.

There are a few of his T-shirts, but they are only here because I brought them from his place to sleep in when he's at away games.

Nothing is in here because he has brought it over. If it wasn't for me having them, there would be no sign of my boyfriend here.

"I guess not," I answer him.

"Want to know what I see every single time I get home?"

I nod, not saying a word.

"I see the clothes that you've left behind because you've taken my shirts, in my closet. I see your small amount of makeup and skincare on my bathroom counter. I see the books that Selena let you borrow on my coffee table, and I see your horrible snacks in my pantry. I see all of that, but I don't see you and I want to."

He's made me speechless.

I knew I had left a few things at his place, but I didn't think it was that much.

In a few short months, I've used his place as if it was mine.

Even with that revelation though, I still deflect.

"My snacks aren't horrible," I mumble out, not knowing what else to say.

A booming laugh leaves Maddox's mouth. "Of course, that's the thing you will hold on to. They are bright red."

"They're hot Cheetos and they are delicious with some lemon and a little bit of *Tapatío*," I argue. Anything to give me more time to come up with an answer to his proposition.

"They're already spicy, why add more?" He's looking at me like I'm crazy, and maybe I am, but I will defend my choice of snack until the day I die.

"Because it adds flavor, I do the same thing with the regular ones. Do not judge me, Bauer."

"I'm not." He pauses for a few seconds, before he starts speaking again. "What if I promise to keep the pantry filled with your horrible snacks at all times, will you move in with me then?"

Now I'm pausing some more.

I don't know why I'm holding back in saying yes.

Living with Maddox would mean spending more time with him, learning more about him and his mannerisms. Moving in together could also mean more possibilities of a future together.

A future that I want with him and him alone.

I was never one to picture a wedding, marriage, family or kids, but ever since I've gotten with Maddox, the pictures started to come.

Images of him playing years from now and me in the stands cheering him on with a little boy on my lap wanting to be just like his dad.

Images of a destination wedding on the sand.

So many images and I want every single one of them.

"You draw a hard bargain, Bauer," I say, a smile fighting to come out.

I see him shrug through the screen. "Anything to have you say yes."

Anything to have you say yes.

I give the man, the one I have a possibility of building a future with, a smile.

Do I think that we shouldn't rush this and wait a little longer to move in together? Yeah, but this could be a good thing and if I'm being honest with myself, I want it.

I want it so damn much, but I need to know one thing.

"What happens when it's the off-season and you go back to Chicago? Do I go with you? Or is us living together only count while you're in San Francisco? What happens if you go to another team?"

Do we end things? Or do I get pushed to the side while he lives his life in another city?

"The way I see it, wherever I live, you live. I move, you move. So, I'll throw a question back to you, are you willing to move with me? Leave San Francisco or California and go wherever I might go."

Yes.

The way that answer formed in my mind was so quick that it even takes me by surprise.

I take a second to really think about it.

Am I willing to do those things?

I have Selena and my parents here; I can't just move and not see them for months at a time.

The more I think about not being able to, the more a few holes appear.

As for Selena, she's only in San Francisco because of Hunter. If he gets traded, she will move with him wherever he lands. She can be here now but next year, she can be across the country.

My parents already live in a different city a three-hour drive away and I see them at the very least once a month. There are some months, I don't see them at all.

And it's not like I have work that I have to think about. I can be a social media manager from anywhere in the world.

I love the city, sure, but it's not like I can't come back.

There is nothing holding me back.

Without thinking about it, I find myself nodding at my computer screen.

"What is that yes for?" Maddox nods, a small smile starting to form on his lips.

"Yes, I'm willing to move with you. It's also a yes to moving in together," I say, giving the answer that has been on my tongue since he asked the question.

"Really?" he says, giving me a boyish smile. I love seeing it on his face so much.

"Yes, really," I say, giving him another nod. "Let's move in together."

The smile on Maddox's face says it all. "Yeah, let's."

It's hours after the call ends, while I'm in bed wishing that Maddox was there with me that I realize that I'm about to move in with a man that I haven't even said I love you to yet.

I'm not scared of the words. I just need to find the courage to save them.

Because I love Maddox Bauer and I will say yes to anything he asks of me.

30

SEPTEMBER 20, 2022

MADDOX

SEPTEMBER, by far ,is my favorite month out of the year.

It has nothing to with the stupid weather or that shit seasonal drink, but everything to do with baseball.

This is the time of the season that can make or break a team. Rosters grow from twenty-five to forty and a good chunk of teams are vying for a spot in the postseason.

Bats become machines, gloves are on fire and the pitching is fucking spectacular.

Did I think the pitching part about myself? Fuck yes, I did.

My pitching has been on point since August, the team winning in each of my starts.

Have there been losses? Of course, there has been, it's baseball. No matter how good your game has been, there will always be a few losses thrown in there.

I may lose a start between now and October, but I won't let it.

Especially when the Miners are half a game away from clinching the western division.

One game and then baseball will be just baseball for a few days until October comes and it's time to put in more work and fight for that world champions title.

First things first though, winning this game and hoping that Los Angeles loses theirs.

I slide on my shoes to head to the stadium when I hear Jen's voice in the distance as if she is talking to someone.

Jen officially moved into my place last week. There was a spurt of home games where we were able to move her things over and when I had to leave, she called Selena and Hunter to help her out.

She still has her apartment, mostly because her lease isn't up until January, but she is officially here permanently.

I never was one to want to live with girlfriends. It was always I had my space and they had theirs, and I liked it that way. Yet with Jen it was different.

I didn't want to have my space or hers. I wanted her, no better yet, I needed her in my space. I needed her here with me, sharing my bed, my couch, my bathroom, everything. It was something that I wanted since we officially got together.

I wanted it all with her and moving her in with me was a way of me getting that.

Thankfully she agreed.

As for how her parents feel about her living with me, well, her mom is happy, and her dad hates the idea.

I have yet to prove to Javier that I'm worthy of being in

his daughter's life, which is fair. I won't get his approval just because I move his daughter into my home. More work needs to be done before we get to that stage.

And we will get there.

After fixing where my slacks land, I leave the bedroom and head to the living room where I find Jen pacing, with her phone to her ear.

"Are you sure you're okay though?" she asks into the phone, her voice having a slight shake to it.

Her back is to me, so she doesn't see that I'm watching her, but when she turns and sees me standing there, her eyes fill with worry.

"Who are you talking to?" I mouth to her.

"Your mom," she whispers and instantly I'm on high alert.

My mom?

Pulling out my phone, I check to see if maybe I missed a call from her, but there aren't any notifications.

I look back at Jen, but she goes back to pacing.

"Oh no, sorry," she says into the phone. "Maddox just walked into the room."

As I watch her pace for a few more seconds, I can't help but to tap at my pockets, looking for something to calm myself down.

Something that I haven't thought of in weeks.

Not being able to handle my nerves anymore, I walk over to Jen, stopping her mid stride and holding out a hand for her phone.

She looks up at me with those brown eyes of hers that

are currently filled with concern for a second or two before conceding and passing me the device.

"Ma?" I say the second I bring the phone to my ear.

Right away, I hear her chuckle but it's not enough to calm me down.

"I told Jennifer not to pass me over to you," she tells me.

Her voice is slower than it usually is, as if she hasn't slept in a few days.

"Yeah, well, I'm your son. Is everything okay?"

So many scenarios pop into my head as I wait for her to respond.

Her surgery to remove the tumors is scheduled for the beginning of November, so maybe it got pushed back further.

Maybe it got canceled completely.

Maybe the tumors are growing again.

There are so many things that could have prompted Jen to ask if she was okay and the look of concern in her eyes.

"Everything is fine," Nora answers and everything in me is telling me not to believe her.

"Are you okay? Are you sick?"

I can imagine her shaking her head at me and maybe even giving me an eye roll.

"I'm fine, Maddox. I just have a little congestion, that's it."

"Congestion? Isn't that something you need to go to the doctor for?" I spit out rapidly.

I know it could be nothing, but given her history, I

would worry even if she sneezed.

"No, it's not," she says, most likely rolling her eyes at me. "It's probably a little head cold or my allergies acting up. It's nothing you need to worry about."

Yeah, that's not going to happen.

I look over at Jen and she still has that look on her face like she's concerned.

Without a doubt, she thinks my mom is lying too.

"Maybe I should call your doctor and make you an appointment just in case," I tell my mom.

She may be right and it's just a head cold, but I'm not going to take any chances.

"I'm a grown-ass woman, Maddox. I'm capable enough to make my own appointments, thank you very much."

"I still think you should see a doctor."

"Boy, I swear to god, I'm fine."

"Then why did you call Jen?"

Jen gives me a shrug like she doesn't know the answer to the question either.

"Maybe because I wanted to talk to her? My son is living with his first serious girlfriend. Maybe I wanted to talk to her and see how she was handling your needy ass."

I let out a groan. The woman is always taking jabs at me, so I guess if she is doing it now, she must be feeling okay and I shouldn't worry.

"Thanks, Ma. I greatly appreciate that," I say to her in a sarcastic tone

"Yeah, yeah. Well, I'm fine and you can tell Jen that too. Play hard today. I will be cheering you on from the comfort of my couch."

"I'll strike out a few batters for you," I say the words that I always said to her while I was growing up.

"You better," she says before she pauses for a second to cough before she comes back. "Okay, well I love you and tell Jen to call me if she can't deal with you. I know I couldn't sometimes."

Jesus, it's one jab after another.

But I ignore it. "I love you too. Call me for anything."

"I will."

When the call ends, I can't help but look down at the phone before handing it to Jen.

I make a vow that no matter the outcome of today's game, I will make a short trip to Chicago to check in on my Ma.

Something about that conversation isn't sitting well with me.

"She coughed a few times before you came in, and it definitely didn't sound like just a cold," Jen tells me, placing a hand on my forearm,

I give her a nod. "Yeah, I heard it too. She also was speaking a lot slower than usual. Said it was a small head cold or her allergies."

Jen gives me a small reassuring smile. "Maybe it is."

I can see it on her face that she doesn't even believe the words as she says them.

Either way, I find myself agreeing with her. "Yeah, maybe you're right."

She must see that my words are just that, words, because she leans up and places a chaste kiss on my lips. As if to relax me.

"Don't worry, she's fine. You'll call her after the game, and you'll see."

I give a nod. "Yeah."

Jen gives me one more kiss. "Head to the ballpark and have a good game. I will be in the stands cheering you on."

This time I'm the one that is leaning down and placing a kiss on her pout. "See you later."

With another smile, I make my way out of the apartment and head to the park.

As I turn into the player's parking lot, I decide to pitch the game of my life.

A game for Ma, because without her, without everything she did to get me to this point, I wouldn't be here. I wouldn't be anywhere near close to who I am today.

She better be right that it's just a head cold or her allergies acting up, because I wouldn't be able to handle anything else.

The universe already tried to fuck with me last year, it better not fuck with me now.

My phone dings as I get out of my car, and when I take it out, I see it's a game notification.

The same notification that I set up to tell me if Los Angeles wins or loses against St. Louis.

Swiping at it, I see the score.

The universe must be on my side because Los Angeles lost. Eight to three.

They lost, now the Miners are half a game away from winning the west.

Time to do as I said I would and pitch the game of my fucking life.

31

Jennifer

THE ATMOSPHERE in the park feels a little bit different today.

It's a lot louder, more exciting. Everyone is on their feet, cheering, not wanting to miss a second of what is going on on the field.

Maddox told me that today was going to be an important game, something about clinching the west. I didn't really understand what he meant by it, so he went into explicit detail as to how baseball postseason works and what winning today's game would mean for the Miners.

He was excited, and given the atmosphere of the ballpark, everyone in attendance is excited too.

According to the announcers, it's a sold-out game and the fact that Maddox is pitching is just icing on the cake.

The boyfriend in question is currently on the mound, pitching to an outfielder from San Diego. The second that the ball hits the catcher's mitt and an out is called, the whole park erupts.

"I've never seen the park like this," I say to Selena and Hunter.

We're currently sitting in a suite, it would have been awesome to sit down in the regular seats but since Hunter's football season is in full swing and we didn't want him to get hounded, we sat up here.

"With the division title on the line and with the way Maddox is pitching, I'm surprised it's not crazier." Hunter voices, swinging an arm around Selena and bringing her closer to him.

"He is pitching pretty great, right? Look at all those Ks he has on the board," I say, like the proud girlfriend that I am.

"It's not great, it's fucking amazing. Everyone is watching that scoreboard and the umpires like a fucking hawk," Hunter says to me.

"Why? The Miners are winning five to zero and nobody from the other team has been able to make it onto the bases."

There have been so many fly balls and plays at first, that I kind of feel bad for the other team.

"Exactly," Hunter says, pointing a finger at me.

"Exactly, what?" I ask him, narrowing my eyes at him.

"We can't talk about it," he spits out, and I swear if my best friend wasn't about to marry him, I would kick his ass for talking nonsense.

"We can't talk about what? You're not making any sense, Hunty. Maybe your football helmet is a little tight."

Hunter narrows his eyes at me and looks like he's about to say something, but Selena stops him.

"You're just going to confuse her more," she says, elbowing him in the stomach.

Selena steps out from under his arm and pulls out her phone.

"So far, this is what Maddox is pitching." She says, holding out her phone for me to see.

She has it open to her search engine and has searched "perfect game in baseball."

"What the hell is that?" I ask out loud, confused even more.

"The type of game where a pitcher pitches that doesn't allow anyone on base. No line drives, no bunts, no walks, nobody on base. Nothing from the other team's end. He has to do all that throughout the whole game in order to get the P word. This is a big thing for a pitcher," Selena explains.

"The P word?" Now she's talking in riddles.

Selena waves her phone. P for perfect. "You can't say it, or you jinx it."

I give Selena a look before looking out onto the field and then the scoreboard.

Huh. I just thought that Maddox was pitching a good game, but it's a lot more than that apparently. So much more.

"So, Maddox is pitching a P word?" I ask my two companions.

Selena nods. "So far, yes. It can change though."

It can change.

That's something that I've learned throughout the

season. Baseball can change so quickly. One single play can mess up a team's lead.

Which is why for the rest of the sixth and seventh innings, I watch the game with so much more concentration. I don't want to miss a single thing.

Every single pitch he throws, I'm on the edge. My nails get bitten to the nubs and my legs keep bouncing up and down.

When the seventh inning stretch comes along, I'm slightly calmer and the same goes for the second half of the seventh but as soon as the eighth inning starts and Maddox walks up to the mound, I'm a chaotic mess.

"Six more batters," Selena says, turning to me and giving me a smile.

Six batters seem like a small amount but six can turn to more very quickly.

Thankfully though, the eighth inning comes with two more strikeouts for Maddox and a ball that was popped up into right field and caught by Aaron.

First half of the eighth inning is done and now we wait for the ninth.

The second half of the eighth has Maddox coming up for his fourth at bat. His walk-up song taking over the whole stadium.

"Please tell me you didn't choose his walk-up song," Hunter says to me with a groan.

"I did, thank you very much."

"It's such a shit song." His face wrinkling up.

"I didn't hear you complain about the song all season

and now two weeks before it's over you decide to?" I narrow my eyes at him.

He shrugs. "I just noticed."

"Well, Jacobi, you can choke on a hot dog."

He lets out a laugh, and we turn back to face the field.

Maddox takes the first pitch and pops it into the stands. The second pitch he takes is a ball, but the third is what gets the crowd up on their feet.

He hits the ball into center field, where the outfielder misses it completely causing it to fall to the floor and for Maddox to end up on first.

I'm always proud of him during the games, but for some reason, with this game, I can't help but to be extra proud.

One more Miner ends up on base, moving Maddox to second, where he stays for the rest of the inning.

When the inning ends, every single person stands up when Maddox walks up to the mound.

From the looks of things, every single person here knows what is happening, what could happen and every single one of them is waiting with anticipation.

Me, I'm waiting with so much anxiety.

Maddox has gone through a lot in the last year and a half. So much that he thought that he would never play baseball again, that nobody would ever take a chance on him.

The Miners took a chance on him, and now here he is, playing again about to pitch a perfect game.

Shit, does me thinking it, mean I jinxed it?

God, I hope not because Maddox really needs this. If

he does this, it will be a way to show everyone that has doubts about him that he is still as good as he was before his unfortunate events. If not better.

Including my dad.

The first batter of the ninth steps up to the plate, and all Maddox has to do is throw a minimum of three pitches and he gets it.

He gets this perfect game.

There I go thinking the words again.

The first pitch is thrown, and the umpire calls it a strike.

One pitch down.

When the second pitch comes, the player swings and ends up hitting the ball up and when it comes down, it gets caught by the third baseman.

I let out the breath I was holding and cheer with everyone else as the second batter walks up.

One out, two more to go.

"You got this, baby. You got this," I whisper into my hands.

Selena hears me, and she comes over to me and wraps her arms around me as if she's giving me emotional support.

I feel like I need it right now.

As Maddox is getting ready to pitch to the second batter of the ninth, my phone vibrates in my hand.

Not wanting to miss Maddox's pitch, I ignore it.

The vibrating stops when the umpire calls out a strike on the first pitch but then it starts up again right before the second.

If someone is calling me twice in a row, it has to be something important.

Turning the phone over, I check to see who's calling.

It's a Chicago number according to the location on my caller ID.

There are only two numbers with a Chicago area code that will call me and one of those numbers is on the field right now.

The other is Nora.

But I have her number, so who would be calling me?

Whoever it might be, it can wait. I need to see my boyfriend finish this game.

Ignoring the call, I pocket my phone and turn back to look at the field. If it's important, whoever it is can leave a message.

Maddox strikes out the second batter and everyone goes wild. He's a few pitches and an out away from a big accomplishment.

As the third batter of the inning walks up, I feel my stomach go into knots.

This could go in a number of ways. I hope to whatever god hears me, that it goes in Maddox's favor.

My phone starts to vibrate again as Maddox winds up for his first pitch, but I don't look down at the device.

All my concentration is on Maddox and that's where it stays as the ball releases from his hand and makes contact with the bat.

I watch as the ball goes up in the air, and as it travels toward right field.

No oxygen enters my body as the ball drops to the ground.

This is it. This is where it all ends.

My eyes are so concentrated on the ball, that I don't notice that Aaron is under it, waiting to catch it until it's already in his glove.

I don't digest what happened until the whole stadium erupts in cheers and celebrations.

Maddox did it.

He pitched a perfect game.

Not only that but the Miners just won the west from what the scoreboard is announcing.

Holy shit, he did it.

Hunter, Selena, and I have our own celebration in the suite and then watch the team celebrate on the field.

With eyes still on my man as he celebrates with his teammates, I decide to finally see what the call was about.

The same number called for a third time and thankfully this time around they left a voice mail.

Pulling away from the noise, I find a little nook and listen to the voice mail.

When the voice comes on, not only does my heart drop to the floor but my eyes right away go to the field and I try to find Maddox.

I can't see him, but he is on the screen, a huge smile on his face.

The second that I tell him what the voice mail says, that smile will disappear.

I should have answered the call sooner.

32

SEPTEMBER 24, 2022

MADDOX

MA WAS RIGHT, it was a cold. A cold that her body was too weak to handle and put her in the hospital.

Doctors told me that even though she is in remission from her tumors, her body is still weak from the medication that any little illness can knock her down.

And knock her down it did.

Mom was watching the game on the couch like she told me she was going to do, but I guess during that time, the fever she had, spiked. She took over-the-counter medication, but her body was so weak that she decided to call the ambulance.

In a way, I'm glad she did because I can't imagine what would have happened if she had gone upstairs and fallen asleep.

When she arrived at the hospital, they called me but because it happened during the game I didn't answer. So, they called Jen.

Mom had asked me when we came to Chicago in July if

we should add her to the list just in case something like this happened. I was hesitant, given that at the time of the question, everything between us was still fake, but if it gave her a peace of mind, I told her to do it.

In a way, I'm happy that we put Jen on the list, because I have no idea how I would have reacted if I was the one that had gotten the call.

I already didn't take it very well.

I had just pitched a perfect game. The Miners had just won the west. I was on the highest high, that I thought no one could touch me.

When I saw Jen walk onto the field, I had this image in my head that I was going to pick her up and kiss the ever-living shit out of her. That we were going to celebrate with my teammates and their families. Then at the end of the night, we were going to take one of the champagne bottles that were handed out and have a celebration of our own.

Everything was already planned out.

But the second I saw her face, I knew something was wrong and that image was never going to happen.

Tears were running down her cheeks as she told me about the voice mail she got.

The voice mail from a nurse at my mom's hospital that said that an ambulance had brought her in.

All celebrations for me came to a screeching halt.

I started to panic, and somehow during that panic, I was able to find Ben and tell him what was going on.

Given the largeness of the game, I was set to do interviews, but he stepped in, so that I was able to leave.

Two hours later, me and Jen were on a flight to Chicago

and now I'm sitting next to the hospital bed my mom has been occupying for four days.

If she was a normal patient, they would have sent her home by now. The only reason she's here is because her doctors are keeping tabs on her and making sure her tumors haven't multiplied.

Now I'm in her hospital room, watching her sleep, something that I've been doing these last few days.

And where I will stay until she leaves this place.

She may not be in a coma, but they do have her on heavy antibiotics to fight the fever that has only started to go down yesterday.

I hear the room door open, but I don't turn to see who just walked in.

A hand lands on my shoulder and gives me a gentle squeeze telling me that it's Jen.

"You should go. You have a game to play tomorrow."

If it was any other time, I would be ecstatic that she knows my rotation schedule, but not right now.

I shake my head. "I'm on family leave until the division games start."

"Oh, I didn't know that," she says, dropping her hand from my shoulder. "At least go home and take a shower."

I'm already shaking my head again at her suggestion. "I'm fine here."

Jen lets out a sigh and comes to stand in front of me, kneeling before me, her eyes filled with concern.

"She's going to be fine, Maddox. Watching her sleep isn't good for you. When she wakes up in a few, she'll probably yell at you to go home."

I shrug at her. "She can yell at me all she wants, I'm not going to be leaving until she does."

"And you tell me I'm a pain in your ass," she mutters, and now I'm the one narrowing my eyes. "You need to rest."

When she says the last part, her tone is more affirmative.

"I said I was fine. How is that so hard to understand?"

When Jen flinches back, I realize that my words came out a lot more harshly than I intended them to.

"I'm sorry," I say, reaching out to place a hand on her face, but she pulls back.

She looks at me with those eyes of hers and has me feeling like an asshole.

"I know this situation pisses you off, it pisses me off too, but don't take it out on me."

She's right.

It may be just a cold that got too aggressive, but I hate that it brought my mom to the hospital, and they won't let her leave. I hate seeing her weak, because never has Nora Bauer ever been weak.

"She's right, you know. I am going to yell at you for staying and not going home." My mom's voice flows through the room, causing both me and Jen to turn in her direction.

Much like all the other times she has woken up, she looks like hell. There are dark bags under her eyes and her face looks like it needs a good lather of lotion or something.

But I do have to admit that she does look better than when we got here a few days ago.

"I'm not leaving until you leave. Take it or leave it."

Ma narrows her eyes at me, as if with her stare alone she can force me to do what she says.

It worked when I was a kid, and maybe it still works a few times now that I'm an adult, but it won't work right this very moment.

We have a stare-down for a good two minutes, just like every stare-down we've had every day she's been here.

And like every single time before, mom loses first.

She's letting me win, I know she is. But she will never admit it.

Ma wants me here, and for that very reason I don't leave.

"Fine, you can stay but the second I get out of here you're taking me to get some real food. A person can only take hospital food so much. I need real food," my mom says, scrunching her nose at the soup that the nurse had brought in earlier.

"Deal," I say to her before I look over at Jen and give her a smile.

She gives me an eye roll but there is a smile fighting to come out.

For the next hour or so, the three of us watch some weird soap opera that I'm sure has been around since I was a kid.

We finally take our attention away from it when the room door opens. I half expected the nurse, since it's around the time she usually does her rounds, but it's not her.

It's mom's doctor. The very same one that has been helping her during this whole brain tumor journey.

He's been on her case since she was brought in. After doing some scans the last couple of days, he hasn't stepped foot in here since then.

I chalked it up to it meaning that if we didn't see him, everything was good.

Now that he's here, I can't help but think that maybe I was wrong.

Maybe no news isn't good news after all.

"Nora how are you feeling today?" the doctor asks, walking to her bedside.

Jen stands up from her spot and comes to stand behind me and watch my mom interact with the man.

Ma gives him a shrug. "Better, but I would really like to go home."

The doctor nods. "I understand. You will be home soon, I promise."

I hear a but at the end. Like he wanted to say more but stopped himself.

Apparently, I'm not the only one that picked up on it, because as I watch my mom, I see her whole body go rigid.

"But?" she asks the doctor, not caring to wait for him to start speaking again.

The doctor doesn't answer, he just looks from my mom then over to Jen and me, silently asking us to leave.

Not going to happen.

"Whatever it is, I will be here to hear it," I tell the man, standing my ground. No way am I going to be leaving right now and definitely not when he looks like he's about to deliver bad news.

He lets out a sigh. "The scans we took yesterday showed an abnormality. They weren't very clear since it was in a location that we weren't looking at, which is why I ordered more scans for you this morning."

I did question why they took mom for more scans, and when I asked the nurse that wheeled her out, she just said it was doctor's orders.

"And? What did you find?" I ask, getting straight to the point.

The bastard has the audacity to look at me and then to my mom ask to ask for permission to answer my question.

My mom gives him a nod yes.

"Nora currently has three tumors that we are keeping a close eye on. Two on her left side and on her right. We found a fourth one right under the one on the right. It's small and covered by tumor three, and because it was hidden, that might be why we haven't seen it until today. Or it could be a new tumor that has formed in the last month or so since our last scan."

The only thing that I can concentrate on is the words 'new tumor. Everything before that and after doesn't register one bit.

"Are there any tests you can do to see if it is a new tumor?" Jen's voice comes through, taking me out of the cloud that I'm in and making the effort of being my saving grace.

The doctor shakes his head. "I wish I can say that there

was a way. I've even looked through Nora's past scans to see if we had missed it on one of them, but nothing comes up. Right now, we can only test if it's cancerous or not and keep an eye on it. I want to see if we can get a few more test in today and see what we are dealing with. It gives me a better idea on how to proceed."

"So, you want to open up her head. That's what you're saying," I spit out.

There's anger in my tone, I can hear it and so can every single person in the room.

Of course, I'm pissed. She can't seem to catch a fucking break. First were the tumors, then the fucking cold that landed her in the hospital and now there's a new tumor that has popped up?

Fuck that.

If my mom lost her hope before, she sure as hell will never get it back now.

"In order to do the test, yes, we will have to perform surgery to not only for a biopsy but to also get a look at it. See its size, and if it's hitting anything major. We need to see things that a scan won't tell us."

This is a repeat of what my mom went through last year.

After she was told that she had the tumors and doctors noticed growth, she went through this exact thing. Her skull was opened and for a few weeks after, she had a bald spot that she would try to hide in any way she could.

That's when they found that the tumors she had, were cancerous.

And it's possible that this one is too.

I stand up, my whole body becoming defensive.

"And what happens if you don't do the biopsy?"

Last time, mom went into depression waiting for the results. She wouldn't leave the house, she wouldn't eat, she wouldn't do anything because of the fear. She had to depend on her neighbor for a lot of things since I was playing.

If she goes through the testing again, she might fall under the same cloud once more.

"We can monitor it. Do scans every few weeks and keep a close eye on it. But given your mom's history, it's best to know what we are dealing with. That way, we can fight this the best way we can."

I look down at my mom and all I see is a blank look on her face. Nothing is telling me what she is thinking or feeling.

She's scared I know she is, especially with everything that has happened these last few days.

"When would the biopsy happen?" I ask.

"Maddox." Jen voices quietly from behind me. "That's not your choice to make."

I turn to the woman that has become one of the most important individuals in my life and see the tears that are starting to form in her eyes.

All of this is scaring her and the fact that I can see it with my own eyes that she is worried about my mom, makes me love her even more.

"She's right," the doctor says, nodding toward Jen when I make eye contact. "It's Nora's decision if we go through the testing or not. We will proceed with whatever choice she decides."

We all stare down at her.

She still has a blank expression, completely zoned out.

Scooting the chair I was just in closer to the bed, I sit down and take her hand in mine.

"Ma, what do you want to do?" I ask her, rubbing small circles against her dry skin.

She doesn't turn to look at me, she just continues to stare out into space as if nothing else around her didn't exist.

"Ma," I say a little more forcefully, and this time she turns to look at me, but her eyes don't tell me anything. The only thing saving me right now is the fact that Jen's hands land on my shoulder. "What do you want to do?"

She holds my stare for a minute. For a solid minute, I look into my mother's eyes and see nothing but the woman that raised me. The woman that gave me her name and everything she had to get me to this point in my life.

I can't lose her.

"No," she says.

Just a simple no.

"No? No to what?" I ask her.

"No to the biopsy. I don't want to know. Not right now at least. We can find out when I get my surgery to remove the other three."

I can tell by her tone that her decision is set, and she won't be changing her mind, but that doesn't mean I won't try.

"But you can find out now. What if it is cancerous and

it grows quicker than the other and you're not here for the surgery?"

"Then I won't be here for the surgery," she says, and I swear my stomach goes into knots just hearing those words come out of her mouth.

"Ma," I try to argue but she stops me.

"No, Maddox. You asked what I wanted to do and that's it. If I don't make it to the surgery, then fine, I don't make it. But I'm not going to stop my life waiting for those test results to come back and neither are you."

Every single emotion that I felt when she was first diagnosed comes rushing back in.

Anger, fear, sadness all find small crevasses inside of my body and make themselves right at home.

I feel like I can't control myself right now, like I need to find an escape.

Giving my mom a nod, I stand up and without another look at the three other people in the room, I do something I haven't done since she was brought here.

I leave.

I leave to go look for something that even Jen won't even be able to get me out of.

33

Jennifer

THE PHONE CONTINUES to ring until it reaches voice mail.

Not once in the forty-five times that I have dialed the number has it been any different.

I can't help but wonder if a phone can overheat by receiving a lot of calls in a short period of time.

I don't know, but if that is the case or not, Maddox hasn't answered any one of my calls or even Nora's.

No texts, no calls, nothing. It's as if the second he left the hospital, he shut off his phone.

I understand why he left, I do. Nora's decision to not get a biopsy and see if this new tumor was cancerous was a hard one to swallow. I've only known the woman for a few months, and I was pissed when she said no, but it was her decision.

He's scared to lose his mom and her deciding not to find out if the tumor is cancerous probably makes him think that he'll lose her a lot sooner.

But if she didn't want to do it, then she didn't want to

do it. From the online search I did while they were getting her ready for discharge, I found that it's not a small thing to do. They would have to cut into her skull to be able to get a sample.

Nora probably had to go through that once already at the start of all of this and didn't want to do it again.

I wouldn't either.

But her making that choice doesn't warrant her only son walking out because of it.

Yet he did.

And now he doesn't answer his phone and I have no idea where he is.

It's been a few hours since he left the hospital room. In that time, Nora got discharged and was able to go home. Thank God, I had the keys to the car Maddox keeps here because we wouldn't have a way home.

Now she's sitting in the living room looking at a blank TV screen all the while I'm trying to get a hold of her son.

My current phone call, number forty-six I think, continues to ring for a few more seconds before it goes to voice mail.

I'm surprised that his voice mail box isn't full by the number of messages I'm leaving.

The beep comes through and for a quick second, I feel like giving up.

"Maddox, can you please just tell me where you are? I'm not asking you to come home, I just need to know that you're in a safe location. Can you please just call me back and let me know? Or call your mom? Something?"

I will take a fucking bird at the window, for crying out

loud. I just need to know that he's safe and not out looking for something he shouldn't. I absolutely hate the fact that my mind automatically went to thinking that he is out there trying to find a high.

That shouldn't even be a thought, since he hasn't said anything about even thinking about taking a hit since July, but given the circumstances, it is.

I want to tell him that I'm here for him like I have been doing in other voice mails, but I don't have enough time.

The words 'I love you' are also on the tip of my tongue but I don't want him to hear those words over a voice mail for the first time.

Ending the call, I give up on getting a hold of him for now. Eventually he'll answer, call back or just show up here.

Maybe I will be able to find him at the apartment. I can go and check, but I really don't want to leave Nora alone.

Pocketing my phone, I head back to the living room.

Nora is still sitting on the recliner looking at a blank tv.

I think she's just trying to process everything that she has gone through in the last few days.

Walking up to her, I place a gentle hand on her shoulder, trying my hardest not to scare her.

"Do you want something to eat?" I ask her, softly.

She looks up at me, giving me a blank stare before composing herself a few seconds later.

Nora shakes her head. "No, I'm not hungry. You get a hold of that son of mine?"

Now I'm the one shaking my head. "No. Every single text and phone call has gone unanswered."

She nods, like this is what she expected. "He'll pick up eventually."

"I'm just worried about him," I say, sitting on the couch next to the recliner.

Nora looks over at me, looking me in the eye for a good minute before she gives me a small smile and breaks the silence.

"I'm worried about him too. I've been worried since this whole shit show started. There were times when I wanted to scream at him, to knock some sense into him, but I can't really discipline a grown man."

I return her smile. "Sure, you can. If there is anyone that Maddox would listen to, it's you."

A small chuckle escapes her, and she just shakes her head. "That definitely hasn't been the case in a few years. If he did, he wouldn't have used drugs as a coping mechanism or gotten suspended or landed himself in rehab. But I guess he did listen to me on one thing."

"And what is that?" I ask with curiosity.

"He went out and found a girl to make him happy. You two may have lied about it in the beginning, but you're both definitely happy now."

I think if I took a picture of my face right now, I most definitely would look like a cartoon character with their eyes bulging out.

She knew?

She *knew*.

Holy crap. Did Maddox tell her and not tell me that he told her?

What do I say? Sorry for lying to you?

Oh my god, is she mad?

I don't know how to deal with this. Now, I'm really wishing that Maddox was here right now, because if anyone is going to get an ass chewing, it should be him.

I try to play it off as best I can.

"Lied? We didn't lie." My voice goes up an octave, and even I don't believe me.

"Do you really want me to believe that I told my son that I wanted him to find a girl that would make him happy and then a week or two later, he has a girlfriend? Sweetheart, that boy knows his way with the ladies, sure, but the dude is not that good."

I'm speechless. Absolutely speechless.

My brain is trying to work overtime trying to figure out something to say, but I come up with nothing.

After a few minutes of opening my mouth to let a few words out, I'm finally able to speak.

"Did you know when we came in July?" I ask, trying to remember if she gave us any clues that she knew our secret.

Nothing comes to mind.

She gives me a curt nod. "I did, but by that point I didn't care. You two were already on the verge of admitting to yourselves that you were more, no need for me to mention anything."

My mind is a little blown right now.

We were pretending to be a couple the majority of the time that we were here, and the whole time she knew it was all a lie.

Well, not all of it was a lie but still, she knew the whole time.

After a bit, I'm able to compose myself enough to give her a proper response.

"I'm sorry, we didn't mean to lie to you. Maddox really wanted you to see him happy."

Nora reaches over the recliner, extending a hand for me to take. When I do, she intertwines our fingers together and gives me a squeeze.

"I know you meant well by it. Do I wish you were real from the start? Sure, but when it comes to something I want, Maddox will do anything to make that happen, even this. In all honesty, I'm happy that he did this, because he did find someone that makes him happy, and I'm happy to see it. Really happy."

Tears spring in Nora's eyes and I can't help but get a little misty eyed myself.

"So, you're not mad that we lied to you?"

She lets out a laugh that sounds exactly like her son's. "No. Things work in mysterious ways, and in the end, it worked out for the two of you. Something I'm happy about."

Hopefully she's right because right now, I don't know what type of headspace Maddox is in.

What if the news of his mom having a possible new cancerous tumor takes him over the edge and not only, he starts using again, but he throws me to the curb?

Anything is possible at this point.

"I'm happy about it too," I say, giving her a small smile and letting a tear escape.

"Don't cry," she says, reaching up and wiping the tear away.

"What if he spirals and starts using again?" I say to her, every single fear seeping out into my words.

"If he does, he has you now to help him get out. I couldn't do it alone last time, but together we can."

"And if he doesn't?"

What if I'm not enough to help get him out of that?

Or maybe I'm getting ahead of myself and overthinking something that won't happen.

"Then you walk. You walk, no matter how much you love him, because maybe then he will realize that he has lost everything and needs to find his own strength before he can hold on to yours."

I wipe at the tears that continue to slip out. "Out of everyone, you are the one person that shouldn't be telling me that."

"I know, and I love my son, but if gets to that point in his life again, it needs to happen."

Nodding, I take her advice. Hopefully it will never come to that.

"Can I ask you a question?" I ask her, once all the tears are dry.

"Of course."

"Why did you say no to the biopsy? Wouldn't it be better to know the results now that way when your surgery comes along, they can take care of it?"

Nora gives my hand a reassuring squeeze. "It would, and I know for a fact that it would make Maddox happy, but that type of thing is a lot to handle. Especially since they cut your head open. Emotionally and mentally, it took a toll on me last time, and I didn't want to go through that again."

I wouldn't either.

It seems like an emotional stress on her.

A response is at the tip of my tongue but before I can say anything, my phone starts to ring.

I go still at the sound, wondering if it's Maddox finally calling me back.

Has he finally come to his senses?

I look over at Nora who gives me a nod to answer the phone.

Taking a deep breath, I pull my phone out of my pocket.

When I see Maddox's picture on the screen, I let out a sigh of relief.

Not wasting a second, I press the green button, answering the call and bringing the phone up to my ear.

"Hey," I say into the phone, my whole body relaxing a bit.

But that only lasted for a second.

"Is this Jennifer?" a deep voice, one that is definitely not Maddox's, says from the other side.

I answer cautiously. "Yes?"

Oh my god, did something happen to Maddox?

That's the only reason that a complete stranger is using his phone to call me.

Something must have happened and now I'm getting the call that nobody wants to hear.

"I wanted to let you know that I have Maddox."

34

MADDOX

Everything around me is spinning.

I don't know where I start and where the room I'm in ends. Every single corner is curved, and the floor seems like it's on a conveyor belt.

Everything is not only spinning but moving.

Maybe the black hole that I've been wishing for has finally come to swallow me up and this is what it looks like.

Or maybe it's the amount of alcohol currently calling my body home that is making everything seem like a carnival ride.

At this point, it might be both.

Even as fucked up as I am, I'm a little surprised that I chose alcohol as my vice tonight and not the little white substance that was calling my name.

I thought about it though. I thought about forgoing the alcohol and going for something stronger. Something more numbing.

I really did.

The thoughts came creeping in and I thought about it for a few hours. I even went as far as reaching out to my old dealer and thought about buying an ounce or two from him.

Was I going to do anything with it? Was I going to use it?

That I don't know.

I want to say that I wasn't going to, that I was just going to buy it and flush it down the toilet the first chance I could, but I don't even believe my own intentions.

Every single inch of me is telling me that I would have bought it and used every single speck of it.

The only thing that was stopping me from doing just that wasn't my mind trying to talk me out of it. It wasn't everything in me telling me that I knew better.

Yeah, I knew better, but I still called the dealer of my own accord.

No, what stopped me was the fact that my old dealer now works for one of the most powerful men in the city of Chicago.

The man that helped me get into rehab.

Dante Rossetti.

I guess he told every dealer that he had on payroll to contact him if I ever called.

And well, I called.

His men found me on a bench on the river drinking two bottles of vodka, bottles I bought when my dealer wouldn't answer the phone when it was time for our meet up and took me to their boss.

When we arrived at his mega mansion, because it was a Saturday and the man has a life out of his strip club, I was drunk out of my mind.

I'm still out of my mind two hours later, and if I had gotten those ounces of coke, I would have been more than just out of mind.

High, and numb are words that come to mind.

Now I sit in what looks like Dante's office, waiting for the man himself to give me the time of day and let me leave.

My phone sits on his wooden desk as it starts to vibrate. The phone is face down, but I don't have to look to see who it is.

Jen.

She's been calling nonstop since I left the hospital. She's also been texting me every chance she gets.

I should respond and tell her that I'm okay, that I will make it home when I feel slightly less drunk, but I leave it be.

She has to be worried about me right now but at the moment, I'm not in the right capacity to talk to her.

I don't think I'm in the right capacity to do anything except drink more of Dante's liquor while he does whatever he does.

Is what am I doing, childish? Absolutely.

I shouldn't be pissed that my mom has decided not to open up her skull to test a tumor. I shouldn't be pissed at all but I am.

I'm pissed not because my mom made the choice but because my chances of losing her just got higher. They got higher, and she doesn't want to do the test that could possibly let doctors save her.

What if the doctors get in there to remove the other tumors to only find that this tumor is inoperable? What if this tumor causes more damage?

So many what ifs and I can't handle any of them.

That's why I'm drowning myself in alcohol because when life decides to throw rocks at me, I sink instead of being able to sail through.

Grabbing the whiskey bottle in front of me and bring it up to take a drink only to realize that it's completely empty.

I guess it's time for a new one.

After grabbing a new one, I must have dozed off because one minute I'm sitting in this room by myself, and the next Dante is here with me.

The room is silent for a minute or two and it's me that is eventually breaking the quietness.

"I'm sorry," I say to him, not knowing how else to start.

"Why the fuck are you apologizing?" he asks as he sits across from me.

I lean my head back on the chair I'm sitting in and look at the man.

"You helped me get clean yet I went out to find a hit the second shit got a little tough."

Like I said before, I'm acting like a child.

Dante nods. "But you didn't take it."

"Because you interfered."

"That wouldn't have stopped anyone that needed something so badly. They would have gone to find someone that would have given them what they wanted. They wouldn't have stopped, but you did."

He's right.

The second that the dealer walked away from our agreement, I could have gone and found someone else that would have said yes.

Instead, I turned to alcohol.

"Have you gone to any meetings since getting out of rehab?" Dante asks, getting me out of my head.

I shake my head. "Haven't had the need to."

"Have you had thoughts about using? Besides today?"

I could lie, I could tell him that I haven't but knowing who this man is and what he does, he might see right through it.

"A few thoughts here and there," I say, taking a drink from the bottle I opened earlier.

Dante doesn't say anything, the man just looks at me as if he's trying to figure me out.

Eventually he speaks. "And when you had those thoughts, you didn't think that you should talk to someone?"

No, because I had Jen.

"I was able to handle them."

Somewhat at least.

I was close to doing what I did today after the street festival.

"You called a fucking dealer tonight. If he wasn't one of my men and I hadn't told him not to sell to you, you would probably be high as a fucking kite in an alley somewhere. Is that your way of handling those thoughts?"

I look at the man talking to me.

My connection to him started before I was even born. According to my mom, the sperm donor that walked out on us was part of the Falcone Mafia family. The same family Dante took over a decade ago.

From what I know, Dante knew the would-be father, even though he was younger than him. Throughout the years, Dante checked in on Ma and me.

I didn't remember meeting Dante until I was drafted by Chicago and even then, our meetings were just friendly encounters.

Friendly enough that he would help me get into one of the best rehab facilities in the country.

I take another swig from the bottle before speaking. "Why do you care so much?"

Ever since Dante offered a helping hand to get me to rehab, I wondered if there was a why behind it.

Sure, he knew my mom from before I was born and checked up on her, but I never understood why he would offer his help to me.

I was just another professional athlete to enter his club.

Why help me at all?

Dante is quiet for a few seconds, as if he's thinking of the right words to say.

After a minute or two, he takes the bottle that I have in my hand and takes a drink.

"Your mom ever tell you how we met?" he says, handing the bottle back to me.

"Never," I answer honestly.

Dante nods before continuing. "She used to be my

babysitter. Every weekend from when she was fourteen to about nineteen, she was at my house. I remember playing games with her and watching movies we shouldn't have. She always treated me as if I was her little brother or something. That's how she met your father. He was at the house one weekend she was there, and I guess they connected. Nora stopped babysitting after she had you. Being a kid, I thought that she was out living life with her new family, you know? I didn't find out until years later that wasn't the case. Once I was old enough, I kept tabs on her. Nora treated me like a little brother, and I saw her as an older sister. I vowed to help her whenever I could and because you're her son, you benefit from that."

I always knew this man had a sweet spot for my mother, I just didn't know how deep it went.

"Me getting you into that rehab facility in Utah and telling my men not to sell drugs to you has a lot to do with who your mother is. That's why I fucking care."

I can see a small bit of anger in his facial expression but given the amount of alcohol that is flowing through my body right now, I could be wrong.

Dante waits for me to say something, but nothing comes to mind.

Eventually he starts speaking again. "Look, you started this because of her illness. You got clean because of her, so how about you stay clean for her. Just because you went to rehab and haven't touched a speck of coke doesn't mean that the recovery is over. Recovery is never over, but you can do the work to make it easier. So do the fucking work."

Still no answer from me, I just take another drink, trying to take in every single word.

Dante is right. Of course, he's right.

From the start of all of this, I knew recovery was going to be hard. I knew that recovery wasn't just going to be a few weeks and then I would be cured. It's why I took the no relationship rule so seriously and even implemented the no sex rule. It's why I told Jen that I was probably going to be recovering my whole life.

But recovery is more than giving myself rules and using my girlfriend to center me when thoughts of using came about.

It's more than just not using and avoiding all thoughts that came along.

I see it now, I see that a part of me was selfish enough to think that just by going to rehab, that would be the end of everything, but it's not.

Sure I was able to get my career back and show everyone in the baseball world that I'm still a worthy player.

But there is more to all of this.

If I overdose and die, the baseball community would be affected by it for a few days, maybe a few weeks, but they will move on.

My mother and Jen on the other hand, if something were to happen to me, it would be with them forever.

I walked out on the two most important women in my life earlier today, all to go searching for something that has a death sentence attached to it.

I need to do better. Be better.

For Jen.

For my mom.

And maybe even for me.

Tired of waiting for me to say something, Dante lets out a sigh and gets up, and starts to leave the room.

It's when he's almost at the door that he speaks.

"I called your girlfriend and told her where you were. You might want to sober up before she gets here."

35

Jennifer

I'VE ALWAYS WONDERED how the one-percenters in this country live. Living in the Bay Area gives me a small glimpse of that, but this is a whole different level.

It's as if someone had an architectural magazine from France, picked this house and had it transported to the backwoods of Chicago.

This place is massive and insanely beautiful and there is so much green.

The only sense that I'm getting that someone actually lives here, and it's not a museum, it's the children's playground that can be seen on the side of the house.

I guess whoever this stranger that called me was, has a family.

That's somewhat comforting, I guess.

Since the number of bodyguards and ultra-secure gates aren't.

This place even has a fancy doorbell.

How Maddox ended up here is beyond me, but when I told Nora where he was, she let out a sigh of relief.

So, I guess it's a good thing he's here. Either way though, I'm going to kick his ass for leaving the hospital, for not answering his phone, and for terrifying me and his mom.

I press the fancy doorbell and hear it ring throughout the house. For some reason, I thought that the second I pushed the button, someone would magically appear to open the door, but that's definitely not the case.

As I wait for a few minutes, I'm starting to think that nobody is home when the door finally opens.

The person on the other side of the door is not who I thought would be opening it.

This place keeps bringing out the surprises.

The woman that opened the door appears to be my age or younger. She's beautiful with shoulder-length hair and doe eyes. Her face looks young, and I can't help but wonder if she's the nanny.

Definitely could be the nanny.

"Can I help you?" she asks, giving me a small smile. She's probably wondering how I got past security.

"Um, maybe. I'm looking for Maddox Bauer. I got a call that he was here?" I say, my words coming out as a question.

The woman raises her eyebrow at me, like she doesn't believe me. She's about to open her mouth to say something, when a voice comes through from behind her.

"It's okay, *amate*. I called her." A voice says.

A few seconds later, a man with dark hair and an olive skin tone appears.

Amate? Like *amante*?

So, she's his lover and here I thought she was the nanny.

The woman looks at the man and gives him a smile before opening the door a bit wider, inviting me in.

When I step through the threshold, it's like I'm transported into the home decor magazine that the house was picked from.

A little boy, no more than two, comes running into the room, calling out mama and running towards the young woman.

Interesting situation they have here.

The man watching what I assume is his wife and son for a second before turning to me and giving me a tight smile.

"It's nice to meet you, Jennifer. My name is Dante, a friend of Maddox."

Dante.

The man that owns the strip club where Maddox almost overdosed.

The Mafia man.

Shit. What has Maddox gotten into?

"Is Maddox okay?" I ask, my voice shaking a bit.

Of course, it's shaking. My boyfriend went off to do God knows what and is now at the house of the head of the Mafia. Just being in this man's presence terrifies me.

Dante gives me a small smile, one that I doubt he gives anyone but his family. "He's fine, drunk but he's fine."

Drunk.

That means he went to find alcohol and not his next hit.

Unless...

"He was just drinking?" I ask, wanting to just reassure myself.

Dante doesn't give me a nod or anything, he just looks at me as if he is trying to figure out a way to answer my question. "Would you like the honest truth?" he asks after a minute.

Would I?

Is the truth going to piss me off even more than what I already am?

Most likely, but I rather know then go into wherever Maddox is blind.

I give Dante a nod, and he gives me one back. He doesn't say anything, he just nods at his wife, excusing us and waving for me to follow him.

Once we are in the massive living room, one that I have to keep myself from drooling over, Dante waves for me to take a seat on the couch.

He doesn't waste any time and gets right to the point. "Drinking wasn't his first choice. He went looking for a hit. Thankfully he went to one of my men, who didn't go through with the deal, and they called me. Found him on a bench drinking out of a bottle, so I had them bring him here."

I close my eyes and try to take in a deep breath. I don't know how to handle this information.

Maddox left the hospital and went to look for drugs.

He could have done so many things, gone to the gym to work out the anger, he could have gone for a walk, he could have talked to *me*, but he chose to do the one thing that put him in this situation in the first place. He chose to seek out the drug that almost cost him his career. The very drug that Dante helped him fight.

His mom needed him at her side, and he walked out and called a dealer.

I'm more pissed now than I have been all day.

There is so much anger flowing through me that I don't know what to do with it.

A part of me hoped, wished, that after the street festival that the urges would go away, that us being together would help him walk through recovery more easily. I guess it was just being me wishful, being *hopeful*.

If this is his reaction to Nora's doctors telling her that they found a new tumor, what would the reaction look like if they tell her it's cancerous?

Will Dante's men say no to him then?

I want to say yes, but I have no idea anymore.

"Can I see him?" I ask Dante.

He nods. "If you want. He was still drinking a little bit ago. That's definitely not enough time for him to sober up."

I'm already shaking my head. "I don't care. I want to see him."

Dante looks at me for a quick second before he nods and stands up from his seat on the couch. "Follow me."

I do as he says and follow him through the house to the

second floor, where he leads me to a set of wooden doors that open up to an office.

My brain wants to take every second and explore the space because it's just as spectacular as the rest of the house, but I try to push that down.

Instead, I try to force my brain to concentrate on the man that is slumped in a chair with a bottle in his hand that resembles the man I love.

In all the time that we've known each other, I've never seen Maddox like this.

He looks defeated and ready to give up.

Nothing like that man that is determined and won't stop until he's at the very top, just to show people is worth supporting.

The Maddox sitting in that chair is one that I never want to see again.

At the sound of the door opening, Maddox turns.

Much like his body is, his eyes are distant and don't have that spark that I'm used to seeing every single time he looks at me.

Something I noticed happen from the very beginning.

Once Dante closes the door behind me, I give Maddox a small smile. "Hi."

He continues to look at me, not saying a word. After about a minute of just staring at each other, Maddox lets out a sigh.

"Let me guess, you're pissed off at me," are his first words.

I guess we are going to get confrontational right away. Awesome.

"If the roles were reversed and I was sitting where you are, I'm pretty sure you would be too. Especially if I had left my mother when she needed me most to go look for a hit."

"Don't do that."

"Don't do what? Call you out?" I'm surprised just how even my voice is right now. I thought I would be screaming at him the second I saw him.

"I know what I did today was wrong." He says, his voice steady but from the look on his face, he wants to puke.

"Do you? Because if you did, you wouldn't be halfway to the hospital to get your stomach pumped. You would be with your mom, telling her that she has nothing to worry about."

He's silent for a few seconds before speaking again. "I'm sorry, okay?"

Three words.

Three words that I should be happy to hear, but I'm not. Those three little words don't feel like enough.

"Not good enough," I say, shaking my head in the process.

From the look on his face, he wasn't expecting that response. He was waiting for me to take his apology and that everything would go back to being good.

That's not even close to what's going to happen.

"What do you mean it's not 'good enough'?" he asks, finally putting down the bottle of whiskey and standing up. His footing is unstable, but he is able to find some balance.

"Exactly what I said. That apology isn't good enough."

Now he looks like he's pissed off, what with the frustrated sigh he lets out. "What else do you want me to say, Jennifer? Dante already lectured me about this. I know what I did was wrong. I'm sorry."

"It's not just about your words, Maddox. It's also your actions. This is life, bad news is around every corner, it's unexpected. You said you're sorry, but those are just words. Those words aren't going to stop you from going out and looking for a hit next time something else happens."

Maddox's face is unreadable, nothing about his expression or even the way he's standing is telling me what he might be thinking.

He doesn't say anything, so I continue. My voice filled with less anger. "I don't want you to say anything, I want you to do. Do something that stops this from happening again."

Again, I'm met with silence. I don't even know if what I'm saying is even getting through to him. It's as if he's looking at me but staring into space at the same time.

Eventually though, he speaks. "Dante said the same thing. That I need to do the work. Recovery isn't just rehab."

I'm liking the Mafia man more and more.

"He's right, it's not. You need to work at it. Now the question is are you going to do it, because I don't know if I can go through you disappearing again and thinking that you're out getting high and going to end up dead."

Just thinking about it makes me want to cry.

When I got the call from Dante, for a split second after he told me that Maddox was with him, I thought the worst possible. I thought that he was in the hospital or worse yet at the coroner's office waiting to be identified.

My head automatically went to all the worst-case scenarios that it took me a second to control myself when he finally told me that he was fine.

Maddox notices that I'm on the verge of tears because he takes a step towards me with a hand reaching for me, but he stops himself.

He thinks that I'm so pissed off at him that touching me wouldn't be a good idea.

It's the opposite, though. I would give anything to have his arms wrapped around me right about now.

"Would you walk away? If it happened again. If I disappeared and Dante wasn't there to stop me from getting my hands on the drugs, would you walk away?"

I hate that he even has to ask that.

I hate the pain that came out as those words spilled out from his mouth.

And I hate that I'm going to cause even more pain with my answer.

I want to say no, I wouldn't walk. I told him that I would be with him, at his side, through everything. But with something like this, I have to think about myself too.

As much as I want to say that I'm strong enough to see him spiral down, I know for a fact that I'm not.

"Yes," I say, tears spilling down my face. "Yes, I would walk away."

I can see the pain in his eyes as soon as I say the words. I hurt him by saying that, but I had to say it.

He gives me a nod. "You said through everything. That

being with me included standing at my side through my recovery, through everything.

"I did, but if this is the path you choose, I have to think about myself too. I can't sit around and watch you throw your life away, Maddox. I've seen all the work that you've done these last few months and it's amazing. You have a choice of keeping it that way, but you have to do the work to do so. I don't want to walk away, but if you don't give me another choice, I will."

"Why?" he asks.

It's a simple question, but it's enough to break me.

"Because I love you, you asshole. I don't want to see the man I love become nothing. I've heard what it was like last year, and I know for a fact that I wouldn't be able to go through that. It will hurt and I will be completely shattered to walk away, but I swear to god Maddox, I will."

Maddox stands there in silence, looking at me like he can't believe what I just said, and frankly, I can't either.

This it's not how I wanted to tell him.

I always had this image in my head that I was going to tell him I loved him while we were in bed. While our legs were intertwined, and our lips were mere inches from each other.

But I guess telling him now is better than not telling him at all.

"Meetings don't seem like enough," he mutters, his voice shaking a bit.

"Then use me. Let me be your anchor when you have thoughts about using. Hug me, kiss me, be with me, talk to me. Go to meetings and use me to help you get through the tough shit. Don't just walk away and sink into the need because things don't go the way you want, or you hear something that you don't want to hear. I'm here for you, your mom is here for you, hell it looks like Dante is here for you. You just need to be here for yourself."

In all the time that I have known him, I never seen Maddox broken. I've seen him nervous, excited, angry, sadden, but never broken. Until now.

Seeing tears form in his eyes, shatters everything in me.

Breaking the distance between us, I walk over to him and place a hand on his cheek just as a tear escapes. "If I lose my mom, I won't be able to handle losing you too," he whispers.

I place my other hand on the other side of his face, making sure he is looking right into my eyes.

"Nora isn't going anywhere. Not anytime soon," I say to him with all the conviction that I have.

"You don't know that."

"You told me once that you had to channel your mom's hopefulness because she wouldn't. Where did that go?" I ask, wiping away the tears that continue to flow out of his eyes.

"It disappeared when I heard there was a new tumor."

"Then let me hold on to it for both of you. Let me believe that Nora will be here for a long time, and you will do the work to make your recovery better."

I lean up and place a chaste kiss against his lips, silently telling him I'm not going anywhere for the moment. I won't go anywhere at all if this all goes how I think it will.

When I pull away from him, he looks down at me with glassy eyes.

"Did you mean those words earlier? The ones about love?"

I nod. "I did. I've felt them for a while, but I didn't know how to get them out."

One of his hands reaches up and wipes at my cheek. It takes me a second to realize that I'm still crying.

"We were never supposed to fall for each other, let alone say those three words," he says, the shakiness gone from his voice.

I give him a nod. "I know."

"Things between us were fake and they were for a few weeks, but everything has been real for a lot longer." He pauses, wiping a finger against my cheek some more. "So real that it has gotten to the point that I don't want to go a day without you. So real that I love you in a way I have never loved anyone before and certainly never will. You, Jennifer Zaragoza, are the love of my life and I will do everything in my power to keep you in it. I will do all the work that I have to make you stay. I will do the work for you, for my mom and for me. I promise."

His fingers ghost against my lips.

He's silently asking for forgiveness and this time around; I will give it to him.

"I know you will and as long as you do, I will be right by your side."

He nods, accepting it. "I love you, sweetheart, so damn much."

"I love you too."

This time when I lean up and meet his lips with mine, there is nothing chaste about it.

If we weren't in a stranger's office, I would make him apologize in another way. I may be adventurous and all but not that much.

When we pull apart, I let my fingers caress his face as I speak. "You have one more person to apologize to."

36

OCTOBER 27, 2022

MADDOX

Maddox

As a kid, I never liked seeing my mom cry.

It wasn't very often that I saw her with tears in her eyes since she knew how to hide them, but when I did, it always crushed me.

There was always this pain in my chest every time I saw her eyes swell up with tears, and I hated it.

I made myself a promise at a young age that my mom would never cry for something that I did.

That promise was repeatedly broken last year.

Every time I saw her, every time I talked to her, every time she begged me to stop, there would be tears rolling down her face.

The chest pain was there for every single one of them, yet feeling that pain wasn't enough for me to listen to her and stop what I was doing.

So, the tears continued.

Since I left rehab, I've seen her with tears once, but those were different, those were happy ones.

When I saw those, I made another promise to myself, if I was going to make my mom cry again it would be because of something happy.

I broke that promise the second I decided to walk out of the hospital.

When I walked into her house after getting lectured by Dante and Jennifer, with the latter vowing to leave if I don't straighten up, I expected the same treatment from Nora.

I expected her to sit me down and lecture me about all the wrong that I'm doing. I expected to hear her yell at me as if I was a teenager again getting home after getting into a fight.

But there was no lecture, no yelling.

I walked into the living room, where she was sitting on a recliner that I had bought her last year when she was diagnosed, and found her with silent tears in her eyes.

She didn't say anything as I walked in and took a seat on the couch next to her.

She didn't say anything as I took her hand and apologized for not being able to handle hearing her say no to the biopsy.

She said nothing when I apologized for leaving.

Her eyes stayed on mine and it crushed me to see the tears rolling down her face and not hearing her say a damn word.

It was when I was done talking that she finally said something.

"Did you?" she had asked and I didn't need any clarification as to what she meant.

I told her the truth. That I tried, that I wanted to use again and that I was close to doing it but that I was stopped. I told her, promised her, that I was going to work on making sure it never happened again.

For a second, I thought she didn't believe me. I know that I wouldn't.

I've broken promises before. What would make this one different?

But she must have seen something in my eyes or in my expression, because she tightened the grip she had on my hand and gave me a sad smile.

"Good, because I don't want to lose my son again. Once was enough."

That was over a month ago, and so far, I've been keeping that promise.

With a grueling postseason schedule, it's been hard to think about anything else but baseball.

The Miners are winning games and now we're in the World Series, only one game away from winning it all.

But today, baseball takes a back seat.

Today, it's all about Nora and making sure she has a successful surgery.

About two weeks ago, Mom got a call moving her surgery up a few days. She was hesitant to take it, because from the looks of things I would be playing.

But when she called me to tell me, I told her to change it, and no matter what, I will be there for her.

The baseball gods were on our side because today

328 | JOCELYNE SOTO

there's no baseball and I was able to be where I was needed most.

Jen takes my hand as we sit, waiting for the doctor to come in and tell us that the surgery is over.

I hold her hands as tightly as I can and try to center myself.

I concentrate on the fact that she's here and that she loves me, all to get rid of the thoughts trying to break me.

I use her presence just like she told me to.

She told me that she would walk away if I used again and without a doubt, I would let her. It would break me beyond repair, but I would let her, because she deserves more than that.

But it's not going to happen. It will never get to that point. I won't give her the chance to walk away, not now, not ever.

Jennifer Zaragoza is mine and will forever be mine, just like I will forever be hers.

So, I hold her hand as tightly as I can and think of our future together. A future with a World Series ring for me and a diamond ring for her. A future with a huge house and a few kids running around while they play with their grandma. A future where we are both happy and don't have to worry about anything.

Jen doses off but I stay awake, not wanting to miss anyone coming in with any news.

It's at the six-hour mark that my mom's doctor, still dressed in his scrubs and surgical cap, comes into the room.

At first, my stomach drops thinking the worst possible

scenarios, but when the older man gives me a smile, everything in me relaxes.

I shake my girlfriend awake so that we both can hear what the doctor has to say.

"Nora is out of surgery and in recovery. The surgery itself was successful. We were able to get the tumors out. All of them."

37

OCTOBER 28, 2022

MADDOX

Maddox

GAME seven of the World Series.

Never did I think that I would get to a point in my career where my team would depend on me so much that they would have me pitch the most important game of the season.

Yet here I am, about to enter the ninth inning of game seven of the World Series.

At the beginning of the season, I was happy to even be on a team. Now, not only did I have the best season of my career, but I've pitched a perfect game and now about to close out the last game of the season.

This is definitely not something that I thought I would be doing this time last year.

I thought my career was done. I thought that after my suspension was over, I would never see the mound again, but I guess I was wrong. Very wrong.

I also didn't think that my mom would still be here or that I would have a beautiful girl in the stand cheering me on, with my number on her back, yet I do.

Never thought that I would play for another team other than Chicago, yet here I am.

People have been calling me the comeback kid and thinking about it, I feel like it's a nickname I deserve.

The sound of the ball meeting the bat sounds through the park. There's a stillness as everyone waits for what the play will be and the second that it meets the center fielder's glove, everyone one lets out a collective groan.

That was the third out. The eighth inning is over and now it's time for me to close out this game.

I've stayed in the whole game, pitched over one hundred pitches and feel as if I can pitch one hundred more.

Ben and our pitching staff wanted to take me out, wanted me to rest, I fought against them. There was no baseball tomorrow, there wasn't going to be a game I had to be ready for. This was it. I was going to stay in the game as long as I could, especially with the tight lead that we had, and the series tied at three a piece.

I was going to win this for us and now it's my chance to do just that.

Throwing my jacket on the bench, I grab my glove and readjust my hat.

It's time to close this game out and get that ring.

My teammates all watch as I make my way out of the dugout. Aaron claps me on the back and Ben gives me a nod.

Three outs.

Three outs is all we need to become champs.

Three outs all depended on how I throw.

The crowd cheers as I walk to the mound, all of them on their feet, all of them anxiously awaiting the outcome.

I grab the rosin bag and chalk up my hands, keeping them dry.

After two practice throws, I'm ready.

The batter walks up to the plate and I get into my stance and wait for the right sign from my catcher.

When I finally get it, I nod.

This is it.

All the turmoil has come down to this.

My mom is going to be okay. I have Jen by my side. I have my career back.

That's all I need.

I wind up and throw the first pitch of the inning.

A pitch for my mom.

For Jen.

For my team.

For the fans.

And for me.

38

CITY OF CHAMPIONS

OCTOBER 29, 2022

THE CITY of San Francisco has another set of champions roaming the streets.

First it was the San Francisco Gold winning the Super Bowl back in February under the helm of quarterback, Hunter Jacobi.

Now, months later, for the first time in ten years, we once again have World Series champions in the San Francisco Miners.

The Miners started the postseason strong by winning the division series in four games, Houston not standing a chance. They stayed on top through the National League Championships and were able to beat out Miami in five games. When they reached the biggest stage in baseball, all eyes were on them.

Ben Kipper, the Miners manager, had a solid team behind him with an even stronger pitching rotation.

At the beginning of the season, it was predicted that

the Miners would not even see a postseason but with a few additions, they were able to define all the odds.

The biggest odd of them all being Maddox Bauer.

Bauer, who had a less than satisfactory season last year, what with a ninety-day suspension for drug use under his belt and being released from Chicago, was better than ever. The young pitcher's acquisition turned some heads at the start of the season but as the games went on, Bauer proved that he had what it took to be a Miner.

Kipper and the pitching staff made changes to the starting rotation back in July, adding Bauer to the mix.

For the second half of the season, the Miners were untouchable. With every pitch, every hit, every catch, they became the team to beat.

Even having a perfect game added to the history books, courtesy of Bauer.

The odds were against them but in the end the underdogs came out swinging and were able to beat New York, claiming the final game to close out the series.

The Miners played a spectacular series and an even more spectacular season.

Congratulations to the Miners organization, to Ben Kipper for a job well done.

To our world series MVP, Maddox Bauer, congratulations on the new title. The city of San Francisco is lucky to have you on their team, Chicago were fools to let you go.

Congratulations again to the new World Series champs, the San Francisco Miners.

39

MADDOX

Maddox

THE CITY IS CALM.

So calm that you would never think that there was a massive celebration that happened a few hours ago. A celebration that had streets filled with people, cheering and dancing on the streets.

People that were happy that their team had just won the World Series at home.

There is something special about winning a title on your home field, that's for sure.

There's also something special about being the winning pitcher of the last game of the season.

After I threw the first pitch of the ninth inning, everything felt as if it was getting lighter with every single pitch that I threw after.

When the first out came in the way of a fly ball, I was ecstatic but didn't show it. I kept myself as composed as possible and moved on to the next batter as if it were any other day.

Batter two came up and he made me work for it.

Every pitch, he would pop back. Fifteen pitches in total but in the end, I was able to get him to swing on a sinker to get him out.

It was when the third batter came up that I felt it. I felt the energy of the stadium inside of me. I felt the pressure that this game had in my hands. I felt every single inch of excitement and I needed to do something to release it.

One pitch.

One pitch was all it took.

I threw the ball, and I saw it the second that it met the wooden bat. I kept an eye on it and I was able to calculate where the ball was going to go.

Right into my glove.

One simple flick of the wrist and the game was over.

All that hard work done with one movement.

That's when all the celebrations started.

With the number of cheers and commotion, I was sure that we were going to set off the earthquake detectors.

So much was happening on the field as hats and shirts were being passed around, but I only cared about one thing.

Getting to my girl.

She had flown back from Chicago with me, saying that she was going to be there win or lose.

I was hesitant since I didn't want to leave my mom by herself after her surgery. After arranging a few things and making sure that the hospital had my number just in case, Jen came with me.

So, the second I could, I looked for her on the field.

I saw her first by the net and the second I did; I was taken back to our first kiss in Sacramento.

It was as if everything was coming full circle.

The second she was in my arms; I didn't want to let her go.

After more celebrations, the on-field award ceremony and a few champagne showers, we came home.

The second we were in our space, our hunger for each other took over and Jen and I had our own celebration.

Now hours later, she's asleep and I'm taking in the dawn.

Last night, I was on a high like no other. A high that I was able to get from something other than a drug and a part of me is happy for it.

Extremely happy.

A happiness that I hold as I watch as the city starts to wake up and the sun starts to rise.

I don't know how long I sit here by the window watching the city, but right before the sun is fully up, I hear footsteps behind me.

Turning slightly, I watch as Jen walks over to me, wearing my jersey, giving me a sleepy smile. She comes to my side and when I open up my arms for her, she wastes no time taking her place on my lap.

"You're up early," she says, cuddling deeper into my arms and her face going against my neck.

"A little too hyped up to be able to sleep," I answer, tightening my hold on her body.

"Good or bad hyped up?" she asks, her breathing coating the skin of my neck.

"Good."

I feel her nod against my shoulder. "Good," she lets out a yawn before she continues. "Have I told you how proud I am of you?"

A chuckle leaves my lips. "You told me a few times last night."

I guess she didn't like my chuckle because it earned me a twisted nipple. "Well get used to it then because I won't stop saying it until I get tired of it."

Grabbing her hand, I bring it up to my mouth and place kisses on her fingertips, before resting it on my chest.

"You can tell me anytime you want. You have no idea how happy it makes me to know that you're proud of me."

"I'm not the only one, you know that right?" she asks, her fingers drawing circles against my bare chest.

I nod. "I know," I say, taking a pause. "I talked to the nurses a little bit ago and they said that she was able to be awake for a bit and watch for a few minutes. Said mom had a huge smile on her face."

"Without a doubt she won't want to kiss a single game next season," Jen says, letting out a little snort.

"She'll probably become the new team mascot with all the games she'll attend," I add.

"She'll set a new attendance record."

We both let out small laughs before we go silent and watch the sunrise a bit more.

After a minute or two, Jen speaks. "I'm really happy you dedicated the game to her. Makes it all that more special."

I nod, resting my chin on her head. "Yeah, I'm happy about that too."

The sun rises completely, brightening up the whole room.

We sit there, looking out the window, just holding each other for a few minutes. When I'm about to suggest we grab breakfast somewhere, Jen shifts herself off me and ends up on her knees between my legs.

"What are you doing?" I ask, feeling a smirk playing on my lips.

"Showing you how proud I am of you," she says, biting her lower lip.

She starts to pull down my boxer briefs and I help her by lifting up my hips.

Once the briefs are discarded, Jen's tongue pops out, swiping at her bottom lip.

She looks hungry and eager to take me in her mouth.

"And how exactly are you going to show me?" I ask, my cock already starting to get hard at the sight of her on her knees.

Jen looks up at me with lust filled eyes and a smile that would have any man crying for more. Thank fuck that man is me.

"By doing this." With her hands on my thighs, she leans forward and runs her tongue against my cock.

I twitch at the motion and when she takes me in her

mouth, still with her hands not touching me, I feel fucking elation.

"Fuck, why are you so damn good at this?" I groan throwing my head back, resting my arms against the armrest of the chair.

"I've just learned what you like," she answers, releasing my cock with a pop. A happy smile on her lips.

"Have you now?" I ask, sliding a hand into her hair and giving her a slight pull.

That sexy smile of hers spreads as she gives me a nod. "I have."

"What else have you learned?"

"That you love watching me ride your dick while my tits are in your face."

Damn, I do love that. It's a sight that I can't get enough of.

With my hand still in her hair, I tighten my grip and bring her face closer to mine, causing our lips to be separated only by an inch of space. She lets out a gasp when I lick her lips and take her bottom lip between my teeth.

"That is a pretty sight, but before we can get to that, you have to do something first," I say against her mouth.

"What is that?"

"You have to come on my face. Then you can be the good girl that I know that you are and sit on my cock to ride me just the way I like it."

Jen lets out a purr before she leans to close the space between us. She kisses me long and hard and when she pulls away, her eyes are filled with sex.

"Yes, please."

"Stand up and lean back against the window," I order.

She does what I say right away.

My jersey is hanging off her naked body, only covering her back since the front is wide open. She had asked for me to wear it last night after we got home and when she woke up, it must have been the first thing she grabbed.

It looks way better on her.

I give myself a few tugs at the sight of her with my number on her back and her body waiting for me to take it.

"You look so damn sexy wearing my jersey." I slide my hand up and down my dick, wishing it was her hand instead.

"Maybe I should wear it more often," she says with a devilish smirk.

"You should, just like that." I stand up and stalk over to her.

The second I sink down to my knees her grin grows even more.

"My riding you might be your favorite sight but you on your knees for me, might be mine."

"Only for you," I say before grabbing her leg and bringing it over my shoulder right before I place my mouth on her pussy.

I had her a few hours ago, but I still need more.

Her moans fill the living room and one of her hands lands in my hair, holding me to her.

Jen rides my face all the while trying to keep her balance.

I taste every single inch of her as I let my fingers dig into her skin, marking her with my nail impressions.

My tongue meets her clit, and she lets out a groan with my name attached.

"Maddox. Fuck, Maddox, please."

Her exclamations have me grinning against her, but I don't give her what she wants. Not yet.

I continue to tease her, running my tongue up and down her slit and even letting a fingertip slide into her entrance.

Finally giving into her pants, I take her clit in my mouth and suck. I suck on her until she is panting my name out in repetition.

I suck on her until she is completely breathless and is trying to pull me off her.

She continues to grind herself against my face and with one more suck, she's right where I need her to be.

With her release on my tongue, I pull away from her and place her foot back on the ground.

She's about to complain, I can see it on her face, but the second she sees me stroking myself she stops herself.

Without taking my eyes off her, I walk backward back to the chair and take a seat.

Like my eyes never left her body, her eyes never left my cock.

She gets pleasure out of this, and if I reached between her legs right now, I would find her ready to go once more.

"Get on my cock," I order.

With weak legs, she walks over to me and climbs on top of me like the pro she is.

The second she sinks down, and I'm wrapped around her pussy, I see stars.

She takes a second to adjust to me and in that time, I bring her face close to mine and kiss her.

I kiss her to show her how happy I am.

I kiss her to thank her for being there for me, for believing me.

I kiss her for supporting me and for loving me.

I kiss her for being mine.

"Have I told you how fucking happy I am that you agreed to be my fake girlfriend?" I say against her lips once she starts moving, letting them slide along the length of her neck.

"Not lately," she says with a giggle.

"So fucking happy," I say before moving my mouth down to her chest and taking a nipple between my teeth.

"Fuck," she says, pulling at my hair again.

"Now you're mine forever."

"Yes," she moans out, bouncing up and down.

"Say the words, Jennifer," I say, grabbing her by the hips and moving her in a circular motion.

"Forever. I'm yours forever."

"Good girl."

She starts to bounce herself on me, her head getting thrown back causing her hair to go all over the place.

Then she looks at me.

She looks at me like I'm her whole world and if I could take a picture of this moment and frame it, I would.

But unfortunately, my phone is nowhere in sight.

This woman has become my everything in such a little bit of time.

She's become more important than baseball will ever be.

This all started as something to make my mom happy and to make people believe that I'm worth taking a shot on, but it has turned into so much more.

It has turned into something that can last forever.

Into something that has a real future.

Jen has become my healthiest addiction. My healthiest drug choice and I will never give her up. I will never let her walk away because of my choices.

I will hold this woman for as long as she will let me.

She holds every part of me.

"I love you," she tells me, leaning her forehead against mine.

"I love you too," I tell her, our breath coming together. "So damn much."

And I will, forever.

EPILOGUE

Jennifer

"C'MON, Jacobi! You're skating like a grandma! Get out that stick you have in your ass and play like you're damn professional!"

The blonde haired girl that's three seats over yells at the glass separating us from the ice as some of the players skate by.

And here I thought Selena was intense, this girl takes it to a whole other level.

Selena, Hunter, Maddox, and I are currently in Chicago at a Chicago Dark Knights game cheering on Hunter's brother, Blake.

It's his second year in the NHL after being called up last year. According to Maddox, Blake is still a rookie, but he sure is going somewhere. Whatever that means coming from a baseball player.

And the blonde-haired girl pressing her face against the glass? Just so happens to be Blake's best friend, Sophia, and the girl looks like his biggest fan.

Kind of reminds me of me and Selena at football and baseball games.

"Are they really just best friends?" I whisper over to Selena, who is sitting next to me as we watch the game.

Selena gives me a shrug. "I've asked the same question. They both say they are but there's definitely something there."

Happy to see that I'm not the only one that sees that even with a plexiglass wall separating them, there's this weird chemistry flowing through them.

I watch as hockey players skate by all fighting for the puck and when the horn sounds in the Dark Knights favor, Blake skates by where we're sitting.

He stops right in front of us, or should I say right in front of Sophia and gives her a wink before blowing her a kiss.

The whole arena saw it, dude even makes it onto the jumbotron. Instead of basking in the attention of a professional hockey player, Sophia rolls her eyes and fake gags.

Damn.

Maybe both Selena and I are wrong and there's nothing going on between them. Or maybe Sophia is laying it on thick so nobody will notice their attraction.

I'm going to go with the latter.

"Imagine the field day people would have if I do that to you," I whisper to Maddox as I lean into his side.

He has his arm thrown on the back of my seat and a baseball hat pulled low on his face.

"People had a field day the one day you didn't wear my jersey number."

That's true. I was trending for a solid three hours because of my outfit choices.

He gives me a lazy smile, the very same one that makes my lady bits tingle.

The same smile he gave me the night that the Miners won the World Series back in October and the one I've loved seeing every day since.

When baseball season ended, everything started it moving at a much slower pace. A pace that allowed me and Maddox to grow as a couple and as individuals.

After the winning game, we flew back to Chicago the next afternoon to be with Nora. We were there for a few days before going back to San Francisco to ride in the city-wide parade to celebrate the team's accomplishments.

I saw the parade that the city threw when Hunter and the San Francisco Gold won the super bowl, and I thought that was crazy. I couldn't be more wrong.

The second that float started to move through the streets, it was complete chaos of the best kind.

Maddox got to choose someone to ride with him, and of course I got the honor. It was absolutely crazy how many people were calling out my name with his or how many people had signs with my picture on it.

Riding in the parade was definitely way better than just being a spectator, that's for sure.

Once all the celebration was over, we flew to Chicago for about a week before coming back to spend some time with my parents.

I told Maddox that we didn't need to, that we could

straight to Nora, but he said that we should, because a lot of things could happen.

So, we went.

At the beginning of our trip, I definitely noticed some tension between Maddox and my dad.

Maddox had told me on the drive over what exactly went down between the two of them when they were last in the same room.

So I was expecting the tension.

What I wasn't expecting was for it to be broken by my dad.

One day the man was displeased to see I was still with Maddox, the next he was acting as if they were best friends.

My dad even started calling him *amigo* and *compa*. I even heard him talking to my *Tia*, Lucas's mom, about how amazing *el muchacho* is.

I asked Maddox one night about it, but he was as clueless as I was.

So, I went to the source.

Somehow, someway, Maddox proved himself to my dad.

I asked and all he said was "*Los ojos mija*, it's all in the eyes."

I told Maddox and he looked at me like I had two heads. He swears that he has always looked at me the same, but if my dad says it's true, then it's true.

Maddox better look at me that way for the rest of our lives together because my dad will notice.

The days with my parents went by fast and when it was time to go, we headed to Chicago.

As much as I wanted to treat heading to Chicago as just another trip, I couldn't. It was a move, especially since I packed up my apartment completely and moved everything either to Chicago or to your place in San Francisco.

Even after a few months, I'm still getting used to the fact that Maddox and I live together. At first, it was fine since he was gone most of the time playing, but as soon as the season ended, it was an adjustment.

A lot of things have been an adjustment.

The biggest of them all was adjusting to life in Chicago, especially with the gnarly winters. I'm used to California winters where I can wear two layers and be fine. Here though, I have to wear at least five and some days I'm still freezing my ass off.

One major plus side about being in Chicago though is being closer to Nora.

Her surgery to remove her tumors was successful. The doctors were able to get it done well before the eight-hour mark that they gave us. As for the new tumor it was benign.

No cancer.

They were able to remove it with the others. Now Nora's doctor appointments are set to make sure that the tumors don't return.

We're all keeping our fingers crossed that they don't.

Nora has been in high spirits during her recovery and according to Maddox, is looking more like her old self every single day.

I can't help but smile every single time I see the mother and son duo interact. It's so damn cute.

As for Maddox, he's put in the effort to work on his own recovery.

During the postseason he started to go to meetings. He said the urges to use were far in between but that he wanted someone that would be there to help him through those thoughts if they came.

I told him I was there for him and responded by telling me that he loved me but it wasn't my job to keep him clean.

Once the season ended and we moved to Chicago, he has gone to a few meetings and from what I can see, they've really helped him.

He's more open about his recovery and talking about what might be a trigger than keeping everything in and letting his thoughts fester.

I'm proud of him.

As for me, I'm still taking care of Maddox's social media accounts, and have a total of four clients under my belt.

I'm happy that I get to do what I told Maddox almost a year ago what I wanted.

Everything is coming to fruition, and I honestly couldn't be happier.

I have my man and my dream job and I still get to see my best friend whenever I want.

Never thought that I would be where I am now this time last year, but all it took was a stranger to walk into the coffee shop and tilt everything off its axis.

Forgetting about Sophia and Blake and the rest of the game completely, I turn to Maddox and lift up a hand to turn his face toward me.

When he sees the smile I have on my face, he gives me one back.

"Have I told you lately how happy I am that you walked into the coffee shop that night and walked me home?" I ask, running my fingers through the thin beard.

He shakes his head. "You have not. That was a special night, wasn't it?"

His grin turns into a smirk as he probably remembers everything that night consisted of.

My mind can't help but follow suit. I think we need to have a repeat.

Anything to have this man's face between my legs.

"It was, and if it wasn't for my mind-blowing sex skills, you wouldn't have come back for more."

He lets out a bark of a laugh, throwing his head back. "Mind blowing sex skills, huh?"

"Admit it, Bauer. I'm the best you've ever had." I say with a shrug.

"I will, only if we can recreate it later tonight," he says in a low sultry voice.

If we weren't surrounded by other people and wouldn't get arrested, I would tell him that we could recreate it right now.

But we don't have a dark aquarium corner. Damn, now I want to recreate that too.

"Deal. I will never say no to having to face between my legs."

Maddox lets out another laugh right before he leans in and gives a kiss that is somewhat appropriate for being in public.

We pull apart and we spend the remainder of the game cheering on Blake and just enjoying life.

Right now, I'm trying to get as much of Maddox that I can get since he leaves for spring training later this month.

When the game ends, Hunter guides us through the arena to the player's section to grab Blake so we can head to dinner.

The number of fans that are outside the locker room area waiting for the players, is crazy.

I've seen fans waiting at both football and baseball games, but these hockey fans are a whole other level.

"Damn. Is it always like this?" I ask Maddox as a few people scream when the first player comes out.

"I guess, hockey was never my thing," he says, bringing his hat down a bit more.

Ever since his team winning the World Series, he's been getting recognized more every day. For the most part, he's okay with it, but there are times, like right now, that he would rather just go through life as a normal person.

I don't blame him. Half the time I wonder if I should be wearing a hat too just to be on the safe side.

A few more players come trickling out and as we continue to wait for Blake, someone calls out Maddox's name.

Looking up, I see that it was one of the Chicago Dark Knights players and he's walking in our direction.

The guy is in a white button-up and wearing a black

suit, not showing much skin but the skin that is showing is covered in tattoos.

So many tattoos.

Damn, that had to be so painful. Especially on his fingers.

"I heard you were back in the city. Had me wondering when I will run into you." The guy smiles over at Maddox before extending a hand when he closes the distance.

"Actually surprised it hasn't happened sooner." Maddox answers by taking his hand and I watch as they give each other one of those bro hugs.

"This your girl?" the guy asks when they pull apart.

Maddox smiles down at me before wrapping his arm around my waist, bringing me closer to him. "Yup. Jen, this is Liam. He's the Dark Knights captain. We were at Notre Dame together. Liam, this is Jen."

"It's nice to meet you," Liam says, holding out a hand.

I take it, trying my hardest not to comment on his tattoos. "Yeah, it's nice to meet you too."

"Want to join us for dinner?" Maddox offers, "We're just waiting on Blake."

Liam shakes his head. "Would love to, man, but I have this dinner for one of my endorsements. I'll catch you next time you're in town."

"Sounds good." With another bro hug, Liam is on his way.

After Blake comes out, we head out to dinner and surprisingly it's an uneventful one.

You would think that having three professional athletes with you, everything would be crazy, but it wasn't.

It's one of the most mellow dinners I think I've had in a while.

Maddox and I get home sometime before midnight and the second the door closes behind us, I jump into his arms wrapping my arms and legs around him.

"Hey," I say, running my fingers through his hair.

"Hi," he responds, a smirk on his face and his hands on my ass.

"I think we made a deal to recreate our first night together." I give his hair strands a good tug before bringing our faces closer together.

"I think you're right. Refresh my memory. Did we start on the couch or the bed that night?"

The smirk he gives me right before he leans forward and places his lips against my neck tells me he remembers exactly what it was.

"Bed. Definitely bed. But trust me you will be bending over the back of the couch tonight."

Maddox just chuckles as he walks us over to our bedroom.

Our bedroom. Now it's *our* bedroom.

Once we're in the vicinity of the bed. I get places on the mattress and neither Maddox or I have the patients to stay dressed.

Clothes start to fly everywhere and start landing everywhere but the hamper.

It's as the final article of clothing disappears and our lips connect that I realize one thing.

My life didn't change when I agreed to be a professional athlete's girlfriend.

No, it changed when I agreed to let a complete stranger walk me home after a shift at the coffee shop.

That night changed everything.

That night we were just two people having fun, in need of a release.

As Maddox slides his tongue against mine, I remember the note that he left me that night.

That night will be embedded into his mind.

It was, without a doubt, embedded into mine and I thank all the gods in the world every single day for bringing this man back into my life a month later.

We're not perfect and there are things that we are still learning about each other, but we have the rest of our lives to be together.

And I yes, I do mean the rest of our lives. Maddox and I may have only been together, officially, for a few months, but I've known for a while now that this fake relationship that we started is made to last forever.

Maddox pulls away from my lips and starts moving his mouth down my body, but before he can get far, I stop him. I slide a hand through his hair and bring his face back up to mine.

The second his hazel eyes meet my brown, I feel every single electric current that ran through us that first night.

"I love you," I tell him, hoping he can feel every ounce of love in my words.

"I love you too," he says and for a second, we just stare at each other.

It's just the two of us in this moment. Two people

brought together by fate. I can see it in his eyes that he's feeling the same thing I am at the moment.

It all started with a dark roast, and it's continuing with a silent vow of forever.

Fake to forever was never something that I thought would happen, yet it did.

And I will take every single bit of it.

THE END.

Want to read Hunter and Selena's Story? Check out Worth Every Second!

Interested in Dante's story? Check out Powerful Deception!

Wondering about Lucas and his story? Do not worry, he is coming! Salutis Meae will be releasing January 5, 2023 and you will learn all about him!

As for Liam and Blake? Don't worry, they are coming too! The Chicago Dark Knights series will start releasing Summer 2023. You will get more Liam in Skating the Blue line and Blake in Hitting the Goal Line!

ACKNOWLEDGMENTS

These two were a mission and a half to get here.

The idea of writing a baseball romance with fake dating came about sometime in 2021 while I was coming up with what I should write next.

At first it was a bad boy baseball player that needed help to show people that he was more than just his image and that idea was all set until I finished Worth Every Second. Jen was never going to get her own book, she was just going to be the secondary character that we only saw for a few seconds, but she cried out and asked for her own book. So she got it.

The the female lead from the original idea was scrapped and Jen came in swinging.

As for Maddox, the more I thought about Jen and who her male lead was going to be the more I wanted someone that had his own demos to fight. Maddox was just to be a new character that we were going to meet for the first time in this book, but like what happened with Worth Every Second, the same thing happened with Powerful Deception.

Maddox jumped out from the pages and begged to be written and what better female to put him with than with Jen?

This story has a lot of elements including the active shooting situation. That situation was actually something that happened to me while I was in San Francisco with a few friends this past summer. The panic was very much real, even if it didn't play out as it did in the book, but it has stayed with me. So I decided that I needed to write about it.

I hope you loved these two because I enjoyed writing them.

Now onto the thank yous.

When I say that this book was a mission and a half, I mean it. I was writing until the last possible minute, even while I was in a different country traveling with a group.

To my Highlights of Morocco Family - Thank you so much for the support that you gave me through our days together for this book. Your encouragement to finish the book helped so much and I hope that if you read this book you know you were only a few feet away while I got my words done. Thank you so much for the words of encouragement every day.

Shauna and Wildfire - Thank you for your tremendous amount of help to promote this book and get it into readers hands. I would be lost without you!

Ellie - you are are most amazing editor out there and thank you so much for working with me and the crazy ass time constraints you have to deal with when it comes to me!

Readers - thank you for your excitement for this book. Without you, I would have scrapped every single word and this book would have never seen the light of day. Thank you for you love for my characters and for your support, it means the absolute world to me.

Now.... Onto the next one!

BOOKS BY JOCELYNE SOTO

One Series

One Life

One Love

One Day

One Chance

One for Me

One Marriage

Flor De Muertos Series

Vicious Union

Violent Attraction

Vindictive Blood

Chicago Dark Knights Series

Skating the Blue Line (coming spring 2023)

Passing the Red Line (coming summer 2023)

Hitting the Goal Line (coming summer 2023

Standalones

Beautifully Broken

Worth Every Second

Powerful Deception

Fake Love

Salutis Meae

ABOUT THE AUTHOR

Jocelyne Soto is a writer born and raised in California. She started her writing journey in 2015 and in 2019 she published her first book. She is an independent author who loves discovering new authors on Goodreads and Amazon. She comes from a big Mexican family, and with it comes a love for all things family and food.

Jocelyne has a love for her mom's coffee and writing. In her free time, she can be found reading a romance novel off her iPad or somewhere in the black hole of YouTube.

Follow her website and on social media!
www.jocelynesoto.com

facebook.com/authorjocelynesoto

twitter.com/AuthorJocelyneS

instagram.com/authorjocelynesoto

pinterest.com/authorjocelynesoto

tiktok.com/@authorjocelynesoto

goodreads.com/jocelynesotobooks

bookbub.com/profile/jocelyne-soto

JOIN MY READER GROUP

Join my ever-growing Facebook Group. You get first looks, sneak peeks and giveaways!

NEWSLETTER

Sign up for my Newsletter!
You will get notified when there are new
releases to look out for, giveaways and more!